THE ORIGIN PROPHECY

LightFall

LightFall

THE ORIGIN PROPHECY

SHIRE-HILL PUBLICATIONS
UNITED KINGDOM

ISBN: 978-1-914483-10-3

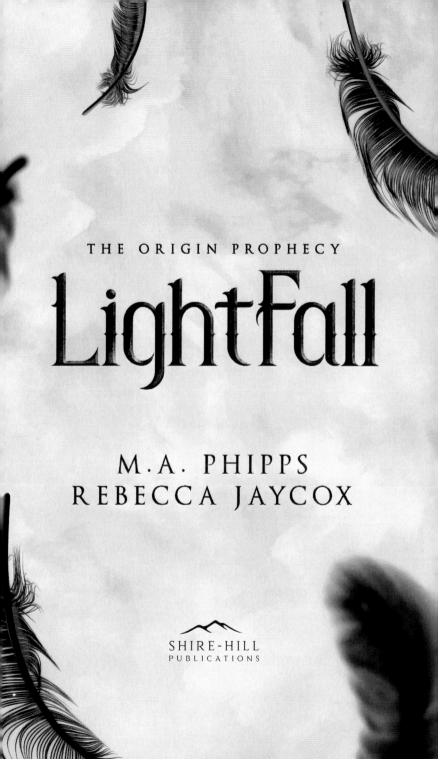

THE ORIGIN PROPHECY

LightFall

M.A. PHIPPS
REBECCA JAYCOX

SHIRE-HILL
PUBLICATIONS

light academies

The Serapeum
EGYPT
Gabriel

Mount Nebo
JORDAN
Remiel

Petra
JORDAN
Serathiel

Mount Sinai
EGYPT
Raphael

Sidon
LEBANON
Amenadiel

Mount Zion
ISRAEL
Uriel

Qumran
ISRAEL
Azrael

dark academies

Megiddo
ISRAEL
Lucifer

The Tower of Babel
IRAQ
Asmodeus

Sodom
ISRAEL
Leviathan

Gomorrah
ISRAEL
Belphegor

Ashkelon
ISRAEL
Beelzebub

Tyre
LEBANON
Mammon

Machaerus
JORDAN
Abaddon

"*Abashed the Devil stood, and felt how awful goodness is, and saw
Virtue in her shape how lovely; saw, and pined his loss.*"

JOHN MILTON, *PARADISE LOST*

prologue

THE WORLD BELOW BURNED. Gabriel perched on the mountain peak like a giant bird of prey, wings folded into her body, her long, black hair snapping in the strong breeze like a flag. She watched the flames wind like rivers of fire through the fragile land. Humans scurried like ants, running from the blaze and the angels battling across the landscape, destroying everything in their path. The earth shook with the force of their rage. How had it come to this?

They were supposed to be brothers and sisters in arms, loyal to one another, and above all to the Creator. Now, they tore into each other like primitive beasts, grooving out lines of destruction in the ground. The newly made humans they were supposed to protect and shepherd were reduced to mere casualties of angelic rage.

Heat built behind her eyes and she blinked, furious. Gabriel couldn't remember tears before humans, before all these conflicting emotions inside her. Before her lover had decided to wage war on the heavens and his fellow angels—all in the name of free will. Her chest heaved as she regarded the chaos below her. If this was free will, the price was too high.

Tensing, Gabriel prepared to leap off and join the fray when a shadow hovered over her. Whipping her head up, she watched as her lover glided overhead, great ivory wings flapping before landing beside her.

The Morningstar. One of the most beautiful angels in Heaven. He turned to her, hair the color of antique gold, eyes the deep blue of the sea rimmed in citrine. His gaze was hungry when it roamed over her face, and she desperately wanted to touch him as she never should have. As if sensing her need, he fisted her long hair, the motion lightning fast, and kissed her. Despite the violence raging around them, despite the pain in her heart, she kissed him back, opening her lips and letting him inside.

He was Gabriel's forbidden fruit, her slippery slide into the seductive world of emotion. Her lust and want and need all wore his name. And her love. Her love for him rivaled her love for the Creator, and she couldn't allow that. Free will was a beautiful dream, an idea that *seemed* to be good and right. But who were they to disobey the Creator? They had a higher allegiance and purpose than indulging here on Earth. Her indulgence in Lucifer had helped lead to this. The death of humans who were so young and just finding their footing in this new world.

But despite knowing what must be done, she clung to him,

memorizing his taste and scent, knowing this would be the last time she'd have him like this. She either had to convince him to stop this madness, or leave him forever and join her fellow angels in squashing the rebellion. Gabriel tore her mouth away, gasping. Leaning her forehead against his, she steeled herself for what she must say, what she must do.

Lucifer tipped her chin up, and she wanted to drown in the blue of his eyes, give in to his temptation and never leave him. But she couldn't—she wouldn't. She beseeched the Creator that she could find the strength to change one of His favorite children's minds.

Lucifer stood, taking her with him, balancing on the icy rock of the mountain. "Look, my love, soon we will be free. Soon, we will make our *own* choices. I will never have to be ashamed again for loving you, for wanting you. For being envious of them and what they are allowed to have that we are not." He flung his arm out in a sweeping motion, and Gabriel regarded the war scarring the land below.

She grasped his hand and brought it to her lips, only then allowing a single tear to escape. He tracked that tear, like a predator honing in on prey. He met her eyes, his expression confused, with a smudge of suspicion forming. Swallowing hard, Gabriel tried to find the words to tell him his dream was impossible, to make him understand they had a higher purpose—no matter how much she loved him. No matter how her heart was rent asunder.

"I love you," she told him, another tear falling. "I love you more than I should, more than *anything*." The confession weighed heavily upon her. Despite her tears, Lucifer relaxed at her words, only to tense again as she said, "And I… I've come to realize how dangerous that is. Don't you see? Look at what we've done." She tasted the ash on the wind and her heart ached.

Lucifer jerked away from her as if she'd struck him. "What have we done, exactly? Love each other? Want more from life than blind obedience and servitude?" he growled.

"We haven't just loved each other, have we? We created a rift in Heaven. I regret my…selfishness," Gabriel said, ashamed she helped cause so much suffering.

"Selfishness? Is that what love is to you? Nothing more than a whim you indulged in?" Fury rode his voice and colored his cheekbones ruddy. "Do you regret me? *Us?*"

His words crushed her. "No, no, I love you. I could never regret you. I regret the destruction we've caused, the death. We've turned on each other—angels fighting angels! We're hurting each other and killing them." Gabriel pointed to the terrified humans, made clear by her raptor vision.

"Them." His voice held quiet venom. "The Creator's new favorites, unbound by blind obedience. Given a choice, while we—superior beings—are slaves to duty, not allowed to love another, to experience the delights of this world. How is that fair or just?"

Gabriel pushed past her pain, reaching for him, but he

dodged her hand. "We *are* superior beings," she said, desperate for him to see. "That means we have a higher purpose and calling. We are their protectors, this world's protectors. We owe our allegiance and obedience to the Creator. We owe Him our love, not our betrayal."

The Morningstar sneered at her, eyes filled with hurt and hatred, and her breath stuttered in her chest. "Yes, I know all about betrayal, my love. And it cuts deep."

"Lucifer, please," she begged. "Please understand, I don't want to hurt you—"

"But you are. You are choosing the Creator over me."

Gabriel winced. "No, I'm choosing a higher purpose. We—"

"We deserve to make our own choices. And if you choose to betray me, then that means we're enemies."

She felt like he'd taken his golden sword and skewered her. "No, we don't have to be enemies. It doesn't have to be this way, please—"

Lucifer's voice was like ice. "You've made your choice. You've chosen to break me." With one final look at her, he dove off the mountain toward the battle below.

Gabriel clutched her middle, pain lancing through her. Pain and regret and horror at what she'd done to him. For a precious few moments, she allowed herself to mourn their love. Then straightening, she shoved all that emotion down and somehow found her calm center. Her sword sang as she freed it from her scabbard and leaped off the cliff.

one

LUNA

SCREAMS FLOOD THE CRAMPED room, growing alongside the flames, the writhing tentacles of fire thrashing in every direction, devouring the creaky metal bed frames and mattresses—reaching out to punish everyone present but me. I know in my heart the fire is my friend. It protects me when everything else wants to hurt me.

It saves me even when the screams make me cry.

My eyelids jerk apart as I'm jolted awake by the jarring impact of the plane landing. The tires skid against the runway, the hissing of rubber on tarmac uncomfortably loud in my just-woken—and still drowsy—state, the remnants of my nightmare fading like the dying tings of an echo.

Weird, I don't remember falling asleep.

As the plane slows to a stop and the engines cut off, the overhead speakers crackle to life. A male voice makes an announcement in Arabic, followed by what I presume to be the same message in English. *"Ladies and gentlemen, welcome to Borg El Arab International Airport. The local time is 9:40 a.m. and the temperature is 28°C. For your safety and comfort, please remain seated…"*

I yawn a few times until my ears pop, releasing the pressure building up in my head. As the pilot's voice drones on through the cabin, I turn my gaze to the small window beside me. A hazy blue sky and stretch of sand patched with weeds await on the other side of the thick glass, offering a first glimpse at my new home.

Alexandria.

I press my fingertips to the warm glass. Despite the strange sense of calm overwhelming my body, I'm not entirely sure how I got here. I didn't even own a passport before yesterday, and the events of the last thirty or so hours are reeling through my head in a muddled fog surrounded by half-answered questions. Questions, which are strangely lacking in fear. All I know is that less than two days ago, I was in a psychiatric ward in central Maine, isolated with no hope of ever seeing beyond the blank gray walls of my cage. Dorothy in my own eternal Kansas.

But now…

My eyes snap to the tall, brunette man a few inches to my left, in the next seat over. He's handsome and on the younger side—no older than mid-twenties if I had to guess—and while he's familiar, I can't recall his name, only that he's my guardian on this trip, which should alarm me but, for some reason, doesn't. I *want* it to bother me. For all I know, he's abducted me and no one knows where I am. Something tells me that isn't the case, but still, why don't I feel afraid? Or more anxious about my first time on a plane? And why can't I bring myself to ask the questions anyone else would in my position? It's as if there's a fog pressing down on my mind, preventing that part of my brain from working.

Sensing my lingering stare, he looks over at me. His amber eyes seem to glow as he speaks.

"How did you sleep?" he asks in a lilting voice as a gentle smile curves the line of his lips. I can't pinpoint where his accent is from. He's definitely not American. If anything, his way of speaking is a strange amalgamation of several different accents, confusing me nearly as much as how I wound up in Egypt. And why.

"F-Fine," I choke out, my answer garbled from the grainy texture coating my tongue from the dry plane air. I must've been sleeping with my mouth open. Clearing my throat, I try again. "Fine."

"Good." His smile deepens as he drags the brown leather briefcase on the floor by his feet up onto his lap. As he opens it and gathers our travel documents, I search his sharp, angular face for answers regarding the muddled hours of the last two days. My efforts cease mid-thought when his fair complexion shimmers with something otherworldly, a halo of golden tendrils slithering across the surface of his skin like thousands of small whips of light.

As my eyes widen, taking in his inexplicable glow, the memory of his deep voice stirs in my ears, drawing forth a flicker of a past conversation between us. I was in that cramped, empty room at the hospital, curled up in a trembling ball on the icy floor, and he was crouched in front of me, speaking in gentle whispers.

"Luna, do you know why I'm here? I'm taking you away from this place."

His hand grazed my shoulder then, but I didn't jerk away from his touch—not like I have with every other person who has tried to get close to me since the incidents began. I wasn't sure what, but there was something about him—something that set him apart from the other doctors who had long since cast me off as a lost cause unworthy of their time or attention. A patient incapable of being helped. That something made me want to trust him.

When I asked him why he wanted to help me, he answered with only three words.

"Because you're special."

Special. That word rings again in my head, although I still don't know what he meant by it. If by special, he meant completely deranged, then sure. I'm definitely special, all right.

The light indicating for everyone to keep their seat belts fastened abruptly shuts off with a resounding ding, and in a flurry of movement, the passengers on the plane all climb to their feet, preparing to disembark. My chaperone follows suit, yanking the faded blue backpack full of my few meager belongings from the overhead storage compartment.

"Ready?" He gestures behind him, holding out his arm in the unoccupied space in the narrow aisle to keep it open for me.

Despite the questions beating against the wall of my skull, I nod and reach out to take my bag from his hand, although I'm not sure I'm ready at all. Every moment since I left the hospital has been like some sort of bizarre dream that I'm sleepwalking my way through, only half aware of what's happening. I can't even remember stepping foot on this plane. Maybe I was drugged. It wouldn't be the first time pharmaceuticals were shoved down my throat in the hope of suppressing whatever inner demons make me do the terrible things that I've done. By now, I'm used to feeling nothing, and that's probably for the best. Every time I start feeling, I only end up having to face what I am.

Dangerous.

If I weren't, I wouldn't have been isolated in a padded room for the past year. Last I heard, the doctors hadn't made any significant breakthroughs regarding my unhinged mental state, so why was I discharged from the ward? And why can't I clearly remember agreeing to leave with this man or bring myself to question him about where he's taking me?

How can I be ready when I don't know where I'm going?

A strange wave of calm washes over me again, dulling my senses and easing my uncertainty and desire for answers, as well as pushing down the fear creeping to the surface like bile rising in my throat. Sedated, I silently trail the man off the plane, letting him guide my steps without question or hesitation like a dog on a leash. As we walk, my gaze drags across the shining white floors and seemingly endless walls of windows, glancing anywhere but at the people around me. I already know what I'll find on their faces. How normal they'll look, their eyes unburdened by guilt.

How I wish I could know what that feels like.

The corridors we progress through are muggy and hot, even with the air conditioners thrumming on full blast through the airport. When we finally reach the line for border control, the heat in the room becomes sweltering as dozens of bodies press in close on each side of us, encroaching on my much-needed personal space. Perspiration beads along my skin, sticking my hair to the back of my neck and drenching my T-shirt and jeans with sweat. God, what I wouldn't give for a shower.

My fingers fumble with the blonde locks that now feel like a heavy curtain draped across my back, bundling them on top of my head and holding them there as I let out a breath. As if reading my thoughts, my chaperone offers me a rubber band to tie my hair up.

At the hospital, we weren't allowed simple luxuries like hair elastics. Most of the residents had their hair shorn short to avoid them finding unique ways to use it as a weapon to harm themselves or others. My own golden tresses were left alone, thankfully, but I know that's only because none of the staff wanted to risk becoming my next victim by forcibly shaving my head.

What the doctors failed to understand is that I never *wanted* to hurt anyone. The incidents... They just sort of happened—like the madness was leaking out of my body and simply latched onto the first available target. I couldn't stop the demons from lashing out, no matter how hard I tried to keep them at bay.

The people who get close to me always suffer.

I fling my hair into a ponytail as the line inches forward one trudging step at a time. With every passing moment, my racing heart picks up speed until my pulse is throbbing in my veins like a physical presence trying to break out of my flesh. When I inhale, the dank air—filled with the chaotic hum of dozens of voices all speaking over each other in different languages—presses down on my lungs, suffocating my already irregular breaths and making me feel even more out of place.

Closing my eyes, I breathe in through my nose and out through my mouth like the counselor at the hospital taught me to do when things begin to get...overwhelming. I can't recall the last time I was around so many people or cooped up in such a crowded space, and the pandemonium of it all is too much to endure. An irrepressible desire to be outside in the fresh air tickles across my skin like an itch.

But then, that peculiar sense of calm courses through me again, and gradually my heart rate slows, and my breathing steadies to a normal pace. When my eyes flutter open, I'm surprised to find myself standing at the front of the line. Strange. I could've sworn we were much farther back. I peek up at the graceful form of the man beside me who grins when I meet his gaze, as if he somehow knows what I'm thinking.

My lips part to speak, but he grabs my arm and escorts me forward before I can utter a word. Clamping my mouth shut, I let him lead me toward the immigration officer beckoning for us to approach her.

The woman, an attractive middle-aged Egyptian wearing a burgundy hijab, holds out an expectant hand for our travel documents. The man offers them to her with an amiable smile.

She glances at my companion's passport first, and as she stamps it, I catch a brief glimpse of his name. Alaric Walsh.

That's right, I remember now. He introduced himself at the hospital.

Another recollection breaks free from the fog in my head.

"Are you a doctor?" I asked, looking him up and down with raised brows. He didn't seem like the other doctors who had all tried and failed to help me since I was committed.

"Yes," he answered in a soothing voice. "But more than that, I'm a friend. You don't belong here, Luna. These people don't understand you."

"There's a problem with these documents." The immigration officer's curt tone shakes my attention away from the memory. She looks at me, her expression stern. "I can see you have an entry visa, but without evidence of a return flight, I cannot admit you. There's also the matter of your Letter of Consent… As you are a minor traveling internationally with an adult who is of no relation to you, it needs to be signed by your legal guardian. This hospital release form is not recognized consent."

My heart drops into my stomach at the thought of what this setback could mean for me. I don't have a legal guardian who can permit me to travel. I'm a child of the state, and Dr. Walsh—*"Call me Alaric,"* I remember him saying now—was my one ticket to freedom from who knows how many more years in that padded room. If I can't enter Alexandria as he intended, does that mean I'll have to return to Maine or be admitted to some other psychiatric ward back in the States? And if I am allowed into Egypt as planned, what alternative awaits me here?

Which path should I be more afraid of?

Either way, I know one thing for certain. I would rather die than go back to a hospital, and if it comes down to the choice between freedom or captivity, I'll make a break for it. I'll run as far and as fast as I can to avoid wasting away in a cage.

"Please," Alaric urges, placing his hand on the smooth, gleaming surface of the black counter. The mischievous glint in his gaze unnerves me. "Could you check the documents again?"

Out of the corner of my eye, I notice his forefinger lift a few inches and hang there, suspended in the air, as if he's pointing at something. His smile, which I had assumed was a permanent fixture, has vanished, leaving his lips set in a serious line.

"That…" The immigration officer trails off, her dark brow furrowing in confusion. "That's odd," she continues after a pause. "I could've sworn it said—"

Alaric's finger drops back to the counter. "As you can see, our documents are in order."

"Y-Yes." The woman looks up at him with wide ocher eyes then directs her gaze back down to the bundle of documents laid out before her. In the space of a few seconds, her dubious expression melts into one of indifferent acceptance. "Of course," she mutters, stamping the pages. "Welcome to Egypt, Mr. Walsh. I hope you and your daughter have a pleasant stay."

I balk at her casual—and wildly incorrect—statement.

Daughter?

Alaric's careful smile returns as we slip away from the counter and continue past the luggage carousel, through customs, and finally toward the exit, following the overhead signs written in English and Arabic to sweet liberation from the stifling confines of the crowded building. The sliding doors swish open at our approach, welcoming us into the dry morning heat. Although there's no breeze, a faint salty aroma hangs in the air, indicating that we're close to the water.

Excitement buzzes through me. I've never seen the sea in person before.

The minutes pass by without either of us speaking as we stand at the taxi rank outside, waiting for the next available cab. Gradually—perhaps thanks to the fresh air in my lungs— that curious fog lifts off my brain. As it fades, freeing me of that invisible restraint, I blurt out, "Why did she suddenly think I'm your daughter?" My stomach twists at the thought of a family—the one thing I've never had the luxury of and can't imagine ever having. As much as I crave a father, this man is a stranger to me, so him feigning the part has me flustered, regardless of how kind he's been since we met. The mere notion of it doesn't make any sense either. Alaric doesn't look remotely old enough to be the parent of a seventeen-year-old—a fact the immigration officer should have noted.

A thousand other questions spiral through my head, but I'm too afraid to ask them. Asking questions never did anything good for me. Silence was always safest around doctors and social workers, even though they were meant to protect me.

"A simple mistake, I'm sure." His tone is innocent, but he keeps his eyes fixed ahead on the bright yellow horizon, avoiding my questioning gaze.

"I'm not buying that," I force out, despite my reservations. "She had two reasons for refusing to admit me, and one simple ask from you and she swung the gates of Egypt wide open."

Maybe Alaric does magic tricks as a hobby or side gig to make extra money. From what I've heard, illusionists are good at sleight of hand. Why else would the immigration officer let me through after stating my documents weren't in order unless she thought she read the provided information wrong? Which Alaric and I both know she didn't.

He considers me for a moment, averting his gaze when a battered black and yellow taxi approaches. As it rolls up beside us, he opens the back door and offers me a nonchalant shrug.

"Let's just say I used my incredible powers of persuasion."

I climb into the taxi and sink into the seat with his cryptic answer swirling through my brain. Alaric slides into the backseat next to me, slamming the door shut behind him. "Serapeum, *min fadlik*," he instructs the driver.

The man in front of me, who smells strongly of tobacco and garlic, grunts and takes off at a breakneck speed that sends my stomach lurching.

Stewing in my own confusion and annoyance at Alaric's lack of a proper answer, I stare out the window, watching the city—a mesh of ancient and modern—whip past in a dizzying, sand-colored blur. Occasionally, I spot the Mediterranean Sea peeking back at me through the staggered gaps in the buildings, but it, too, flashes by before I can get a good look at the sparkling surface reflecting the sun. Disappointment rises in me, extinguishing what little excitement had managed to break through my shroud of doubt and unease. Nothing new there. My life has been a constant shift from one place to another like I'm nothing more than a piece on a chessboard—a pawn surrendered to an invisible enemy in a game I never asked to play. Why should my move here be any different? I've never had any say in what happens to me, which is why I don't waste my breath questioning these things anymore. Others will always dictate my fate.

But what fate does Alaric have planned for me? And why did he let that lady believe I'm his daughter?

I roll my teeth over my lower lip, considering the nagging

thought biting at me like a mosquito in the heavy heat of the summers in New England. "Back at the hospital...you said they didn't understand me." Although I don't turn to look at Alaric, I can sense his perceptive eyes watching me.

"Few can."

"Because I'm crazy?" My voice catches on that word. I've always hated it. I hate how it's come to define who I am.

Warm fingers wrap around my shoulder, comforting me much like the same action did two days ago when we met—the bright-eyed doctor and the broken girl.

"You aren't crazy, Luna. You just don't know what you are."

What I am?

This question scratches at the seam of my lips, but I can't find the courage inside me to ask it. My voice wobbles when another thought pushes through in its place. A dangerous thought. A thought that terrifies me to my core. "Where are you taking me?"

"Someplace where you will be among others like you. Someplace where you will be safe."

Safe from what? From myself?

Nausea churns my stomach as I gauge the deeper meaning behind his statement. "So, another hospital," I realize with dread.

His soft voice fills my ears as his slender fingers squeeze my shoulder again. "No, not another hospital," he promises.

The cab comes to a screeching halt, throwing me forward. The seat belt locks, and I wince when the rough fabric strains against my chest, cutting into my neck. Beside me, Alaric's posture is poised and eerily still, as if the sudden stop hasn't had an effect on him.

"We're here," he says in a buoyant tone, offering me an encouraging smile.

My brows knit together as I glance between his bright, joyous expression and the mound of rubble waiting outside. The only elements still intact that I can see from the taxi are a statue of a sphinx and a random pillar, but even those don't provide any clues or context that would suggest this could possibly be our destination.

I wrinkle my nose. "These are ruins. There's nothing here."

With a low chuckle, Alaric pushes open the door. "Just because you can't see something doesn't mean it isn't there. Come on."

He slides out of the taxi, and I follow closely behind despite my hesitation, standing off to one side of the road as he pays the driver, who takes off in a burst of speed a moment later without a second glance back at us. When Alaric appears beside me, I narrow my eyes at him, trying to figure out what he's up to and whether or not I should be afraid. He laughs again at the disgruntled look on my face.

"Now…" He leans in until his mouth is right next to my ear. "Look closely. See beyond the ruins before you. Only then will you understand why we're here."

I cock an eyebrow, unsure what he means. "See beyond?"

See beyond it how?

"Just trust me," he murmurs, his tone pleading.

With a sigh, I relax my shoulders, relenting. Focusing, I skim my gaze across every rock and every broken stretch of wall. As I take it all in, the air in front of me ripples, warping like a mirage in the heat until the ruins before me vanish behind the distortion. In their place stands a magnificent cream and gold-colored building towering at least one hundred feet above me—a conglomerate of pillars, decorative arches, and domes, which cripple the surrounding landscape with their beauty.

I stumble back in awe and trip over a rock, the ground rushing upward to meet me. Alaric catches me with a hand on my arm before I land flat on my ass. "How did you do that?" I gasp.

Smirking, he sets me back on my feet before proceeding up the staircase where only moments ago there was nothing but sand. He pauses halfway up the steps to glance back at me. "I didn't unmask it. *You* did, Luna. You just had to want to see it."

"See what? What is this place?"

The amber eyes watching me flick upward toward the ornate doors at the top of the staircase. "A school. For special people like you."

There's that word again.

"Special how?" *What are you talking about?* I want to scream. *A school for what?* My hands ball into fists at my sides, my palms hot and slick with sweat. The one question I couldn't bring myself to ask before tumbles from my quivering lips in a whisper. "What am I?"

Alaric gives me a careful smile then turns, continuing his slow ascent up the stairs. As the doors at the top swing open at his arrival, his voice echoes down the slope of steps and burrows in my ears, touching the deepest depths of my soul, like a hand carefully shaking me awake from a dream.

Disbelief ignites in my gut like a flame as a single word sets my world on fire.

"Nephilim."

two

CALEB

THE CLEAN SCENT OF citrus trees in full bloom surrounds me as I stroll through the lush Hanging Gardens. I've always loved the Gardens. The jewel-bright colors both stimulate and soothe my senses. I wander here when I need a break from my friends or my latest hookup. Or when I've been surrounded by humans and their special brand of chaos and need to recharge.

The Tower of Babel looms over the scattered ruins. To the human eye, Babylon is nothing more than a rotting husk from an ancient civilization adjacent to Hilla, a small city never able to achieve the wonders of Babylonia. Archaeologists constructed a fake gate of Ishtar for tourists, even though the real gate stands next to it, flawless in its navy-blue beauty, although invisible to the mortal eye. Its alternating rows of bulls and dragons are etched with breathtaking detail. The one they display in a mortal museum is a well-crafted copy. I never grow tired of looking at the real one, this stunning ode to the goddess of love

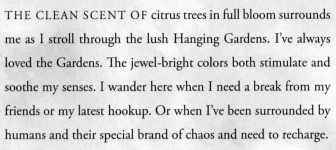

22

and war made by human hands.

Carefully concealed with angelic magic, the Tower has been preserved, perfect and untouched by time, along with other parts of the city. Like a handful of other ancient sites around the world, it houses one of the seven academies for Dark Nephilim, children of the Fallen bloodlines.

The midday sun floods the Gardens with heat, despite the pools of water nurturing the fruit trees. I step out of a puddle of shade into bright sunshine, my bronze skin absorbing the rays. With a lazy hand, I push back my black hair. It's grown a bit shaggy, but I find that women like to run their hands through it. And shit, I like it a little messy. What's the point of being a rebel if you don't enjoy looking the part?

A stunning woman captures my attention in a grove of trees to my left. She stretches her long-limbed figure to pluck a tangerine from a branch. Her white dress clings to dangerous curves. I stop, giving her a wary stare. Her presence here can't be a coincidence. Damn it.

Ishtar turns toward me, her scarlet lips curving into a slow smile that makes me want to step back. To mortal eyes, she appears as the epitome of seduction. But she hasn't earned her immortal reputation as a goddess of love and war by accident. She is the academy's professor of persuasion, teaching the Dark students how to wield their mental powers with precision and responsibility—although she does that last part begrudgingly. Even she has to follow the rules.

Raising my hand in a brief salute, I hope to pass her by. As a first generation Nephilim, Ishtar's power is strong. She's almost achieved immortality through her Fallen blood—almost. It may take another thousand years but she'll die. A fact I know that she resents. Hell, I resent it, too. My father was a second generation Nephilim and my mother human. Although my powers rival a second generation's, I'm a third. That means I'll live a long damn time, but I won't get forever. Despite all the power I possess, I'll eventually wither and die just like my mother.

"Darling Caleb," Ishtar calls to me, voice husky and sweet. I shiver at the sound and the way it kisses my skin. I hate that she can affect me, but she affects everyone, so I don't feel like too much of a chump. "I'll walk with you. I'm ready to return, anyway."

I pause, like the obedient student I am. Well, the Dark teachers don't encourage blind obedience, but they do demand respect. And only a fool disrespects Ishtar. I offer her a warm smile.

"It's always a delight to be in your company," I say as she draws up beside me.

She's chosen Babylonian-style attire today, the gauzy white fabric of her dress draped and folded around her lush figure, and held securely at one shoulder with a beaten gold pin, emphasizing the time period in which she flourished.

"Liar," she scolds, musical voice teasing as she slips her hand into the crook of my proffered arm. "I make you want to piss yourself."

I scowl. "No one but Lucifer could make me piss myself." Then I give her a genuine grin. "But you come pretty damn close."

A surprised laugh escapes her lips. "To compare me to the Morningstar is a compliment indeed." Her onyx eyes search mine, her brown skin gleaming in the strong sun. Her blue-black hair cascades down her back in gentle waves. "You've been to see your mother?"

I stiffen. Her question is innocent enough, but I know she disapproves. Not that I give a shit. She may be a badass bitch, but even she doesn't get to interfere in my relationship with my mom.

"New York was fun," I reply, keeping my pace steady. "Mom's got a new job. And Queens is surprisingly cool. So many gorgeous ladies to play with." And play I did.

"Practice your mind tricks, did you?" Ishtar asks, amused.

"No, I don't need mind tricks to get laid. I'm a smokeshow. And like all the Darks, I believe in free will. Human or not, I'm not robbing anyone of theirs." My anger overrides my respect and cautious fear of the woman beside me for a moment.

Instead of the rebuke I expect, she pats my hand. "Spoken like a true Dark. I may hate the rules preventing me from showing the world how truly powerful I am, from keeping me from ruling over these lesser mortals, but to rob someone of their choice is to go against everything the Fallen stand for."

Not that we Darks aren't above manipulating human minds when we need to—like when mortals see something they shouldn't. And I know some feel it's fair game to mess with humans when it doesn't directly involve them. That's a fine line that will lead to punishment if you land on the wrong side, though. And punishment sucks. Yeah, I heal fast, but it still doesn't mean broken bones feel good. Or the lash of a whip.

And of course, it's always fun to play with the Lights. Stuck-up assholes.

I'm beginning to relax when Ishtar says, "When are you going to give up this unhealthy relationship with your mother?"

I bite my lip hard, straining not to resort to violence. I could get some good jabs in, make her bleed, but in the end, she'd break my spine to teach me a lesson. I glare at her. She's tall, but at a couple inches over six feet, I'm taller.

"Never," I say flatly. "I love her. She took care of me when my dad didn't give a shit. He was happy to play and then just ran off. I'm not going to abandon her." Mom knew exactly who she was raising, and instead of dumping me in the nearest orphanage because she couldn't handle it, she loved me. She prepared me. And when the Dark Nephilim came to take me to my primary academy, she let them. Not because she didn't care, but because she knew it was best for me.

"She'll die long before you. Don't you want to spare yourself pain?" Ishtar counters. "This attachment anchors you too strongly to the mortal world."

My laugh is bitter. "I'm part mortal and so are you." Her eyes cut into me and I flinch, but continue, "I'm anchored whether

I like it or not."

She digs sharp nails into my arm and jerks my chin down to meet her eyes with her free hand. Her black eyes are fierce. "You're better than humans. Remember that. *We're* better."

"I *like* humans," I say and it's the truth. I love their messiness and their creativity. I even love their pain. They're like mayflies, trying to make the most of their short lives.

We resume walking and Ishtar snorts. "I like them, too, but they're not my equals. Never forget that you're superior to them, no matter how much they amuse you. Remember your bloodline."

"As if I could forget," I say, resentful. I never forget my bloodline.

Alexander the Great. My grandfather. He's also a first generation Dark Nephilim. After he tried to conquer the world, the Lights entombed him somewhere. Since he's like Ishtar, he would still be alive. But we brokered a truce with the Lights to avoid another war, and he's not coming back. That's what you get when you try to take over the world and go against the original agreement between the angels and the Fallen. Alexander had a good run, though, he almost made it. I wish I knew him. Maybe he wouldn't be a dick like my dad.

We walk past the stone lion tourists flock to. There are a couple of them out this morning, although with the political situation in Iraq, they're rare. Ishtar and I remain invisible to their eyes with a simple illusion that renders us as nothing more than part of the landscape. The lion stands tall and proud, and I trail my fingers over the smooth rock.

The Tower sprouts up ahead, shaped like a round, tiered cake built of fired brick that grows narrower as it reaches for the heavens. The masonry work is intricate, the carvings detailed. It's a stunning achievement, even if it is Nimrod's middle finger to the Creator. Nimrod might be a first generation Dark Nephilim, but he's also a bit of an asshole.

Ishtar speaks again, breaking our silence. "As you might already know, tensions are running high between us and our Light brethren."

I chuckle. "Aren't tensions always high between us and those goody-goody pricks?"

She arches an imperious brow. "This is different, Caleb. Some of us tire of hiding. We've chosen Earth as home, and we'd like to be completely free here."

I look at her, slightly alarmed. Yeah, total freedom sounds like a blast. To be able to show my powers and just walk around letting it all hang out, but I don't like the idea of humans getting hurt. My mom getting hurt. And if the Lights and Darks go to war, that's what will come out of it.

"What's happened?" I demand. I was only gone for two weeks. Did my entire world go to shit in that time?

Ishtar's smile is sly. "Nothing. Yet."

My unease grows as we climb stone steps worn smooth by thousands of years and thousands of pairs of feet.

"I hope you understand that I'd never condone harming humans," she says, and my brow raises. "They serve their purpose, and they are endlessly entertaining, but despite all their advancements, they're still like children. Greedy, only thinking of the now. Gold and war and destruction. Look at what they've done to their own lands?" She makes a sweeping gesture with an elegant hand.

Beyond our little oasis is a region torn by years of war and strife and terror. I can't argue with that, so I remain silent, waiting for her to get to the point. My gut churns.

She tosses her silky mane back, and I catch a whiff of honeysuckle. It's intoxicating like her, but she's too scary to ever let my mind wander down that path. She'd eat me for breakfast and pick her teeth with my bones.

And though you'd have to drive a spike in her eye to get her to admit it, I think Ishtar is still hung up on that Light jerk, Gilgamesh. I was accidentally in a room with them once, and the pheromones were flying so fast, even I wanted to smoke a cigarette.

"We were made to rule them," Ishtar continues, bringing me back to the here and now with a hard bump to my shoulder. "They need a firm hand to show them their folly. We could stop this foolish hiding, take our rightful place as lords of the Earth, and all prosper."

"That's a great dream, but the Lights won't ever agree to that. You're talking war. How do you plan to win without killing half the planet?" Shit, humans have no issue offing themselves now in conflicts. I can't imagine a global-wide slaughter. No matter how appealing freedom is.

Her smile turns triumphant. "Alexander the Great."

The enormous wood doors before us swing open of their own accord, spanning at least two-stories high, and the ringing voices and bustle of the academy spill out around us, but I might as well be deaf to it, my attention wholly focused on the goddess next to me.

I sneer. "Um, isn't he entombed somewhere, trapped, basically rotting away until death pays him a visit? I don't think he's going to win this one for us."

Rage shivers along the corners of her mouth, and it takes everything in me not to step back. Okay, so I might have been too much of a dick with that statement, but I get tired of bitter Darks talking about waging a war against the Lights. And yeah, if Alexander were around, he might succeed—he almost did before. But he's not.

Ishtar snarls, "Foolish child! Do you think you know everything? In your eighteen years, have you accumulated the wisdom I possess? Do you proclaim to know more than *me*?"

Each statement is like a slap I deserve. A few Nephilim exit the cavernous doorway, giving us a wide berth, as if they can smell the tension. I ignore them as does the furious woman staring me down, eyes like chipped stone. Without thinking, I move into a defensive stance, setting my feet wider apart. If she comes after me, I'll be ready.

I keep my voice calm as I say, "No, I don't claim to know shit, but I've been told my whole life that my grandfather is lost to us. *You've* told me that."

Her face shutters, the rage vanishes, and she shrugs. "I have the wisdom to admit I was wrong."

I startle, my own anger subsiding. "What do you mean you were wrong?"

Ishtar reaches for me again, slipping her warm hand back through the crook of my arm. We cross the threshold into the cool interior of the Tower. It's crowded here, the ground level housing classes for first-year students as well as the administration offices. The ancient architecture has received an update with some creature comforts and modern technology, but the ornate style is still stamped on everything.

Narrow, tall, arched windows allow sunlight to spill over the gray marble floor shot through with silver veins. Just like the rings of a tree, the first ring around the academy is a wide corridor with doors leading into the second ring, where classrooms are found, and the administration offices await in the third ring. The surface of the stone walls are painted a bright blue with mythical creatures marching in rows across its surface. Above the painted wall runs a stone relief, carved in meticulous detail, depicting the Fall and the war between the angels.

My brow arches as I wait for Ishtar to continue when she surprises me yet again. "The Lights have suggested an exchange program to help ease the tensions between our people and bridge a better understanding of each other."

My mind spins as I stare at her, confused. "What? An exchange program?"

Ishtar nods, a slow and satisfied grin curving her lips. "Yes, a Dark Nephilim will spend a year at a Light Nephilim school. We get to choose the school and the student, of course. And Asmodeus has already approved my selection."

A sinking feeling drags at the pit of my stomach. Although I already know the answer, I ask, "And who's the sucker you've chosen?"

Genuine mirth colors her laugh. "You do have a unique way of describing a wonderful opportunity, lovely boy."

"Getting treated like shit by a bunch of stuck-up Lights is an opportunity? Pass."

Her black gaze clashes with mine, and I still at the predatory gleam reflected there. "You'll not only embrace this opportunity, child, you'll thank me for it."

I scowl, both dreading and anticipating her answer. "Why?"

"Because I'm sending you to the academy at Alexandria, and guess who we've discovered is imprisoned deep within the bowels of the Serapeum?"

"Alexander," I breathe, stunned.

"Yes, and you're going to help us free him."

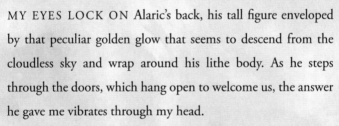

three

LUNA

MY EYES LOCK ON Alaric's back, his tall figure enveloped by that peculiar golden glow that seems to descend from the cloudless sky and wrap around his lithe body. As he steps through the doors, which hang open to welcome us, the answer he gave me vibrates through my head.

"Nephilim."

A few years before I was committed, I took a *History of Religion* class at a Catholic school I was enrolled in during a brief stint with a foster family in Boston. My guardians at the time thought force-feeding me Bible verses would help to suppress my inner demons, like some weird, new-age exorcism. Unlike with the other classes I had to take at that school—and at every other school I ever attended—everything the teacher told us resonated with me like I had heard it somewhere before, a distant memory I couldn't quite bring into focus. My teacher's lessons plunged me into a constant state of déjà vu, and yet I

 33

couldn't explain my fascination with the subject matter.

Especially any part about angels.

From what I remember, the Nephilim were the offspring of angels and humans and were viewed as an abomination by God. But rather than punish the angels for their deviancy, God chose to punish the humans by inflicting them with the worst penalty He could think of.

Mortality.

Or so the stories said. I never had cause to believe any of it was true…until now.

But do I believe it, even after what I've just seen? Maybe this is all a fantasy I've concocted, and the reality is that I'm still at the hospital, living out some grand delusion in my head from the confines of my padded cell. That's the only explanation that makes any sense.

Alaric disappears into the depths of the school, and the imposing doors remain open behind him, as if urging me to follow. The soles of my worn sneakers smack against the cream-colored stone as I race up the wide steps after him.

At the top of the stairs, my feet slow to a stop, and my eyes crawl over the towering entryway. The gilded doors, which stand several stories high, are decorated with protruding shapes depicting an image of angels engaging in battle. Carved clouds separate them into two groups—one above and the other below—and every angel wields a weapon as the world beneath them is consumed by an eddy of swirls my gut tells me is fire.

I glance at each of the angels in turn, but my attention is drawn to one face more than the others. The beauty of the Fallen angel emanates from the shimmering golden surface, and for a moment, I'm hypnotized by his gaze, which looks up at the heavens with rage and remorse. The pain driving his actions seems to leak from the metal, tempting my fingertips to touch his sculpted cheekbones. As my skin grazes the hard interpretation of his, there's a split second where I almost understand what he's feeling.

A gasp parts my lips as the echo of receding footsteps reaches for me through the still open doorway, dragging my thoughts back to my pursuit of Alaric. A long hallway with a high, vaulted ceiling stretches before me, and at the distant end, I spot him.

"Wait!" I yell out, sprinting over the threshold. My hurried steps resound off pristine white tiles cut through with streaks of gold that sparkle in the midday sun filtering in through the narrow stained glass windows lining the walls. The panes channel the light into starbursts of color on the floor. As I race forward, closing the distance between us, I catch glimpses of the statues situated on each side of the path. Seven made of white marble on my right, seven made of black on my left—facing one another across the wide path like opposing chess pieces. Fourteen in total. The statues are angels, some male, others female, but they're all vastly different in their portrayal, with such incredible detail I can't help wondering if they represent real people.

Not people. Angels, I correct myself. Assuming what Alaric has said about this place is true, and I haven't jumped off the metaphorical cliff into full-blown hallucinations.

Alaric glances back over his shoulder and smiles at me with a look that suggests he knew I wouldn't be able to resist following him. He waits patiently at the far end of the corridor, allowing me a chance to catch up.

Once I'm standing beside him, my natural tendency to not question anything in my life fades away. To hell with keeping quiet. None of this, from why I'm here to the mere existence of this place, makes any sense, once again forcing me to doubt if I'm not actually back in the hospital and all of this is just some figment of my imagination. I'm not sure which I'd prefer—the comforting but disappointing notion that I'm normal but crazy or the idea that there's something more to what I am. That, although my entire life might be a lie, there's also some answer as to why I've done the horrible things I've done.

"This is…all…some sort…of joke…right?" Every word escapes me in a pant as I bend over, my hands on my knees, out of breath. Spending a year in a psychiatric ward certainly hasn't done me any favors with fitness. "You don't…*really* think…I'm a—"

He shakes his head. "I *think* nothing, Luna. I *know*. Just like I knew from the second I saw you that you weren't disturbed like all those ignorant mortals believe."

"Mortals?" I straighten, arching a dubious brow at him as a choked laugh escapes me. "You say that like you aren't one."

An amused, crooked grin forms an endearing dimple in his

left cheek. "Half actually. Like all our Nephilim brethren unless we want to get technical with percentages. Our life spans only differ depending on what generation we are. The more diluted the blood, the weaker the ancestral link, and the farther from immortality one is. Of course, anyone with angelic blood will still portray powers. It's merely the strength and lifespan that will differ."

I draw in a faltering breath then push it out through my nose. "Is this some kind of weird test to check my mental state or something? You're not making any sense."

"With time, everything will," he assures me with a chuckle. "Right now, you're in shock, and your body is coming down off the Calm. It's to be expected that this would all seem disorienting."

More like batshit crazy.

I'm debating whether Alaric is as off-his-rocker-bonkers as I am, but I keep those thoughts in check. Clearly, this guy believes what he's spewing.

"Calm?" I ask, wariness creeping into my voice.

Alaric averts his gaze and gestures toward a steepled wooden door behind his right shoulder. Beyond it lies a manicured courtyard filled with species of flowers I've never seen before in my life, in person or in any book. Petals of glimmering gold and silver surround us while others burn with the flaming color of fire. I take it all in as we walk side by side, staying under the cover of the encompassing cloister.

Several moments pass before Alaric breaks the silence. "When we landed in Alexandria, did you feel peculiar at all? As if you'd been asleep for a while and like everything was sort of hazy?"

I think back to when I woke up on the plane, remembering how fuzzy my memories of the previous two days were, and how everything felt like some sort of strange dream I was wading my way through, as if I was waist deep in muddy water. It wasn't the first time I'd experienced such a sensation given how medicated I was at the hospital, and yet, the apprehension that normally went hand in hand with the experience wasn't there this time. Despite the disorientation that muddled my head during the journey here, I wasn't afraid, even though the logical side of me kept insisting I should be. The worst I felt was a grating uncertainty.

"That's called Calm," he explains, clamping a hand on my shoulder. "It helps make the transition process to an academy less daunting for new students, especially those who've had no previous experience being around other Nephilim or were raised to believe they were human, like yourself. It takes away that initial fear. This is, after all, quite the revelation, and yet, it's not as surprising to you as it should be, is it?"

My mouth opens and closes again. He's...not wrong. If he had told me all of this back at the hospital, I probably would've thought he was as crazy as I am. But now, with that instinctual terror and doubt stripped away, I'm not finding what he's said as inconceivable as I should. Could it really be possible? Could

I be a Nephilim? Or am I so desperate for an answer to explain why I am the way I am that I'll believe anything at this point?

I shake my head. Good intentions or not, I can't ignore the sting of betrayal I feel at his words. "So, you drugged me?"

Shrugging away from his touch, I stop walking and stare up at him, the accusation written all over my face. He's been kind, and because of that, I wanted to believe he was different. I *needed* to believe he wasn't like all the doctors who viewed shoving pills down my throat as the only cure for my condition…whatever the hell that is. I don't know anything for sure anymore.

"No," he murmurs, "but I understand why you'd think that. It's more like I used my powers of persuasion to alleviate any worries or anxieties you had."

It occurs to me this is the second time he's used that phrase: *"powers of persuasion."*

"Like how you made that woman at border control think I'm your daughter?" I knew he did something to convince the immigration officer to let us pass. I just didn't know what, or how exactly, he managed to do it.

He nods. "Just like that. I can make others see what I want them to see, and I can make them feel whatever I want them to feel. All Nephilim have their own special abilities. Those happen to be some of mine."

His words tumble through my thoughts as I consider the idea of what he's explaining to me. Every syllable presses against the walls of my brain, offering only one explanation

I'm able to process.

"So...it *is* like magic." My suspicion that he dabbled in tricks of illusion wasn't too far off track after all.

Alaric chuckles. "Something like that. In time, you'll discover how it works for yourself."

He turns and carries on down the stone path, past rows of vibrantly colored flowers and manicured shrubbery. I watch him go, debating if I should follow. Wondering if I even have a choice in the matter.

Pausing at the turn ahead where the cobbled walkway veers off to the right, Alaric waves a hand in beckoning. "Come. There's someone here you should meet."

My chest swells with doubt, but behind it, I sense an overriding calm that I now know Alaric planted there for... what, exactly? To make me believe him? To help with my integration here? To make sure I wouldn't have another outburst that could endanger someone like what happened with my last foster family and the countless others before them? To avoid a repeat of my past incidents? Considering where Alaric found me, he must know that much about my life.

The thought of my past surfaces in the back of my mind, but I push it away before it can choke me. If only Alaric could take away those dark memories, then I'd accept his weird sorcery, no questions asked. Who knows, maybe this place could teach me how to do that. He said it himself—all Nephilim have their own special power.

Maybe mine could help me forget.

Driven by that hope, I trail Alaric through the cloister into a long-stretching corridor of an adjacent building. At least half a dozen wooden doors branch off from this hallway into what I assume must be classrooms. The bits and pieces I catch from the booming voices on the other side of each one confirm that suspicion.

Ornate, carved pillars stand at the end of the passage, framing a set of glass doors leading into what appears to be a surprisingly modern administration office given the aesthetic of the rest of this place. Considering how many times I've transferred schools, I've gotten a vibe for what these offices look like—even if this academy exceeds all expectations of what I've come to expect from even the stuffiest private establishment.

A woman with gleaming chestnut hair twisted into a fashionable braid smiles as we step into the office. Like Alaric, a golden light outlines her body.

"Morning, Evangeline. Is she in?" Alaric jerks his thumb toward a black door in the corner bearing a silver crest of a G in the middle of a shield with wings extended out to each side. Inscribed into the wood around the emblem are tiny feathers, which seem to drift to the floor.

The woman behind the desk—Evangeline—beams up at Alaric with longing in her sapphire eyes. A faint blush stains her cheeks, coloring them a flattering shade of pink as she practically sings, "She sure is."

I cast a sidelong glance at Alaric, wondering if he notices how obviously in love with him this woman is. I've been locked up for the past year and suck at even the most basic social encounter, and even I'm able to see it.

"Great." Pressing a hand to my back, he crosses the office, guiding me toward the black door. The fingers of his free hand curl into a fist as he raps his knuckles three times against the polished, dark wood.

From the other side, I hear a muffled, "Enter."

Alaric inches open the door and pokes his head through the gap. "Headmistress."

"Ah, Alaric," a coy feminine voice says. "I was wondering when you'd turn up again. What news from the outside world?"

"I actually have a new student for you." He pushes the door open the rest of the way to reveal a pristine, spacious office. The furnishings are elegant but sparse—clean and organized with everything in its rightful place—and in the middle of the floor stands a large, wooden desk lined with gold trim, just like everything else I've seen here. Behind the desk, a youthful woman stares at me with wide brown eyes so dark they almost appear black. Only when the light from the window catches her face do I notice the caramel tint to her irises.

"Luna," Alaric continues as the woman rises from her seat, "this is Gabriel. She's the headmistress of this academy."

Gabriel? As in the angel from the Bible?

I gape in disbelief at the statuesque woman before me, my

eyes trailing from her long, ebony hair to the light burning across her ivory skin like a sweeping mass of golden flames. Her features are severe, as if they've been cut from glass, but she's beautiful—more stunning and regal than anyone I've ever seen before in my life. She reminds me of the statues I glimpsed in the entry hall, and despite the fact that she's likely been around longer than the entirety of the human race, she looks to be no older than her late twenties, trapped forever in eternal youth.

I stare at her, unable to tear my gaze away even as her brilliance sears into my retinas. How anyone can stand to look at her blinding radiance for more than a few seconds is baffling.

The flutter in my stomach only grows wilder when she takes a step toward me.

"H-Hi," I stammer, unsure what else to say. How are you meant to greet a renowned angel who's been alive for thousands of years?

Her lips pinch into a tight, reserved smile—an expression I've come to expect from school principals. "Welcome to Alexandria." Her hawk-like eyes turn from my face to Alaric's. "Alaric, may I have a word?"

Gabriel struts toward the window on the right side of her office, which overlooks another lush, vibrant garden. After so long cooped up in my room at the hospital, I'm drawn to the idea of exploring the outdoor spaces offered at this school. Assuming I don't mess things up, get expelled, and end up right back where I started.

When Alaric approaches Gabriel, she grabs his arm and pulls him close to her side.

"Where did you find her?" She says the words under her breath, but I hear every one as clearly as if I'm standing beside them and involved in their conversation instead of being the subject of it. Her gaze burns orange in the light streaming in through the window.

"A psychiatric hospital for adolescents in Maine. Everything you need to know about her is in here." Alaric opens his briefcase and hands Gabriel a large brown envelope containing my medical records, transcripts, and, if I had to guess, a detailed account of my incidents.

"Just…be gentle with her," he whispers. "She's not had the most stable upbringing."

I bristle at the cautious edge to his tone.

"Duly noted." Gabriel takes the envelope from his hand and tosses it across the room onto her desk with a lazy flick of her wrist. Clearing her throat, she fixes the full brunt of her gaze on my face again.

I tremble under the weight of her stare, which narrows the longer she takes me in. When she finally breaks her hold on me, it's as if all the air has been sucked from my lungs, leaving me breathless and lost for words.

Is this her special power? To intimidate her victims to the point of them nearly losing consciousness?

"I'll have a class syllabus prepared for you, which you can

fetch from my assistant, Evangeline, in the morning, along with your uniform and textbooks." Gabriel's voice is a languid monotone. "In the meantime, perhaps Alaric could show you to the dorms."

Her raven hair falls in a curtain across half of her face as she returns to her desk and pulls something from the top drawer, sliding it across a stack of papers. As soon as Alaric retrieves the object, she shuffles the stack with an agitated vigor. When he picks it up, I note it's a small golden key. Taking her silence as our cue to leave, Alaric pushes me through the open doorway. "Come on, Luna," he mutters. Then, in a slightly louder voice, "Gabriel, until next time."

Evangeline offers a polite wave as we leave, but Alaric doesn't seem to notice. Poor girl. With one hand on my back, he ferries me out of the office and into the hallway beyond where we hook a right toward another set of ancient-looking wooden doors. We pass through them into yet another courtyard that leads us into yet another building.

Just how big is this place?

"You seem on edge," Alaric notes as he directs me toward an immense split staircase at the end of our current path, taking the side branching off to the left, and then up a smaller, tucked away set of spiraling marble steps a bit farther down the passage. "What's on your mind? I *am* a doctor. You can tell me anything, and it will stay between us. Doctor-patient confidentiality and all that."

Oh, I don't know. How about this is a lot to take in and all seems absolutely insane? And I would know. I am insane.

I glance back in the direction we came from. "Was that who I think it was?"

"That depends. If you're asking me if the Gabriel you just met is one of the seven Archangels and the Messenger of God, then yes. She is who you think she is."

"Huh. I thought Gabriel was male."

A sigh breaks the rising silence between us. "Religious texts are not always accurate. Have you ever heard of Chinese whispers? Every time a story is told, the details are altered until the original is barely present in the latest telling. Besides, the texts were all written by men, and I'll be the first to admit, we tend to have fragile egos. My gender has a terrible tendency to paint itself as the superior and prominent half of our species. As such, all angels were depicted as male."

"Oh." Another question occurs to me then. "Where are her wings?"

Alaric coughs into his fist to mask a laugh. "Hidden. But I assure you, she has them." His reaction makes me wonder if it's not polite to ask about such things, especially when he says nothing else on the matter.

When we reach the top of the stairs, he leads me down a long hallway, then down another, before turning a corner and signaling to a door a few feet away on the left with the number 317 carved into the rich mahogany surface in gold.

"Here we are. It will take some time to adjust, but this school really is the best place for you. People out there… Let's just say, it's not safe for our kind to be alone and exposed among mortals."

Exposed. The thought forms a lump in my throat.

Alaric fishes out the key Gabriel gave him from his pocket and shoves it into the embellished brass lock. A few seconds pass with his hand on the key, but he doesn't turn it, instead glancing at me out of the corner of his eye.

"I understand this is a lot to accept." His voice is soft and low. Calming. Is he using his gift on me now? Is he robbing me of feeling the full extent of everything I would otherwise be experiencing given the absurdity of what he's telling me? "You've been through so much in your short life already that couldn't be explained by rational thought. But you lived through those traumatizing events, and more than that, you *survived* them. Now, it's time for you to thrive."

Tears blur the edges of my vision as the inescapable hand of shame tightens around my throat. "If you're talking about what I did—"

"None of that was your fault. Everything you did was an unfortunate side effect of not knowing what you are. This place will help you figure out who that is."

He rotates the key, unbolting the door. My gaze sweeps over the bright interior of my new home—the room furnished and complete with all the essentials I'll need, like bedding and an alarm clock on the side table—before darting to Alaric's retreating figure. He quietly heads back the way we came without so much as saying goodbye.

"Are you leaving?" Panic makes my voice unsteady.

"I'm afraid I have to," he says. Although he's stopped walking, he keeps his back to me. "My job entails that I leave for varying stretches of time, but I'll be back before you know it. And when I am, you can tell me all about how you're getting on here. Sound good?"

"Okay," I whisper, although I'm not sure how I feel about him abandoning me. I'd hate to think that Gabriel will be the only familiar face I'll have in this place.

She might be an angel—as weird as that is to admit—but there's something about the way she acted during our meeting that doesn't sit well with me. Her behavior was too reminiscent of the doctors who were so quick to declare me mentally unfit for life around other people.

"What *is* your job, anyway?"

Alaric's gaze drifts over his shoulder to me. "I travel the world in search of possible Nephilim."

"Like me." It's the first time I've said it aloud. The first time I've dared to believe this could all really be happening.

"Yes," he says with a cautious smile, his eyes glowing with an emotion resembling sadness. Or fear. "Just like you, Luna."

four

CALEB

ISHTAR LEADS ME TO her office in silence, opening the iron door for me, which was once black, but is now green with age. I sink into the gold embossed settee she's placed for students. Along one wall, books cover the entire surface. Books written on vellum and papyrus. Books human scholars would kill to possess. Along the other wall, sickle-shaped swords and spears crafted from iron hang over a wooden shelf displaying ancient pottery and miniature carved figures that are hand-painted.

My eyes snag on a figure of Ishtar herself. Ha! The artist got her expression wrong. I've never seen Ishtar look that serene.

The Mesopotamian goddess seats herself behind a modern desk complete with a sleek laptop. Her eyes clash with mine and she grins.

"You've been good long enough," she muses. "Ask." She waves an imperious hand.

"Are you sure he's really there?" I demand, my mind reeling.

"How do you know? How can I free him?"

I don't think the headmistress of the Serapeum, Gabriel, will allow me free rein of her academy to search for one of their greatest enemies. *Oh, hey, pardon me, has anyone seen my gramps? You know, the guy who almost conquered Earth? Oh, he's under there. Why, thank you. Maybe you're not a total prick.* Yeah. Not.

She nods. "We're certain."

"Who's we?" I ask, craving more information. That's part of what we're taught here in the Tower. Ask, ask, and then ask some more.

Ishtar tilts her head, her expression carefully blank. "What is that delightful phrase mortals use? Oh, yes. It's above your pay grade."

Unease flickers through me once more, stronger this time. That's not a very Dark answer to give and leads me to believe an Archdemon has a hand in this. There are seven Archdemons who rule the Fallen and the Dark Nephilim, and they're all powerful, but Lucifer still runs the show. The Morningstar is content with his place on Earth, but not all the Archdemons are. Some resent the ban from their birthplace. And some Nephilim, like the goddess in front of me, also resent their secret, shadowy existence. Asmodeus is the head of our academy, her beauty as fiery as her temper. She's never outright preached rebellion— well, she has already participated in the biggest rebellion in history—but she and Ishtar do get along like thorns on roses.

But if Lucifer isn't on board with this plan, then I shouldn't be either. Ishtar observes me under hooded lids, but I don't let my discomfort show, hoping my silence will prod her into revealing more information.

A heavy sigh escapes her lips. "Darling boy, stop worrying. You trouble yourself for no reason. As Alexander's grandson, do you think I'd put you in harm's way? You know how we value bloodlines here, and his is strong as are you." Her stare is flinty. "And besides, Alexander was a friend of mine. He almost did what I could not, what I dreamed of. I wouldn't dishonor him by treating his kin like a lamb to be sent to slaughter."

I hear the truth in her words, but how much truth? Yes, the Dark and Light Nephilim prize bloodlines, no matter how diluted. And yes, she's a regular fangirl for my gramps. She might even secretly have his name tattooed on her ass, but I know she's not being open with me. She's already admitted it.

Her voice turns low and rich, like dark chocolate melting over strawberries. "Don't you want to know him, Caleb? Don't you want to learn from him? Think of all the things he could teach you." Her mouth twists into a scowl as she spits the last words, "He would never be so careless with you the way your cursed father is with his offspring."

I feel like she's sucker punched me. Ishtar rarely criticizes my father, although she doesn't think much of him, believing he hasn't lived up to the legend of Alexander and is rather useless, other than as a sperm donor. I know I have a trail of brothers and sisters out there, but I don't know who they are. Apparently, that's a condition my pops made with the Archdemons, a deal they only honor to avoid us creating our own little army and accidentally exposing all angelkind to the humans. Secrecy above all and what not. When his children are brought to one of the seven Dark academies, they aren't to be told they have family at any of the schools. Our blood doesn't sing to one another because the Archdemons put a blood bind on us, so we can't identify our family. In fact, the bind repels us from one another, so we don't accidentally get horizontal with a sibling. That would be disturbing. Of course, I only know this because Ishtar once let it slip that dear old Dad didn't want his kids to unite against him and hunt him down. Yeah, he should be afraid. I'd love a family reunion where I could take a turn beating his ass.

Whatever Ishtar's truth may be, my truth is I do want to know my grandfather. I *long* for it. And yeah, maybe Ishtar is playing me like a prized violin, but I don't think even she's crazy enough to go against the Morningstar, despite her extremist views. The Lights and Darks have both done shitty things to each other. Why should Alexander be punished his entire life? Sure, he tried to take over the world, but he's suffered enough for his folly.

Giving a slow nod, I say, "Okay, I'll do it. But how do you expect me to find him? No one in that place is going to volunteer info, and I doubt the student body even knows he's there. They're too busy stroking each others' harps and dreaming about their wings. And if they know I'm Alexander's grandson, I doubt they'll let me within ten feet of that school."

A huff of laughter slips past Ishtar's lips. "I do so love the colorful way you put things. Stroking each others' harps, indeed." Her face grows serious once more. "Caleb, you should know we don't give bloodline information to the Lights. They have no idea who you are. You have many gifts, lovely boy, like all the Nephilim, but you have a very special gift that you wield with precision. One that will be very useful in this mission."

I grin. "Oh, you want me to break into people's minds." Now that I think about it, that *is* the obvious answer, and I'm very good at it. My smile fades. "I got mad skills, but I don't know if I can break into a first generation's mind or an Archangel's," I admit, thinking of Gabriel, who runs the academy in Alexandria. From what I hear, she's an ice queen who is more than capable of taking your head with her sword. A total badass.

Ishtar braids her hands together on top of her desk. "I have faith in you, Caleb. And besides, you don't necessarily need to break into an angel's mind. All you need to do is plant the seed of curiosity in a vulnerable student and tend the seed and see what grows."

I chuckle. "That's easy. And fun," I add. Normally, I'm pretty responsible with my powers, but against Lights, I don't really feel the need to hold back. They've never exactly thrown kindness my way.

Ishtar stands and I follow. "Good. Now that that's settled, go pack your things and say goodbye to your friends. Meet me in the Hanging Gardens in one hour. Don't be late."

I hurry to the door when she throws out, "Oh, they're going to make you wear a uniform."

Whirling around, I stare at her. "Are you kidding me?" I glance down at my faded jeans and soft, black T-shirt and scuffed boots.

"Sheep dress alike, darling," she says, grinning, and I groan.

Ugh, Lights. Assholes.

I fist bump my best friend, Rafe, with one hand while I adjust my backpack on my shoulder. Then I grip a small roller suitcase. I have a lot more stuff, but I don't know how long this goodwill exchange program will last. Best to pack light.

"Man, you're really going into a Light school? With those holier-than-the-Creator little shits?" Rafe asks, scowling. His bright green eyes fill with disbelief as he shakes his head.

Rolling my luggage across the main foyer, I shrug. "Yup, keeping the peace and all that. Good will to all the little Nephilim."

Rafe snorts. "Fuck that," he says. "It'll be boring as hell here without you. I'll have no one to compete with for the top spot."

I can't suppress my smug grin. I'm not just a pretty boy—I've got a brain and plenty of talent. I share the top spot at the Tower of Babel Academy with Rafe and my friend, Shalina. All three of us occupy that position at different times as if we're all in an endless game of musical chairs.

"I'm counting on Shalina to kick your ass to Heaven and back," I counter, surprised when a slight flush creeps up his neck. "Dude, you and Shalina?" Shalina is my friend but she isn't Rafe's. They share a healthy loathing for each other—or at least I thought they did. Well, I guess all that tension had to go somewhere.

"Shut it," Rafe snarls. Then he pretends to look at his watch and grins. "You better hurry, or you'll be late, and Ishtar will kick your ass."

I flip him off and he chuckles. "Later," I say.

Rafe's expression sobers. "Be careful, Caleb. I don't trust those Lights."

I nod. "Will do." We bump knuckles one more time, and I walk through the massive front doors and down the long trail of stone steps, my suitcase bouncing behind me.

The afternoon sun sizzles and I squint, cursing myself for not wearing my sunglasses. I trod across ancient, uneven stone until I reach the Hanging Gardens and the sweet, fresh air there. Ishtar isn't alone. The tall, severe figure of Hammurabi stands next to her. He looks every inch the Babylonian king this morning, despite his modern clothing. His black beard hangs in neat curls, and he wears a capped turban around his head banded by a circlet of gold. His hawkish features are harsh, but I know more than a few females in the academy who lust for him. He's a goddamn honey pot. In all honesty, he plays by the rules, so I'm always taken by surprise he's on team Fallen. He and Ishtar have locked horns more than once because of her "I deserve to take over the world" views. But he's a total warrior and I admire him. Between training with him and Ishtar, my combat skills are well-honed.

He nods at me. "Caleb, Ishtar tells me you are to be our representative in this…diplomatic endeavor."

I wink at Ishtar. "She picked me because of my charm."

Hammurabi crosses his arms over his massive chest, frowning, but I just flash a grin. "Caleb, this is a serious matter. Tensions are high between our factions, and the fact that they've offered this olive branch means a great deal."

I grow serious. "Yeah, I know. I won't let the Tower of Babel Academy down. I'll do you all proud."

"I'd whip you within an inch of your life if you let us down," he says casually, and I hide my flinch. Did I mention Hammurabi is old school? I mean read his code of laws.

"I hardly think that will be necessary, old friend," Ishtar counters, rolling her eyes.

Hammurabi glares at her before shifting his gaze back to me. "You're a very bright boy, Caleb. So while you will do your best to succeed on this diplomatic mission, you'll keep your eyes and ears open, yes? This may be a genuine offer from the Archangels to soothe tensions, but just in case there's treachery afoot, you are to remain vigilant and report anything suspicious you see or hear. Understood?"

I dart Ishtar a quick look under my lashes, but her face remains blank. Hmm, I doubt the Babylonian king knows about Alexander. That's not a super comforting thought. Then again, he's not exactly Ishtar's main confidant.

I nod. "Yes, sir."

One big hand slides into a sheath hanging at his hip, and he pulls a dagger free and holds it out to me. My eyes narrow as I take in the beauty of the weapon. The hilt consists of gold with patterns of mythical creatures engraved upon it, their eyes decorated with jewels such as lapis lazuli, carnelian, and jasper. But that's not the most fantastic thing about the dagger. Etched into the gleaming steel is Enochian script. I can recognize it, but I can't read it. Both the Archangels and Archdemons keep their native tongue guarded like the Mona Lisa, unwilling to share it with us Nephilim. Eyes widening, I stare at Hammurabi. My mind blanks as I search for words. He can't be offering me this, can he? Shit.

A grin breaks his fierce exterior. "So, you do know what this is?"

"I…uh…yes," I fumble. This dagger is a weapon from the Fall. They're forbidden now, locked away or destroyed, so I have no idea where Hammurabi got his hands on one. "But why—do you think I'll need that?" I glance at Ishtar for explanation, but she stares at the knife, her lips twisted in a sneer.

"I still can't believe this was in the museum at Babel this whole time, and I didn't know," she says, shaking her head as if to clear it.

Hammurabi's smile disappears, his face smoothing into an

expressionless mask at her words. His stillness at her casual comment makes me uneasy, but then he focuses on me, his mouth flattening. "I hope you won't need it. This is a last resort. No one must discover you have this—no one, Caleb. Understood?"

I give a frantic nod, still shell-shocked. I take the dagger from him, a near silent hum emanating from the metal and invading my ears. It's light and agile, but it feels as heavy as iron shackles around my soul. This weapon can harm an angel, Dark or Light. I mean, if I punch an angel hard enough in the face, I might hurt them, but they won't bleed. But this? This will make them bleed like a mortal. This dagger will cause serious damage. I swallow hard.

"Not to sound like a dumbass, but where am I going to hide this thing?" I ask. "If I'm caught with this, the Lights will execute me for sure, peacekeeping efforts be damned."

Hammurabi nods toward Ishtar and says tersely, "Show him."

Ishtar bristles at the command but takes out a black silk drawstring bag from the pocket in her gown. "Give it to me." With almost relief, I hand over the dagger. She slips it into the bag and draws the string shut, only now I can't see the bag at all.

Shaking my head, I blink rapidly. Ishtar holds her palm open, as if she balances something, but all I see is empty air. I reach out for her hand, and my fingers brush against silk. Startled, I yank my hand back and they both laugh.

"Concealment spells," Ishtar says, smiling. "This bag takes on the exact appearance of its environment and suppresses the power of whatever object it carries."

"This is the shit," I say, and Hammurabi frowns at me, but I ignore him. With careful hands, I place the dagger in the folds of clothes in my roll-on luggage. After I finish, I look at Ishtar.

"It's time," she says.

"Until we meet again, Caleb." Hammurabi gives a shallow bow and marches in the direction of the Tower.

"So, um, you sure you want to take me? I can totally get there on my own. I mean, *he's*—"

Ishtar's glower shrivels everything below my belt, and my jaw snaps shut with an audible click.

I can almost see frost form in the air when she speaks. "He is of no concern. As your teacher, it is my duty to see you to Alexandria."

She marches farther into the shadows of a fruit tree and holds out an elegant hand. I step into the deep puddle of shade and grasp her fingers. And then we step *into* the shadows.

The Shadow Road swallows us whole, and we land on a dirt path, our surroundings smeared, like charcoal drawings. The Road ahead and behind us is barren and desolate and cold. I suppress a shiver as I walk beside Ishtar. We pass marker after marker, all identical to each other—if you don't know what you're looking for. To travel the Shadow Road is a Fallen gift, although not all of us can access it. If the bloodline is too diluted, the Road does not recognize you. When training to use it, I accidentally ended up on the Great Wall of China. I don't know who was more shocked, me or the tourists when I popped out of thin air.

Ishtar finds the marker she's searching for, and we step off the Road into the scorching sun of Alexandria, directly in front of the Serapeum. I raise my eyebrows as I observe the opulent academy, its cream-colored, marble exterior gleaming against the azure sky. It's blinding in its purity. I snort.

"Do you think it needs a touch of white? Subtle, aren't they?" I ask Ishtar.

A cruel smile plays upon her lips. "Subtlety was never their strong suit."

We make our way up the steps when the gilded, towering doors open, and a tall man strides out. People say Gilgamesh looks like those statues the Greeks used to make celebrating male perfection or some shit. I don't know about that, but he moves like an athlete, and I bet he packs a mean punch. He smiles at me in greeting, a friendly gesture that morphs into something unreadable as he turns to Ishtar.

I glance at Ishtar and have to stop my tongue from rolling out of my mouth. I thought she'd be all warrior goddess, but she's emitting seductress like it's a homing beacon for any male in a hundred-mile radius. Her scarlet lips are pouted, and an artful hand on her hip pushes out her rather amazing rack. However much he may not want to be affected, Gilgamesh is not immune. I see heat flash in his eyes before he shuts it down. The tension and silence stretches and stretches between them until I'm in desperate need of a cold shower. Ugh, I'm stuck at a Light school where I'll never get laid, and these two decide to eye fuck in front of me. I hate them both.

I clear my throat, not caring if I piss off Ishtar, just desperate to get away. "Um, I'll just leave you to it," I say, hooking a thumb toward the academy's entrance. "Gilgamesh, take your time with...*catching* up. I'll just be up there. Waiting."

I give a furious Ishtar a salute and hurry up the stairs, not caring whether Gilgamesh follows, or the two of them tear each other's clothes off or just tear into each other. It could go either way. I just got here, and I'm already sick of the drama between the Darks and the Lights because I know this will be my daily life with the Light students, well, minus the sexual tension. I just have to think of Alexander. My grandfather is what matters. Freeing him is my focus.

I hear Gilgamesh's voice behind me, calling out for me to stop. I turn and put my game face on. He wears a look of apology, and Ishtar is nowhere in sight. Man, I'll probably catch hell for that stunt later.

"I apologize, Caleb," he rumbles. "That was...unfortunate. And unprofessional, frankly. Welcome to the Serapeum Academy. We're so happy to have you join us." He holds out a hand.

Happy, ha! I glance at his hand warily, like it's a snake waiting to bite me. Finally, I sigh and shake it. Welcome to the Serapeum Academy, indeed, Caleb. Not. It's going to be a long year.

five

LUNA

MY FINGERS TUG AT the starchy collar hugging my throat before moving to the tie hanging around my neck like a noose. The silky material is the same red as blood—*"A symbol of our celestial bloodlines,"* Evangeline told me when I went to pick up my schedule from the office this morning. Along with my schedule and the textbooks I would need for my classes, she provided me with a bundle of new day-to-day clothes and the uniform I'm expected to wear during school hours: a crisp, white button-up shirt, ruby skirt, and matching tie embroidered with the insignia of the school.

This isn't the first time I've had to wear a uniform, but as I glare at myself in the full-length mirror fixed to the back of my dorm room door, I struggle to recognize the person looking back at me. For so long, I've avoided mirrors out of shame and refusal to face my deep-seated trauma, afraid to face the monster I knew I'd find staring back. Seeing the guilt in my eyes

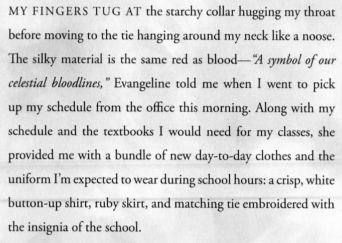

only makes the horrors of my life that much more real.

Swallowing, I glance away from my reflection, my gaze catching on the small white box on my desk. My teeth sink into my lower lip as the memory of my encounter with Evangeline earlier comes rushing back.

After collecting my textbooks and uniform—and after muttering a soft "thank you" to the older Nephilim—I set off back in the direction of the dorms to prepare for my first lesson of the day. I barely made it halfway down the adjoining hallway when Evangeline burst out of the office, shouting, "Luna, wait!"

Startled, I turned back to face her, noting the small white box clenched within the cage of her fingers.

"I almost forgot," she said, rolling her eyes as she bopped herself in the forehead with the palm of her free hand. She then held out the box, which I eyed suspiciously. "From Alaric. He dropped it off this morning."

Confusion marred my brow. "I thought he had already left Alexandria," I muttered.

Grinning, she shrugged a delicate shoulder. "So did I. But there he was at the crack of dawn, sitting on the edge of my desk, waiting for me." A dreamy look passed over her face at the recollection, and a lovelorn sigh parted her lips. Blushing under my scrutiny, she offered me a bashful smile before clearing her throat. "Anyway, he insisted that I get this to you."

"What is it?" Frowning, I took the box from her hands, handling it with the care of a bomb disposal technician.

"I'm not sure. He just said that he thought you might need it."

My heart hammered against my ribcage as I carefully pulled the lid off the box and peered inside, my left eyebrow hooking upward at the sight of the cell phone nestled within, lying in a bed of red and white tissue paper. A folded note was tucked in beside it.

Luna,

I know how lonely this must all be for you so if you ever feel the urge to talk or need to vent about something, I'm here. You can call or text me anytime, day or night. I've programmed my cell number into the contacts. I hope to hear from you soon.

Affectionately,
Alaric

As I slip out of the memory, I consider his offer. I've never had someone to talk to before, not really. Not when all the adults in my life up to this point abandoned me the moment they realized I was trouble. But Alaric—he knows what I am. He knows about my past, every dark, awful detail, and has reached out to me in spite of it all. Maybe he will be different, like I first felt at the hospital, even if I'm too afraid to hope for as much.

Maybe I should give him a call later…to thank him for the phone.

A quick glance at the phone reaffirms my decision when

the screen lights up, buzzing with a text notification. Plucking it from the box, I swipe my thumb over the screen and peer hesitantly down at the message.

Good luck with your first day of classes. -A

My chest tightens, and a smile tempts the edges of my lips. I don't think anyone's ever wished me luck before. I nod to myself, resolved. I definitely need to call him. But right now, I have to get to class or I'll be late. Placing the phone back in the box, I collect the pile of leather-bound books from my desk and head for the door, stepping out into the empty hallway, prepared as much as I can be for my first day as a student of the Serapeum Academy for Light Nephilim.

It's still so unbelievable to me. When I woke up this morning, I half-expected everything, from the plane ride to meeting Gabriel, to be nothing more than a dream. A vivid dream, but a dream. On some level, I suppose I still do, like I'm waiting for the other shoe to drop.

Perhaps because I don't really know what it means to be a Nephilim, or what this school expects from me. All I can hope is that this place will teach me how to control whatever impulses have led me to do the terrible things I've done. And who knows? Maybe, in the process, I'll find the one thing I ever really wanted.

A home.

I follow the spiraling steps nearest my room to the bottom floor of the girls' wing of the dormitory, retracing my path from yesterday and this morning. The student residences intersect at a massive split staircase, which I hurry down before continuing onward through one of the academy's many courtyards to the building of classrooms, which luckily isn't too far given the vast size of this place. The door to my first class, *History of the Fall 101*, is the second to last on my right. *An introductory class,* I realize with dread, double-checking my schedule with a pained wince. Great. I might as well wear a sign on my head that reads *Newbie Nephilim* in large letters.

The space on the other side of the heavy wooden door is modern like the office, which is surprising considering the rest of the school looks like the inside of a centuries old cathedral or temple. Twenty desks are arranged in four rows of five, facing a dry erase board, which spans most of the wall situated at the front of the room. Beside it stands a tall, muscular man with broad shoulders who looks like he could be the poster boy for the Olympics. His sleeves are rolled up to his elbows, exposing the rich golden skin of his sculpted forearms, which strain as he writes in a book propped against the crook of his opposite elbow. Dark umber eyes scan the room, flicking from the students down to the book, as his mouth, framed by neatly trimmed ebony facial hair, soundlessly mutters every name.

Like Alaric and Evangeline, this man has a strange golden glow vibrating around his body like an outline of pulsing light. It's nowhere near as strong as Gabriel's, but still bright enough I'm tempted to hold up my hand to shield my eyes from his glory.

Palms sweating, I cross the room, tightly gripping my books, which threaten to slip from my grasp at any moment. My meek voice barely penetrates my trembling lips.

"Excuse me."

The man looks up at me, flashing pearly white teeth. "Ah, you must be Luna. I'm Gilgamesh. I'll be your teacher for *History of the Fall*."

He holds out a hand for me to shake, but I can't bring myself to take it. At least the few times Alaric touched my shoulder or back, he never encouraged me to reciprocate the gesture. If these people know what's good for them, they won't expect me to, either.

Gilgamesh lowers his hand and offers me a kindhearted look that seems to say, *Don't worry about it.* He then breaks my gaze and waves his hand at the desks. "Just sit anywhere. Oh, and try not to be too anxious. We're all here to help one another."

Keeping my head down, I make my way toward the back of the room where I spot two empty seats. The other desks are already occupied—I must be one of the last to arrive—and although Alaric insisted the other students are just like me, I can't find the nerve to lift my eyes and confirm that. I've been through the whole new school thing enough times to know that I never fit in.

My skin burns as I walk toward the empty desks. I can sense

it—the other students staring at me. They don't mask their curiosity or even attempt to lower their voices. At least the kids at my other schools had the decency to pretend they weren't talking about me.

"Hey, is that her?" one girl says to her friend in a British accent as I shuffle past. Out of the corner of my eye, I glimpse yellow-blonde hair.

"Must be," the other girl answers in a deep Southern twang. An American, like me. "I'd steer clear," she adds in a tone of indifference, as if she finds the whole mystery of who I am to be unworthy of her time. "Yasmin told me she overheard a few of the teachers talking about her, and one of them straight up said she's crazy."

The hair on the back of my neck bristles when she utters that word—that awful, hateful word. Sinking my teeth into my lower lip, I hug my books even tighter to keep a hold on my emotions. I can't lose it, not now. Not when I only just got here.

I fix my gaze on one of the two unoccupied desks in the back row and slide into the empty chair. As I place my books on the floor under my seat, I glance up to find the two girls staring at me like I'm an animal in a zoo. They're both pretty in that airbrushed, magazine cover kind of way, but look a few years younger than me. As I glance around the room, I note that I seem to be the oldest student in this class. Wonderful. There's nothing quite like being surrounded by a bunch of immature gossips who all think they're better than you. As I shift my focus back to the duo, I realize that, like everyone else I've seen in this place, their skin beams with noticeable outlines of light.

I turn my hand over on top of my desk and peer down at my own non-glowing skin. If I'm a Nephilim, then why don't I have an aura like they do?

"Really?" My eyes flick upward, settling on the blonde girl's pinched face. Her lips purse as she tilts her head. "She looks normal enough to me."

"Yeah." The other girl, the American, flicks a loose lock of rusty brunette hair over her shoulder. "Apparently, she killed a few mortals and burned down a building and a bunch of other crazy shit. They even tried to have her exorcized."

Sucking in a sharp breath, I fist my hands into my lap and look back down at my desk.

Block them out, I urge myself. But I can't. Every word they say reaches my ears with ease—cutting at the threads holding together my already questionable sanity. They chat as if the subject of their conversation isn't sitting only a few seats away.

"No way." The shock is apparent in the British girl's voice.

As is the scathing disdain in the brunette's.

"Yup." I can almost hear the smile in her tone, as if she's taking pleasure in my discomfort.

My jaw tenses as I fight the temptation to scream out that she doesn't know what she's talking about. She doesn't have a clue what it's like to be me.

"All right, everyone." Gilgamesh claps his hands, silencing

the students' chatter and drawing everyone's attention to the front of the room. "Eyes on me. Ellie and Lisbeth, that means you, too."

The two girls whip around in their seats, but not before the brunette sneaks in a venomous sneer at me. I crumple beneath her leering gaze.

"First, we have a new student joining our ranks, so let's all do our best to make her feel welcome." Gilgamesh gives me a slight nod of acknowledgment but doesn't bother introducing me to the class. It strikes me as odd, considering what it's been like every other time I started at a new school. Then again, he's probably aware of my history and knows I don't do well with being put on the spot.

Hey, maybe being the crazy girl can work to my advantage this time and get me out of any mandatory class participation.

Gilgamesh turns his back to us and grabs a marker from the tray at the base of the dry erase board. Ripping off the cap, he writes the word *Recap* in large, elegant script.

"Today, I'm going to backpedal a bit and go through what we've learned so far about the Fall. This is a good opportunity for those of you who haven't been taking notes as this *will* be on the midterm." He casts a knowing glance over his shoulder at a deeply tanned male student sitting in the second row by the windows. "I'm looking at you, Jared," he says, arching a thick eyebrow.

The boy hunches his shoulders and sinks into his seat as the other students laugh at his expense. Gilgamesh seems to take no notice as he hastily scribbles a word on the board. My lungs tighten as my eyes rake over each letter.

Creator

"In the early days of humanity, all the angels lived in Heaven under the rule of the Creator. They were charged with protecting the newly made humans, for the Creator loved them dearly. Almost as much, if not more so, than the angels themselves."

A few students sitting in front of me yawn, and the wisps of their auras flatten into a lethargic slumber, their visible boredom suggesting they've heard this lecture a thousand times before. Their indifference agitates me as I cling to Gilgamesh's every word, entranced by the story of their ancestors. *My* ancestors. He paces in front of the board, recounting the details of a time I always thought was fiction.

"This angered one angel in particular who envied the humans for having free will and desired the same freedom for himself and his brethren. Can anyone tell me who that angel was?" His dark eyes jump from student to student until someone finally raises their hand.

Gilgamesh points to a red-headed girl in the front row.

"Lucifer Morningstar," she answers.

"Correct." Gilgamesh spins back toward the board and quickly scrawls a few more keywords for the class. Although I know I should be taking notes, I'm too transfixed by his story to move.

Looks like Jared and I will be failing the midterm together.

"So," Gilgamesh continues, "Lucifer rebelled against the Creator, and that rebellion led to what we know as the Fall. Now, just before the Fall, during the Great Battle of Heaven, the angels became divided into those who followed Lucifer in his quest for free will, commonly known as the Fallen, and those who sided with the Creator, who we all know as the Faithful. When the battle ended with the Fall, the two groups' differing desires led to their abilities and wings transforming to reflect either the darkness or light, with their bloodlines carrying on that change as a permanent reflection of their choice. Thus, one race was torn into two, with angels loyal to the Light and demons to the Dark.

"*But...*" He enunciates the word, his voice dropping an octave. "Despite their differences, the angels and demons still had one thing in common. Regardless of which side they chose, they all spent a significant amount of time on Earth— the Fallen reveling in their new freedom while the Faithful continued doing the Creator's bidding and looking over the newborn human race as intended. On both sides, many even went so far as to mate with the humans during that period, creating a new race of creatures known as the Nephilim, who were predisposed to favor the darkness or the light depending on their bloodlines."

My ears prick up at the mention of Nephilim. Gilgamesh

meets my gaze across the room, flashing me a quick, hooded look, as if to say, *Yes, Luna. This is your history. It's real. Embrace it.*

"These offspring were half-mortal but incredibly powerful due to the celestial blood in their veins. However, many didn't know how to wield it, and since the humans who mothered and fathered the Nephilim were unaware of the existence of angels and demons, they incorrectly assumed their mates and their resulting children were like them: ordinary. As such, they were completely unprepared for the reality of raising a Nephilim child—a task made infinitely harder for many when the Creator called the Faithful back to Heaven and forbade them from having any direct involvement with their children. The Creator also proclaimed that all Nephilim would reside here on Earth and that they would be bound by the limitations of their mortal blood, regardless of their parentage. Their lives would be long, but they would one day expire. This was the punishment for the angels' intimacy with the humans they were charged to look after, which the Creator viewed as a threat to their loyalty and love for Him. If so many had not already been lost to the Fall, the Creator might have even cast the guilty out of Heaven. Instead, He chose to be merciful, imparting a new law on his Faithful children. From that point on, any physical union between the Faithful and humans was forbidden.

"And so, the ignorant humans were left to care for and subsequently grew to fear their half-angel offspring. The Fallen, who remained on Earth, did their best to hide their own children from human eyes, but exposure was inevitable and left them all open to persecution. In those days, due to their notable differences to the humans, the Nephilim were either revered as gods or put to death, an impressive feat considering these were first generations who, as we all know, can't be easily killed." An amused grin tugs at his lips at this comment, and the class lets out a collective chuckle, as if they're in on a joke that's flown over my head. If I had to guess, I'd say, based on the boastful look on his face and his renowned role in early human history, Gilgamesh is probably a first generation, which means he was there when all these horrors occurred.

No, he wasn't just there. He survived it.

A shudder rolls over my skin when his gaze darkens and his voice takes on a solemn note. "This went on for many long years, and it's said the Fallen and Faithful wept for seven days every time one of their children was burned alive or beheaded."

Tears blur the edges of my vision as Gilgamesh's narrative takes a familiar shape in my head. As an orphan, I know what it's like to be cast aside, like many of those Nephilim were. The only difference is, nowadays, they don't murder you for having a problem that defies rational thought, as Alaric phrased it. They just lock you up in a loony bin where life passes you by as you waste away.

Alone and forgotten.

I blink the moisture from my eyes and watch as Gilgamesh writes the number seven on the dry erase board. He circles it twice—once in black marker and then again in gold.

"Out of love for their children and concern for their safety, both sides eventually agreed to a truce. With the Creator's blessing, seven of His favored Faithful were allowed to return to Earth and work with seven powerful Fallen to oversee the fledgling Nephilim and establish fourteen schools as safe harbor—seven of Light, seven of Dark. Together, they formed a council of Archangels and Archdemons, and each became responsible for one of the schools, built with the help of the eldest Nephilim with the intent of training the future generations and keeping them safe from the humans who would seek to destroy them out of fear. And thus, the angels' and demons' focus turned away from war and settled on the measures needed to avoid the exposure and destruction of our kind. Now"—he spins on his heel again, facing the class—"can anyone tell me where the seven schools of Light are located?"

The brunette who sneered at me raises her hand. "We have the primary academies at Mount Nebo and Petra, then the secondary academies at Mount Sinai, Mount Zion, Qumran, Sidon, and here, at the Serapeum in Alexandria."

"Very good, Lisbeth," Gilgamesh praises. "Any volunteers who can tell me where the Dark academies are located? How about you, Jared? Let's see how well you've been paying attention."

Jared jerks upright in his seat. "Uhh…" He hesitates then slowly counts off on his fingers in French before answering in perfect English. "The primary academies are in Sodom and

Gomorrah. Then there's the secondary academy at Megiddo…"

"That's right, keep going," Gilgamesh urges with an encouraging nod.

"Ashkelon," Jared mutters. "Tyre, uhh… Machaerus, and—"

"The Tower of Babel," a deep voice finishes from the hallway.

A sharp inhale fills the silence in the room as all eyes fall on the boy at the door. He's dressed in the same uniform the rest of us wear, but where our shirts are white, his shirt and pants are as black as the obsidian hair crowning his head.

He stands propped against the door frame with his arms crossed—shirt sleeves pushed up to his elbows—and a gloating smile twisting his lips. The overhead lights bounce off his bronze skin as dark mischievous eyes scan the room. Whispers erupt around me, but I don't take note of a single word the other Lights say. All I can focus on is the aura enveloping the newcomer's body—the rich shades of dark blue and purple entwined with black, like tiny wisps of shadow reaching out to entice me.

Gilgamesh lifts his chin and snorts. "I see you've finally decided to join us. Come in and take a seat."

The boy straightens and struts into the room as if he doesn't have a single care in the world. He looks a bit older than the other students in this class—probably closer in age to me, seventeen or eighteen by the looks of him—and as he walks, he leans into each step with a confidence I can only dream of. He certainly doesn't have any of the new student awkwardness

I always seem to exude. Even the mutterings of the students around us don't seem to faze him.

"Is he…" Ellie whispers.

"Oh, my God," Lisbeth gasps.

Gilgamesh claps in an effort to draw the class's attention back to him. "Everyone, this is Caleb, and he's coming to us from the Tower of Babel Academy. He'll be spending the year with us."

Lisbeth jumps up from her seat and slams her hands down on her desk. "But he's a *Dark*," she hisses with a vehemence in her voice I don't quite understand.

My mind wanders back through Gilgamesh's lesson, remembering what he said about the angels taking sides during the Great Battle of Heaven and how that choice carried on through their bloodlines after the Fall. This new student must be one of these Dark Nephilim he mentioned.

And so what if he is? What's the big deal? Surely, by now, after so many years, the Darks and Lights have learned to co-exist.

"That's enough." Gilgamesh's booming voice makes Lisbeth shiver, and she falls back into her seat as if her legs have been swept out from under her. "We are welcoming Caleb to our school in the spirit of friendship. I expect you all to treat him with the same civility you would impart on each other. Now, let's move on."

The lecture, which had me captivated before, fails to hold my focus once the transfer student—Caleb—sits down. The only empty desk stands less than three feet to my left.

Swallowing, I peek at him out of the corner of my eye, bewitched by the shadows licking over his skin. They're eerie and haunting but astonishing. Beautiful. Unlike with the Light Nephilim, I don't feel an overwhelming need to look away, like I'll be blinded by his aura if I don't. If anything, my eyes want to linger on his face and devour that darkness forever.

Caleb looks over at me, and my cheeks flush with heat once I realize he's caught me staring at him. A sly grin hitches up the corners of his mouth as he angles himself across the side of his desk. Holding up a finger, he signals for me to lean in—like he wants to tell me something. Entranced, I do as he beckons, closing the distance between us.

When our faces are only a few inches apart, he looks me up and down with disgust.

"Take a picture," he scoffs. "It'll last longer, *Light*."

I blink, stunned by his scathing tone and the venomous way he spits that last word, hurling it like an insult. Embarrassed, I turn my gaze to the front of the classroom. But no matter how hard I try to concentrate, I fail to take in any new information for the rest of the lesson.

All I can think about is the Dark Nephilim boy beside me and his beguiling aura.

SIX

CALEB

MY EYES SLIDE TO the gorgeous blonde beside me. And she is gorgeous, despite being a Light. Her hair is an unusual shade of gold, not ditzy blonde like the hostile girl sitting in front of me who keeps trying to shoot daggers out of her eyes at me. Bring it, little girl. I'll tear your mind into pieces.

Goldilocks doesn't seem hostile, but she was staring at me like bacteria under a microscope. I feel a little guilty about my snarky comment. I'm not usually an asshole to women, and she appears…fragile, for lack of a better word, like I genuinely wounded her with my words. Ha! Like a stuck-up Light would give a shit about what I have to say.

Gilgamesh drones on and on about basic Nephilim stuff—why am I even in this class?—when honest-to-Lucifer bells chime, the sound clear and sweet. This place is such overkill. I miss the clear, aggressive war horns at the Tower of Babel. That sound said move your ass or be punished for being late.

Goldilocks stands up, the motion slow and hesitant. Despite my harsh words, she kept peeking at me the entire class as if she couldn't help herself. Hmm. Time to use that curiosity against her. I stretch to my feet, ignoring the scowls and glares thrown my way, my laser focus on my prey.

I follow her into the hall. "Hey," I call, and she pivots on one foot, surprise on her pretty face. "Sorry I was a dick before." I tug at my scarlet tie. Ugh, I'm wearing a bloody tie. At least my pants and shirt are black, unlike the red and white freak show going on around me. Thank God for small miracles.

Her hazel eyes widen. "Um, th-that's okay," she stammers. Her smile is sheepish. "I didn't mean to stare. I just... I'm new here, too."

It's my turn to be surprised. A Light apologizing? That's a first. Maybe the apocalypse really is coming. As I study her, I realize she's too old to be a first-year. I'm eighteen, and she's got to be close to that. She should be in my grade or maybe one lower. All Nephilim—Dark or Light—are assigned a primary academy at the age of seven to learn the initial steps of control then a secondary academy at fourteen where we hone our skills and figure out our special abilities. Before that, it's up to our parents to keep us in line so we don't go kaboom. But because of assholes like my old man, there are a string of orphans dotting the globe, placed in group homes run by the older, more experienced Nephilim who aren't teaching at the academies. There, the young Nephilim are watched over until they're of age to go to school. But I'm getting the vibe none of this applies to Goldilocks, so, why has she been enrolled so late? What's her deal?

I wave a dismissive hand. "Don't worry about it. Sucks to be new, right? So, you know my name, but I don't know yours. Doesn't seem fair."

She shuffles her feet. "Luna," she says, her voice so low I strain to hear it. "It's kind of nice not being the only new person."

Is she for real? My eyes narrow, seeking deception, but she radiates sincerity. "Yeah, but you're a Light. I'm sure everyone is falling all over themselves to be your friend. Getting ready for Ascension and all that." I scoff.

She frowns as if she's confused by my words. "Ascension?"

Stunned, I study her for a moment, but either Luna is the best actress in the world, or she has no fucking clue what Ascension means to Lights. "Are you serious?" Try as I might, I can't quite keep the bite from my voice. Luna flinches, ducking her head, and I give myself a swift mental kick. "And there I go, being a dick again. I didn't realize how shiny and new you really are."

Luna bites her full lower lip. Lucky lip. "Does...everyone know about Ascension?" She doesn't specifically say Dark Nephilim, but she doesn't have to. I bristle for a moment before she hastily adds, "I don't mean to offend you. No one's really explained anything to me."

Relaxing, I assess her. There's something so appealing about her. I'm not sure if it's her shy sincerity or the uncertainty that marks her every move. But it makes me want to be her friend, protect her. Suspicion creeps in, and that cynical, survival part of my brain wonders if this is a trap. Gabriel picks a hot blonde to follow me around and keep tabs on me. Maybe gets me to confess Dark secrets against those kissable lips. I'm a lot of things, but I'm not a sucker.

I send my powers toward her, like black, smoky threads unwinding from a spool. If she's working for the headmistress, I'll know it soon enough, and maybe I can plant a few suggestions in that vulnerable mind of hers. Finding the shield of her mind, I try to push through, but I am abruptly shut out, like a steel door slamming down. It jars me, and I shake my head. What the hell? I try again, this time forgoing subtlety for force, and once more hit an impenetrable barrier. *Shit.* How in Lucifer's name is Luna doing this?

My eyes dart to her, standing there, fidgeting, and I realize I've been quiet too long. "Yeah, everyone knows about Ascension. When all the good little Light Nephilim get their wings."

Her eyes grow impossibly huge. "Wings…"

The reverence in her voice makes me want to roll my eyes. "If you believe that line."

Confusion mars her smooth brow. "There's so much I don't know about all…this." She gestures vaguely to our surroundings. "Could you…" A blush stains Luna's cheeks and my brow raises. "Could you, maybe…help me? No one else has bothered to speak to me, not…"

She trails off, and I hear what she isn't saying in the silence. *Not like you have.*

I try one last attempt to break into her mind and test her truthfulness, but it might as well be the Vatican vault for how well it's fortified. She seems to tremble as she waits for my answer, hope shining in her eyes. God, I want to help. I want to tell her all the dirty secrets the Lights hide away from her. But I can't. I don't trust this feeling. I don't trust her.

Suddenly, her innocence seems manufactured and the hopeful look in her eyes calculating. Anger bursts through me. I refuse to be manipulated by a Light. Or allow one to spy on me. I sneer at her, and she withers like a dying flower.

"I don't think so. Best stick to your own kind," I say. Ignoring the hurt on her face, I push past her and make my way down the hall.

Why couldn't I crack her mind? It doesn't make sense. Has Gabriel placed a protection spell on her? I guess she could be a second generation and unusually strong, but that doesn't seem to fit. It's more likely she's been sent to spy on me. I take a sharp turn down the corridor and enter a cloister—one of many here. They need more cloisters like they need more touches of gold. Overkill.

To my left, the lush garden shows brilliant green under the hot sun with bursts of violet and pink and blue blossoms. Marble benches are placed in strategic positions under fig trees. It makes me miss the Hanging Gardens at Babel, but I crush that encroaching homesickness like the destructive weed it is.

Light students flow around me like I'm a boulder in the middle of a stream, and they might sully themselves if they crash into me. God, I hate these assholes, but they do provide ample opportunity to test my theory. I hop up on one of the low walls and lean against an arch, one knee drawn up to my chest and close my eyes. Taking a deep breath, I cast my net wide. Thoughts and distant mutterings flit by me.

Can you believe they let a Dark in here? He's disgusting…

Think Gabriel will take him hostage?

Guys, we should get together later and beat his ass…

I can't believe I had to sit near a Dark. Now, we have two freaks in class…

Relieved my powers still work, I hone in on that last thought. My lids flicker open as I seek out the source of that voice. It's that bitchy brunette from class. Oh, little girl, you mess with the wolf… A predatory grin spreads across my face as I slip into her mind and plant a small suggestion.

As she talks to her bottle-blonde friend, she begins scratching her side, discomfort growing on her face. She digs her nails harder and harder into her skin until the blonde clutches her hand, face askance. "Lisbeth, what the hell is wrong with you?"

Lisbeth looks positively panicked, and I squash my growing smile. "I don't know." She lifts up her shirt and squeals. "God, look at this rash! What is it? It itches so badly." She jerks her wrist from the blonde's grip and digs her nails into her smooth, unblemished skin.

"There's nothing there, Lis," her friend says, trying to grab her wrist again.

Those stupid bells chime, and the brunette takes off down the hall, her friend at her side, trying to calm her hysteria. I wait until the sound of students hurrying by dissipates before I allow a slow, satisfied grin to cross my face. I haven't lost my touch after all. That was easy.

I slide my feet to the ground, making my way to my next class, not in any particular hurry. It's my first day and I'm a Dark. I bet all my teachers' opinions are already properly low of me, so I'm sure they don't expect me to be able to find my way or give a shit about being on time. They'd be right about the latter. Though Hammurabi's words about representing the Dark Nephilim the right way puts a little spring in my step.

My thoughts drift to Luna and my glee evaporates. Why couldn't I read her thoughts like the other students? Is Gabriel interfering, or is it something else? And what had the bitchy brunette thought before? That there were *two* freaks in class. As I push open the door to my next class, I wonder who the other freak was she mentioned.

seven

LUNA

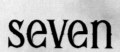

THE FIRST FEW WEEKS of the fall term at the Serapeum pass by without incident. Unless you count Lisbeth and Ellie and their minions doing everything in their power to make my life hell. Those girls are only freshmen by normal high school standards, but they're veterans when it comes to mental warfare. They put mortal bullies to shame.

I've tried my best to ignore their attempts to get under my skin, but the effort is exhausting. Not to mention, it's an unwanted distraction from figuring out what my powers are—a goal that has consumed me throughout the month I've been here and with which I've made absolutely zero progress.

After calling Alaric to thank him for the gift, I realized how easy the Nephilim is to talk to and, despite the distance, we've formed a friendship of sorts, texting on a near daily basis and catching up over the phone at least once a week. But whenever I press him for more information about when I'll learn what my own special talent might be, he simply urges me to give it time. That I'll learn who I am through my lessons here. I want to believe him, but so far, my classes have mostly just been lectures about our history as Nephilim and what we're not allowed to do—not what we can. Sure, what I'm learning is interesting, but on a personal level, every day I feel a bit more disconnected from the subject matter, like I'm back in a mortal classroom where this is all fiction and none of it applies to me. It'd be easier to believe Alaric's repeated assurances about what I did before I was committed if I actually understood what I was capable of.

Even Ascension—which I've been curious about ever since Caleb mentioned it—doesn't hold the same draw for me as it seems to for everyone else. Granted, I haven't spent my whole life daydreaming about gaining my wings, like some of these students clearly have based on the way they constantly harp on about it. My perspective on the idea is that of an outsider.

On the rare occasion our teachers do discuss Ascension, they merely preach that devotion to the light will lead to entry into Heaven and full angel status granted by the Creator Himself, where the Nephilim will finally be able to join their Faithful ancestors and achieve immortality. Of course, they always clam up when the students ask for specific examples of when this has actually happened, as if the act itself is private and not to be spoken about in any real detail. Add to that the fact that all our teachers are first generation Nephilim—not to mention some of the most prominent figures from history—and have yet to Ascend themselves, and it makes the whole concept seem questionable. If I'm honest, the whole notion sounds like propaganda—an incentive to convince the Lights to behave the way the Archangels in charge want them to. Even Alaric couldn't give me any real details when I asked him about it one night over text, claiming the experience is personal and unique to each Nephilim, not unlike mortal spirituality. As much as I like him and feel a certain growing kinship between us, his answer felt rehearsed, like he's merely regurgitating what he's been told.

Who knows if any of it is true?

Classes aside, the Serapeum Academy has been like most of my other schools, isolating and lonely. Friendless. Most of the time, I rush out of class before Lisbeth or Ellie can find new ways to torment me or convince one of the older Nephilim students to do the job for them. It never takes much convincing. Despite us all having celestial blood, to everyone here, I'm an outcast. A freak of nature—an imperfection in their otherwise perfect world.

And here I had assumed Lights were supposed to be good.

I haven't spoken to Caleb again, although I desperately want to. Every day, we sit next to each other in the few classes we share—no one else wants to sit next to the Dark or the crazy girl, forcing us to occupy the sole remaining seats—but he never looks at me, even though I'm always sneaking glances at him whenever I think he's not looking. I'm not sure what it is, but there's something behind his standoffish exterior that makes me sense we're the same, despite him being a Dark. And not just because we're both pariahs by the Lights' social standards, but because there's something about the shadows lapping over his skin that I recognize within myself. That I *feel* in the buried, unreachable depths of my own soul.

Not that it matters. What I think or feel is irrelevant if he refuses to talk to me. *"Best stick to your own kind,"* that's what he said. I don't fully grasp this feud between the Darks and the Lights, but if sticking with my own kind means turning into someone like Lisbeth or Ellie, I'll pass.

I'd rather be alone than be anything like them.

My fingers curl around the spines of my textbooks, hugging the heavy bundle close to my chest. On weekends, there's not a whole lot to do here, and it's not like I have any friends to pass the time with, so I spend those free days alone in my room or exploring the school, which is never-ending in its vastness. An unsent text on my phone awkwardly asks Alaric to come visit one weekend, but I've yet to work up the courage to send it, so today, I'm on the hunt for the library, which my teachers have claimed is legendary. According to my lessons, the Library of Alexandria was believed to have burned down centuries ago, the treasures within lost to flame, when in reality, unbeknownst to humans, the Archangels moved what they could salvage here—to the Serapeum where it would be protected by magical barriers, hidden away, and kept safe from the reckless destruction of mortals.

The teachers at this school—all first generations—never pass up any opportunity to moan about how rash and irresponsible mortals are, as if they aren't half-human themselves. I've yet to catch the snobbery running rampant among the other Lights, which only fuels the doubts I've had since Alaric told me the truth about what I am. I certainly haven't seen any evidence that would suggest I'm unlike the very same mortals the Nephilim here seem to detest. It's as if they believe themselves to be a superior species, which is illogical considering everyone here, aside from Gabriel, has at least one mortal ancestor somewhere in their bloodline. Even a child born of an angel and a Nephilim would still be part mortal—a first generation and powerful sure, but mortal, their blood watered down by the human connection through their Nephilim parent. Without humans, we wouldn't exist at all, not that the other Lights would ever admit that, especially when they make it a point to keep to our own kind to avoid further dilution of our celestial roots. Based on what I've heard in class and in passing, it was inevitable some notion of supremacy among the Lights would form over time, pitting them against the inferior humans who they see as responsible for their weakening bloodlines. From that viewpoint, I suppose it's easy to buy into an idea like Ascension when you already have an inflated opinion about yourself and where you belong in the world.

The hallways are empty as I search for the library. Many of the students who know and have healthy relationships with their parents, human or Nephilim, have gone home for the weekend—an escape I won't be partaking in any time soon. It's kind of hard to go home for a weekend when you don't have a home to go back to.

Considering where the school is located and that many of the Nephilim hail from the other side of the world, I was surprised to hear that any of them go home at all, apart from when the academic terms end and classes break up for holidays. I mean, who wants to take a flight lasting who knows how many hours only to then make the lengthy return trip to school less than two days later? Sounds tiring and not at all worth the effort.

At least, that's what I thought until I heard about the Blessed Road. That's one good thing about being an outcast—no one seems to take any notice when you're eavesdropping on their conversations.

Per my new knowledge, Nephilim, Light and Dark alike, have methods of traveling that are beyond the scope and understanding of mortals. I'm not really sure how the Blessed Road works, but when I asked Alaric for details about it, he compared the Road to a highway with exit points scattered across the planet. It's hard for me to imagine, but apparently it's faster than traveling by plane or any other form of human transport. When I then pressed him about why he didn't just use the Blessed Road to bring me to Alexandria instead of flying, he said the Road will only open for those who are aware of what they are, which, at the time, I wasn't. He had also muttered something about the possibility of my brain imploding if I saw something like that without having the proper time to process my being a Nephilim, and that statement was enough to shut me up on the matter.

The sun beats down on me as I pass into one of the courtyards sprinkled across the academy grounds. Although the light is warm, a shiver crosses my skin, leaving me cold and feeling exposed and alone. I can't stop thinking about how nice it would be to have someone to traverse this new landscape with—someone to help me make sense of what I am and this bewildering world I find myself in. While Alaric has been a source of comfort and is always available to lend a friendly ear, he isn't physically here. He has responsibilities that keep him busy.

But Caleb... I was foolish enough to think he might be that person, a friend even, but clearly, my first impression of him was sorely misguided. He's as disgusted by my existence as everyone else in this school, although his rejection of me is more painful somehow. Perhaps because I've made it a point not to get close to anyone since...well, the first incident that threw my life into disarray. He was the exception—the one person my own age I was ever tempted to try to get close to.

And not just because he's nice to look at—a fact my inconvenient teenage hormones have taken notice of—but because there's something there, in the billowing indigo and violet shadow outlining his body, that speaks to me in a way the brilliant radiance of the Lights hasn't yet.

Ironic, considering I'm supposed to be one of them.

I finally stumble across my destination in one of the western annexes. Immense, wooden doors framed by glimmering golden symbols lead the way into an extravagant room spanning the height of at least four stories. The walls are covered in tall, arching windows, and shelves full of books stretch from the floor up to the sky-scraping ceiling, which is painted to look as if Heaven itself gazes down on the library below with shining approval.

The structure is mesmerizing—like a painting brought to life—made all the more enchanting by the white marble floor, which reflects the details of my surroundings in its glistening surface.

At least twenty round tables fill the room, clustered around several rows of free-standing bookcases, which section off the space and create cozy patches of darkness I'm tempted to lose myself in. As I weave between them, I wince at the thunderous echo of my steps on the marble. My heart catches at the thought of drawing unwanted attention, but thankfully, the library is empty, apart from a few seemingly studious Nephilim, who make it a point to ignore me as I lumber past.

I make a beeline for a door in the corner, intrigued by the sign hanging over it printed with a single ornate word in gold leaf. *Exhibits.* I flatten my palm against the brass push plate and lean my weight into the wood, nudging it open. The hinges creak as if protesting my entry.

Behind me, the door swings shut as a breath of quiet awe

rushes out of my lungs. The space is poorly lit—there are no windows in this room—and the minimal light from the low burning lamps ignites the dust particles in the air like floating embers suspended in time. Glass cases stand in clean rows like sentinels awaiting their orders, housing relics showcasing the history of the Nephilims' past.

I abandon my books on a small accent table beside the door and approach a miniature sculpture of the library that sits in one of the nearby cases. According to the placard, the model represents what the original structure looked like from the outside before it burned down all those years ago and its contents became a part of the school at the Serapeum. In another case, metal ornaments resembling skeletal wings fill the full breadth of the display, framing a shining golden breastplate. It's only when I glance down at the placard that I realize what I'm looking at is armor that was worn during the Great Battle of Heaven that led to the segregation of the angels and subsequent birth of the Lights and the Darks. Beside it lies a sword brandished with a familiar symbol I'm certain I've seen somewhere before. When the connection registers, it dawns on me which angel this sword and armor belonged to.

Gabriel.

The long, steel blade extends into a bronze hilt, the guard crafted to resemble two outstretched wings identical to the silver insignia branded on the door to her office. A glowing gem lies embedded in the pommel, matching the brilliant golden aura that shrouded her body the one and only time we crossed paths.

A low hum permeates the air, like the vibrations of a tuning fork, and I blink, breaking my gaze on the sword. Turning from the case, I move onto the next one. This display contains hundreds of preserved moths—all of the same species, size, and brown coloring. My eyes skim across the collection then fall to the sign beneath the glass, tracing over the accompanying epitaph.

To protect our children from human wrath,
the Dark and Light shall come together to offer salvation.
And with the lives saved, we will remember those lost.
The precious ones we build this for.

"For the moth will eat them like a garment,
And the grub will eat them like wool.
But My righteousness will be forever,
And My salvation to all generations."

ISAIAH 51:8

Beneath the inscription and Bible verse is a long list of names and dates spanning back thousands of years. Comprehension darkens my thoughts as I remember Gilgamesh's lesson about the Nephilim who were murdered in the early years of our species. Each of these moths must represent one of those lost children—a tragedy that served as the foundation for which the schools of Light and Dark were established.

The case is cool to the touch as I press my fingertips to the front of the glass. My eyes narrow, honing in on one of the moths, noting the different shades of brown interlaced with black and white adorning the arrow-sharp line of its body. Its wings are stretched out to the sides with the stiff precision of an airplane in flight.

My nails drum against the glass—*tap, tap, tap*—as if coaxing the moth to wake from the slumber of death. The longer I stare at it, the more I can envision it moving—its frail body returning to life and escaping the cage of this glass mausoleum.

An unexpected urgency twists my gut, and I find myself silently begging the moth to shake free from the confines of the pins holding it still. Maybe because I feel as trapped as that moth—imprisoned by the horrors of my past.

My fingernail taps again. A faint flicker. No, it was just a trick of the eye.

As I stare into the case, the whisper of a deep, masculine voice rises out of the hush and begins whispering nonsensical words in my ear. I whip around, tearing my gaze from the moth, a breath catching in my throat, but no one stands behind me. No one else is here. The room is empty.

I'm still alone.

Swallowing, I turn back toward the display. The instant my eyes return to the moth, the voice resumes its echoing hiss, this time in my head, filling my entire skull with its presence. The sound seems to simultaneously cut through and surround me, bouncing off every surface in the large space, while also lingering impossibly close.

"Anastēson auton. Ho skotos dia sou diarreitō."

My eyes snap closed at these words, and my palm flattens against the glass. A shiver crosses my skin as the voice purrs again.

"Anastēson auton. Ho skotos dia sou diarreitō."

I nod, driven by its unknown direction. Hearing a disembodied voice would shake any normal person, but for me, it's just another sign that I'm as deranged as everyone thinks.

The voice speaks once more, but this time, there's no mistaking its meaning. I don't know how I can suddenly understand what it's saying, but every word is clear, like the voice is translating on my behalf, so I can comprehend what it wants.

"Resurrect it. Let the darkness run through you."

A shudder of apprehension rolls over my body as my fingers press against the case, led by something outside myself I can't control. The voice speaks again, reassuring me.

Calming me.

"I am a friend. Trust me. You have the power."

Silence falls like a curtain at the end of a stage production, suffocating all sound apart from a faint flutter on the edge of hearing—like wings beating in the distance. Eyes flitting open, I peek down at the moth, both stunned and unsurprised to find it alive. It struggles against the pins for a moment, then breaks free, hunting for an escape. The glass crypt offers none.

A loud bang to my right tears my focus from the display,

and blinking, I meet the gaze of a third-year Nephilim girl I vaguely recognize as one of Lisbeth's friends. She stands in front of the door, gaping at me with a hand clamped over her open mouth. The books she was carrying lie scattered across the floor by her feet.

"Y-You…" The girl stumbles back a few steps, her vibrant, seafoam-green eyes wide with fear.

I furrow my brow, bemused by her terror, as she glances between my face and the glass case beside me. When I follow her line of sight to the display, I notice the moth is no longer moving. The poor thing has returned to its grave.

"Blasphemy…" The word penetrates her lips in a faltering breath, just loud enough to draw my gaze again. Her pale, stricken face twists and she glares at me with disgust, as if I am a Biblical plague on this earth. "Blasphemy!" the girl says again, shouting this time.

"Wha—" A single step toward the girl sends her barreling from the room before I can get the full word out.

The door to *Exhibits* whips back and forth behind her like a white flag waving in surrender, each swing as furious as the glowering expression she wore, her visible revulsion seared into my mind. Between each swing, I catch a glimpse of the girl racing through the spacious room beyond, clutching a cell phone to her ear.

"Great," I mutter. *Just what I need.*

Sighing, I trudge toward the door, stepping over the

abandoned books on the floor and collecting my own pile from the small table with a lazy swipe of my hand. The cavalry is probably already on its way—I should leave while there's still a chance to enjoy the rest of my weekend harassment-free.

Stalling, I cast a glance over my shoulder at the case where, for a fleeting moment, I was able to give that moth life.

Alaric was right, I realize with a laugh. Bitchy, high-school diplomacy aside, I do belong in this world. It wasn't a mistake.

I really am a Nephilim.

A thrill rushes through me at the thought, and as I push open the door, that voice returns for the briefest of moments, following me in my shock and glee. It caresses my shoulder like a pat on the back, offering its congratulations.

"Well done," it murmurs.

With a smile stretching across my face, I walk from the shadowed museum back into the warm glow of the main room of the library, for once in my life feeling powerful instead of weak and afraid of what I am.

eight

CALEB

SHOVING MY HANDS IN my pockets, I head toward the famous Library of Alexandria, or what the Serapeum Academy managed to salvage from the great fire, which is actually most of it, unbeknownst to humans. They moved the library here to be safe and away from the stupidity of mortals. It's the one place in the academy I admire, vast stores of knowledge throughout the ages at my fingertips. The Nephilim are an ancient race, and I love spotting us in texts when the concept of civilization was brand new, and humanity was just discovering their full potential. The library also offers shadowy alcoves to read in, providing relief from all this white and gold. Today, I want to read everything I can get my hands on regarding Alexander the Great. I might find some clue, even amongst mortal accounts.

Frustration knots me. I know it's only been a month, but I've learned depressingly little about where my grandfather could possibly be. Mind surfing the Light students has yielded zero results and has been mind-numbingly boring. A lot of hatred for yours truly, the usual school gossip of who's sleeping with whom, and of course, every Light's obsession: Ascension.

And to my surprise, a lot of these Lights have a disdain for humans in the same way Ishtar does, although they'd never admit they share a common ideal with a Dark. They might not want to subjugate humans, but they sure do believe they're superior, despite their mortal blood.

And then there's lovely Luna. That's a nut I still haven't been able to crack. We sit next to each other in the handful of classes we share, and in each one I feel her eyes on me when she thinks I'm not looking. I hate to admit it, but I want to look back, and not just because she's a smokeshow. Yeah, I'm still convinced that something shady is going on there, but I can't be certain she's Gabriel's puppet, either. She seems so…lonely. Lost. From what I can tell, she doesn't have any friends. She hurries from class the moment it ends, and from what I've observed, those little first-years—Lisbeth and Ellie—have fun tormenting her. For the life of me, I can't figure out why. Is this all real or part of an act? Aren't Lights supposed to be all goody-goody and shit? At least to each other, I mean.

They have no problem being total dicks to the Dark Nephilim. And I have no problem dishing it back to them. Spoiler alert— I'm going to win that battle. I'll give them visions that will make them tear their eyes out if they push me too far. I hate bullies.

I put a little swagger in my step as I stroll down the endless corridors, stretching out my powers to catch any piece of conversation that might prove to be useful. But I don't have high hopes. I'm going to have to up my game and start targeting teachers, and that'll take a bit more finesse. And a bit more time.

As it is, every time I'm out and about, Light students avoid me, giving me a wide berth and looks full of loathing. Even after the teachers have preached about togetherness, there has been zero change in attitude. Shocking. As thoughts flood my way, my eyes narrow. This isn't exactly what I've been searching for but it *is* interesting.

I can't believe what she did in the library...

I didn't know Lights could do that. That's Dark shit...

I knew she was a freak. All those stories and now this...

Holy shit, Luna performed a resurrection. That's forbidden...

She doesn't belong here—she's jeopardizing our chance at Ascension...

Luna needs to be taught a lesson, crazy bitch...

I stumble at these thoughts, my feet slowing. Luna performed a resurrection? Raising something from the dead is strictly forbidden among the Lights because only the Creator has the right to wield that power. Only He has the right to creation. Resurrection is a Dark trait. And even then, we *don't* do it. We have no business meddling with life and death. Breathing life into inanimate objects doesn't count, although the Lights still look at it as creation. Oh, the blasphemy. My heart speeds up. What *is* Luna? And why would she be so foolish as to bring something back to life in front of witnesses? She can't be that naive, can she?

Then that last thought catches me like a punch to the gut. *Luna needs to be taught a lesson, crazy bitch…* My eyes scan the hallway as I pick up speed once more. There, up ahead, I see Lisbeth and Ellie and two guys I haven't seen before—or maybe I have, and I just haven't been paying attention. Making friends hasn't been my goal, after all. They're big dudes, and anger simmers in my chest. Four people to teach one girl who's a buck twenty a lesson? They're real brave, these pathetic excuses for Nephilim.

They hurry around a corner, and I resist the urge to break into a run. There are too many people around, and I'm outnumbered by Lights who would have no problem attacking me if they thought I was going after one of their own. The last thing I need is mob mentality kicking in. I consider myself a grade-A badass, but taking on more than five Nephilim at a time would be a struggle, even for me. Inside my head, I hear Hammurabi scoff, declaring he could take on ten Nephilim and not break a sweat.

I round the corner, but the dumbass quartet are nowhere in sight. Shit. The long hallway is nearly empty. I guess the library isn't a super popular place to be, so I throw caution to the wind and sprint. The few Lights I pass all shoot me wary looks bordering on frightened. It's not a bad thing being feared, as my classmates are about to discover.

Guilt nags at me as I run. Guilt that I rejected Luna and failed to notice the extent of how badly she was being treated.

She's not my responsibility—I'm not her protector—but still, the guilt sloshes in my stomach like acid. I've been so focused on Alexander I didn't even pick up the signs that my Goldilocks is hiding some serious Dark powers. Ishtar would kick my ass if she knew how blind I've been. Luna isn't my mission, but I should have been paying attention.

I hit the corridor in front of the library, my boots thumping on the marble floor, the sound echoing to the tops of the tall ceiling. I pass the great library doors, and I see them not too far off, for once thankful for my bright ivory surroundings that make it difficult to hide. Luna's burnished gold hair is hard to spot, as she's surrounded by Lisbeth and Ellie and the two hulking boys. The anger that has been simmering boils over into full-blown rage when I watch as the spiteful brunette shoves Luna against the wall and delivers a backhanded blow to her face. The rest of them descend on her like wolves, and my vision washes in red.

I'm almost upon them when one of the guys looks up, a shocked expression on his face, as he finally realizes there's a bigger predator in their midst. My elbow finds his nose with a satisfying crunch, and I slam his head into the stone wall with a sickening thud. He slides to the floor, out cold. Dumb, dumber, and dumbest all freeze for a moment as Luna gazes up at me, stunned. I take precious seconds to see if they've hurt her, but aside from her dazed expression, she doesn't appear to be injured.

"You," Lisbeth hisses, bringing me back to the here and now.

"Me," I snarl, barely avoiding the blow her other male companion aims my way. I grin. Now, it's time for the real fun to begin.

My power lashes out of me like dark whips, wrapping around the minds of my victims with vengeful glee.

Ellie hops up and down screaming, "Get them off, get them off me! Oh, God!" She yanks at her clothing like a madwoman, and I step around her. Blondie then drops on the floor, rolling around.

Lisbeth screeches, "Why am I bleeding?" She swipes her hands under her eyes, holding them out in front of her, wailing, "It's coming out of my eyes. Out of my eyes. I can't see!" She sobs.

I smile and then focus on the last man standing. He falls to his knees, his eyes distant on some faraway horror. Suddenly, he curls in on himself like a baby. I step over him, finally reaching Luna.

Her eyes blink up at me, impossibly huge in her face. It's like she sees me, but she's still stuck in her own nightmare, and this one isn't an illusion. I keep my movements slow and deliberate as I bend down, making sure she can see my hands. I don't want to freak her out more than she already is.

"Hey, Goldilocks," I say, keeping my voice soft and even, but loud enough she can hear me over the screams and cries of the three asshats behind me. "You're safe now. I won't let them hurt you, but we need to get out of here, okay? I have to release them at some point."

A small headache nags me, reminding me of how much power I'm expending to keep three Nephilim trapped in a loop of terrors. I don't mind the pain. After what they tried to do, a splitting migraine would be totally worth it.

Luna blinks up at me. "Goldilocks?"

Her bewildered and unexpected reply startles a laugh from me. I wrap one finger around a strand of her silky hair and show it to her. "Yep, you can't deny who you are. I'm going to help you up, okay?"

"I… Yes," she says, allowing me to take her hands.

I lift her to her feet with ease and keep one of her hands tightly clasped within my own. Her skin is soft and smooth, and I run my thumb over hers, hoping that small gesture of comfort helps. I take her back to the library, knowing we can get lost in the shadows there.

When we enter, it appears mostly empty, but I don't plan on staying out in the open. I hurry past towering rows upon rows of books, the smell musty with knowledge, to my favorite secluded spot that features two deep amethyst velvet armchairs in a dim nook. This is the philosophy section, and for whatever reason, students avoid this area. Maybe it's because I've claimed it as my spot, but I wonder if the Lights don't like to read about morality too much. They might have to question their choices and beliefs. Oh, the horror.

With gentle hands, I sit Luna down before I collapse onto my own seat. Sweat beads on my forehead. I've been steadily sending illusions to those three idiots, and it's wearing on me like sandpaper. Closing my eyes, I snap the tethers connecting my power to their minds. Relief floods through me and I sigh. When I open my eyes, I find Luna studying me as she so often does in class when she thinks I don't notice.

Her eyes dart away, and a flush sweeps up her neck and along her cheekbones. I suppress a grin. When I notice her slight tremble, my grin morphs into a frown. "Are you okay?" A bitter laugh escapes me. "Well, four assholes just tried to jump you, so that's a stupid question, but they didn't hurt you, did they?"

She shakes her head, gazing at the floor. "Thank you…for helping." Her voice is so soft I barely catch her words. "I know this doesn't mean anything. I don't expect you to change your mind about…"

She trails off, and guilt claws at me as I remember what I said when we met. *Best stick to your own kind.*

Shit, she's killing me. I scoot my chair around, scraping the mahogany legs against the marble. Luna glances up, eyes rounded. I take her cold hands in mine, trying to warm them. She stares at my fingers as if she's never held hands with a guy before. Hell, maybe she hasn't.

"Look, I'm sorry I've been such an ass. It's just that—Lights— my experiences with Lights have been pretty shit. And I know that's not your fault, but when you tried to be nice to me…" I release another heavy sigh. "I thought you were playing me. And that pissed me off. I thought this whole thing you've got going on was an act, and you were trying to lure me into some sort of trap."

Shaking her head again, she whispers, "Thing I have going on?"

I wince at the confusion in her voice, hating myself a little. "The innocent, new girl thing. I mean, you're kinda old to be a new student, so it threw me off." I shrug. "Everything about you threw me off."

Her eyes rise to meet mine, and the unexpected anger I find takes me by surprise. "I can't fit in anywhere."

I grip her fingers harder, my own anger bubbling to the surface. "Hey, if people treat you like shit here for no reason, you don't want to fit in." My eyes bore into hers, and she drops her gaze.

Releasing one of her hands, I lightly grasp her chin, forcing her to look up at me. This close, I notice the ring of gold around the hazel of her irises. "I don't fit in here, either. Everyone hates me, and I haven't done a damn thing to deserve it but exist. Everyone hates me but you, that is. Know what I say?" I ask, and she shakes her head for a third time. "Screw 'em."

A giggle escapes her, making me smile. "Screw 'em," she repeats.

"Now you're learning," I say, letting go of her chin, my hand clasping her free one once more. "Luna, do you want to tell me what happened?" I know what happened, but I want her to open up to me. I want my suspicions confirmed.

She glances away, biting her lip and then turns to me, shrugging. "I don't know. They've been like this since I got here.

They think I'm a freak." She gives me a helpless look. "So much for hoping this school would be different."

The mournful note in her last words catches at me, and I decide not to press her further. She's just been traumatized, and I want her to trust me. And I honestly don't think she understands the implications of what she's done, which is even more intriguing. If she's displaying Dark tendencies, how did she end up at a Light school?

Luna is a mystery I desperately want to solve, but she's not my reason for being here. Alexander is. But that doesn't mean I can't use an ally. I genuinely like her, and I can't toss her back to the wolves after saving her. That's not my way.

"Well," I say, "you've got me. That is, if you still want to be friends after I was such an ass."

She gifts me with that timid, sweet smile. "I'd like that." Then curiosity reflects in her expression. "What did you do to them?"

My lips curve into a satisfied smile. "Nothing they didn't deserve." I rise to my feet, pulling her up with me. "Come on, Goldilocks. I'll walk you to your room."

nine

LUNA

A GROAN ESCAPES MY lips when my alarm goes off first thing Monday morning, each blaring beep like a drill bit cutting into my temples, carving a path straight to my brain. My hand smacks down on the clock, hitting the snooze button. I'm still drained from what happened this weekend—the only saving grace of the whole ordeal being my newly born friendship with Caleb.

I'm not sure what I would have done if he hadn't turned up. When Lisbeth and Ellie cornered me with their friends, it was as if I suddenly forgot how to move. My feet were rooted to the spot as my mind was pulled back to every other time I'd been accused of doing something terrible.

That's the part I still can't figure out. Why were they so upset by the fact I brought a stupid moth back to life? I'm sure the other Nephilim at this school can do far more impressive things than revive a dead insect for less than a minute. And yet, the way that girl looked at me in the library museum before running off to find her friends… There was an unmistakable fear and repugnance in her eyes, like I had just personally wronged the Creator.

I sit up, running a hand through my hair. Yesterday, just after I resurrected the moth, there was a moment when I finally believed I fit in here. That I wasn't possessed by evil like I'd always been told, and that I really was born with some greater power that made me different. Special, just like Alaric said when we met.

But my encounter with the other Nephilim has made it clear that my life is a pendulum, always swinging back and forth between the hope I belong and the grim reality that I never will.

Swiping my phone off the bedside table, I click on the screen and open the messaging app, bringing up my conversation with Alaric. The message I typed last night stares back at me, judging me, from where it sits in the text box, unsent.

Have you ever resurrected something?

.

Frowning, I tap the delete button, erasing the words.

A knock on my bedroom door makes me jump, and I bolt from the bed, my heart racing as I inch toward the threshold. Are Lisbeth and Ellie waiting on the other side, here to finish what they started? I cast a wary peek through the peephole to find a brown eye blinking back at me. A breath of relief fills my chest as the eye pulls away to reveal Caleb's face.

"Knock, knock, Goldilocks. We're gonna be late," he calls through the wood in a sing-song voice.

I unlock the door, crack it open a few inches, and poke my startled face through the gap.

A grin tugs up one corner of Caleb's mouth as he gives me a quick glance up and down. "Love the hair."

My hand flies to my head, still mussed from sleep, the golden strands sticking up in wild disarray.

My cheeks flush as I slam the door in his face. "I… I'll be out in a minute."

Stumbling toward my dresser, I pull out a fresh uniform then race to the bathroom where I tame my wild mane of sleep-tangled hair and scrub my teeth. Thank God all the rooms in this place come with private en suites. Sharing a bathroom with a judgmental psycho like Lisbeth or Ellie is just about the last thing I need.

Once I've freshened up, I grab my books off my desk and throw open the door to find Caleb waiting in the hallway, lounging against the beige stone wall directly opposite my room. His eyes find mine, making me blush again. The downside of being a pariah? I've not had much experience being social with boys. Or anyone for that matter, at least not my age. My only interactions lately have been with Alaric—and always only via phone call or text—but I haven't wanted to burden him with what's been going on here or make him worry, hence my growing habit of deleting my messages to him before I hit send. He got me out of the hospital, and for that, I'll always be grateful, but he's an adult with a life far away from this school.

What I desperately want is a friend. Someone my age, *here*, who understands me the way only another teenager can.

"G-Good morning," I stammer, swallowing the dry lump in my throat.

Great start, Luna. Way to stay awkward.

Caleb stands upright, his lips curled into a lopsided smile that leaves me a little weak in the knees. The aura surrounding him pulses, the tendrils of shadow reaching out in warm greeting. My pulse quickens. He must be happy to see me.

"Ready to head to class?" he asks.

I fall into step beside him as we walk down the corridor, taking the fastest route to the large staircase marking the meeting point of the boys' and girls' dormitories. The other students stare as we pass, grimacing and shooting us both equally dirty looks, which I brush off and try my best to ignore. From the hushed whispers filling the halls, I gather word of what happened at the library this weekend has spread. I'm not surprised. I've been enrolled in enough schools to know how quickly rumors can travel, especially when the student body is smaller. And, in this case, when intent on their hatred.

As we follow the white marble stairs down to the ground floor and carry on through the adjoining courtyard, sticking to the cool shadows of the cloister, I risk a glance at Caleb. I'm no stranger to being at the center of rumors and bullying, but what about him? He seems incredibly level-headed and calm about all of this, but he also grew up in this world, aware of what he is. Before transferring here, he probably had more friends than enemies.

Now, he only has me. Me, the broken girl who's spent her whole life drifting from one foster home to another, socially isolated and unaware of my heritage. What kind of friendship can I realistically give him? I don't even know what friendship is.

"You don't have to walk with me, you know. I mean…if you don't want to."

Caleb raises his eyebrows. "I said I wanted to be friends, didn't I? Well, here I am, being friendly."

I want to believe him, but the part of me that's so used to being alone isn't sure if I can. Or if I should.

We continue for a moment in silence until he nudges my shoulder with his. "It's okay if you're worried. But, just so you know, you don't need to be. Those assholes won't bother you again. I'll make sure of it."

I shudder at the memory of my attackers, cowering on the floor, lost in some terrible hallucination Caleb inflicted on their minds—a Dark ability, I'd wager, based on their confused reactions. As awful as it was to watch, I don't feel any pity for their pain. If anything, seeing Caleb defend me like that only strengthened my desire to trust him.

At least I don't have to worry about either of us getting punished for whatever he did to them. If Lisbeth or Ellie went to a teacher or the headmistress, there would be questions about how the fight started, and I've been the victim of enough bullies to know the last thing they'd do is purposely get themselves into trouble. Especially since Gabriel seems like the type to suss out the truth and then punish the liars for their attempted deception.

"What about you?" I blink, looking up at him.

His dark eyes fix on mine. "What about me?"

"The things they say about you…" I trail off, clamping my teeth down hard on the inside of my lower lip. Surely, he must hear what the other Nephilim whisper about him in class when they aren't talking about me. I shake my head. "I'm not the only one they're terrible to."

Caleb stops dead in his tracks once we reach the academic building and signals for me to follow him into an empty classroom. As the door shuts behind us, his gaze slides to my face.

"Listen, I've grown up with this prejudice. I'm used to it. And believe it or not, it goes both ways. This segregation between the Darks and the Lights is old news." He waves a hand between us, as if to illustrate his point.

"I don't understand it," I mutter.

His biting laugh cuts through the room, making me shiver. "What, you mean the preachy, self-righteous lectures in *History of the Fall* haven't made it abundantly clear to you how much the Darks and Lights hate each other? Color me shocked."

As Caleb rolls his eyes, the darkness around him vibrates, projecting what he's feeling. Anger. Irritation. Injustice. I'm tempted to reach out and soothe the shadows—soothe *him*—but I don't know the first thing about comforting anyone. Hell, I don't even know how to comfort myself.

Besides, he knows and understands the rules of our kind far better than I do. Caleb and the other Nephilim seem to view our existence in black and white—two separate sides with their own ideas of what's right or wrong. Despite being a Light, I feel trapped in the middle, where all I'm aware of are muddied shades of gray. Nothing about this world makes sense or resonates with me the way I'm guessing it should.

"I don't know. It's just…I'm a Light, right?" The words escape me in a strangled breath.

Caleb hesitates. "Yeah? And?"

"So"—I shrug—"as a Light, shouldn't I feel some sort of divine devotion to their cause or something?"

How can I ever belong anywhere if I don't even know what to believe?

He worries his lower lip between his teeth, scanning my face as he considers my question. "It's more complicated than that. We aren't born with these prejudices against each other—they're learned. Because every new generation is exposed to these opinions, it's easy to see why there's still a divide, but being one or another—Light or Dark—doesn't automatically brainwash you into those ideologies or force your loyalty. Take the Darks, for example. We're all about thinking for ourselves. We'd never pressure anyone into doing something they don't want to do or to fight for an idea they don't believe in."

"And the Lights?" My voice is a tremulous whisper.

"Have different views than we do, and the academies do a

damn good job of ensuring we all stay on our respective sides. They keep us apart to avoid sparking another war. Not that Darks and Lights ever want to play nicely."

And yet, Caleb is here. Enrolled at a Light school.

"If that's true, then why leave the Tower of Babel?"

A smirk warps his lips, and he reels back, impressed. "Someone was listening my first day of class."

A flush creeps up my neck. "I just mean…why would you come here if you knew the Lights would treat you this way?"

The smile slips from his lips, and for a long moment, he stares at me, saying nothing. Leaning back against the nearest wall, he crosses his arms. "From what my teachers told me back at the Tower, this whole exchange program is just a political move. Tensions are high, as they always are,"—he mutters that last part under his breath—"and the Lights want it to look like they're doing everything in their power to keep the peace."

That would explain why even the teachers don't seem too thrilled about Caleb's enrollment at the Serapeum. They're civil enough to him—more so than the students, at least—but it hasn't escaped my notice how on edge they always are in his presence, like they're waiting for him to cause some sort of problem. I guess it's hard for me *not* to notice when people have looked at me that way my whole life.

"You didn't answer my question." The accusation in my tone takes us both by surprise, and Caleb gapes at me, his eyes wide.

"I don't know," he says. "Boredom, I guess? Morbid curiosity?

They needed someone, and I have thick skin. I knew what I was walking into. Although…" He pauses, clearing his throat. "Certain aspects of this place are definitely better than others."

The smile returns to his lips and he winks.

Oh. He means me, I realize.

My cheeks burn with the heat of a thousand suns as I shift my weight from one foot to the other, embarrassed.

As silence floods the room, it occurs to me that, although there's no physical barrier between us, I can sense the divide Caleb spoke of. I've seen it in the glances of the other Light students when they look at him like he's less than they are, even though he's so much more. It was there today, and it will continue to be there every time someone gossips about us in passing, even though I don't care what they think.

Regardless of how much I like Caleb or how much he likes me, the world and our history wants to keep us apart.

A tightness grips my chest at the thought. "Does that mean we're breaking some kind of unspoken rule by not hating each other?"

This friendship between us might be new, but I don't want to lose Caleb because of some stupid societal rule that says we shouldn't be mixing.

The darkness brimming along his skin expands outward like ghostly appendages reaching out to embrace me.

His smile deepens. "Maybe," he says, his tone mischievous. "But you know, I've never been big on following the rules."

ten

CALEB

I LEAVE THE EMPTY classroom and then stroll into *Nephilim Powers 100* across the hall, Luna trailing in my wake. Not because I'm a sexist bastard, but because I want to take the brunt of the venomous glares. I can handle it better. And unlike lovely Luna, I couldn't give two shits if I don't belong here. Goldilocks is all the friend I need, and she was quite an unexpected and unplanned for friend.

My first assessment of her was spot on. She is totally innocent about this world, and that makes me fear for her. She didn't seem to understand why Lights would freak out about her resurrection trick, which leaves her underbelly exposed for attack. Luna can't protect herself if she doesn't know the rules.

As I slide into a chair behind a long, high table, I silently vow to do my best to give her the basics so she can build some defense. I can't be with her twenty-four seven, and I have my own mission to contend with.

 119

Luna slips into the chair next to mine, causing a collective wave of silent hatred to roll over us. I just smirk at my fellow classmates, daring them to start something. I won't lie—I'm itching for a fight. Not so much for me, but for Goldilocks.

The door swings open, and our teacher for *Nephilim Powers 100* steps in. Lucifer's sake, they have me in a 100 class. Like I can't run laps around everyone in here. When I briefly met with Gabriel, she explained it was so I could gain a deeper understanding of Light powers and so her younger students could understand Dark powers better. Whatever. Mostly, I feel like a zoo exhibit.

Vesta—otherwise known as the Roman goddess of fire—steps in front of the classroom and smiles at us, a perfect, welcoming, practiced smile. I'm always surprised she's a Nephilim; she's so subdued, even for a Light. Her copper hair is pulled back in a neat twist, and she wears a lab coat, which strikes me as absurdly funny.

"Children," she begins as she always does. I guess we are children to her given how long she's been around. "Today, we are going to focus on something basic. Something that reveals our essence as Nephilim."

I feel Luna perk up beside me, and I suppress a grin at her eagerness. Damn, she's cute. I know what's coming, and I'm a lot less excited, but I enjoy her enthusiasm. This is literally a whole new world to her.

I was lucky. Yeah, my deadbeat dad bailed, but Mom knew

what I was. I was never afraid of my powers or how I didn't quite fit in with the other humans. Mom told me what she could of my heritage, promising me that one day I'd go and be with my own kind. As a kid, that terrified me, and I remember crying a lot, not wanting to leave her. But as I grew older, I longed to go to an academy, and while Gomorrah was a great primary school, the Tower of Babel proved to be everything I ever wanted. It also helped me strike a balance between belonging to the Darks and the mortal world—to Mom.

I glance at Luna's face, shining with curiosity. She never got any of that from what it sounds like. And she deserves a hell of a lot more than the experience she's getting here. This should be a time of wonder and celebration for her, not bullying and distrust and cruelty. My Goldilocks deserves more than that. It makes me want to try to talk Ishtar into having her visit Babel.

Vesta's lilting voice interrupts my thoughts from treading down that dangerous path. "Today, we are going to create flame. All Nephilim carry the fire of creation inside them, whether Light or Dark." She gives me a pointed look, and I resist the urge to roll my eyes. "Caleb's fire will look different than yours," she says to the rest of the class, "but that doesn't make it any less beautiful, as it is all gifted by the Creator."

I arch a brow. Huh, Vesta just told these Light kids that my flame is as beautiful as theirs. I don't know whether to applaud her audacity or scoff at her bullshit. Not that my fire isn't scorching, but I doubt Vesta believes it's anywhere near as good as a Light's flame.

Luna gazes at me under her lashes. "As much as I'm dreading this, I'm also looking forward to seeing your other powers. I bet your fire's amazing," she offers, voice bashful. She waves her hand at me, as if tracing an invisible outline. "Everything else is." Those last words are so soft I barely hear them, but I do hear them, and I can't help the wide grin spreading across my lips.

"So brazen, Goldilocks," I murmur. "I knew you thought I was hot." I grin harder as a dark flush rises from the collar of her shirt to sweep over her face.

"Th-that's not what I meant! I…" She bites her lip, looking mortified.

I tilt my head, leaning a little closer. "So you don't think I'm hot?" Luna grows even more flustered, and I enjoy every moment of her blushes. I wink. "It's okay. I think you're hot, too."

Luna's mouth drops, and Vesta clears her throat. I glance back at the front of the class and shrug at my teacher. I'm a rebel. Duh.

"Now that everyone is paying attention," Vesta says, and I ignore the wrathful looks of my classmates. "Search deep inside, find that spark, the essence that makes a Nephilim. Your bloodline. Find your fire there." She looks at me once more. "Caleb, since you're an advanced student, why don't you go first? Demonstrate to the others how it's done, hmm?"

Huh, I didn't expect her to trot me out like a show pony. I better perform.

"My pleasure," I say. I whirl my fingers and flick out my wrist, exposing my palm. Heat singes my blood, building and begging to be set free. Ebony fire laced with the deepest purple bursts to life about two inches from my skin. The flames grow taller and split, until two figures writhe above my palm, dancing to a beat only I can hear. Luna gasps, and although her face is pale from nerves, I see her lace her fingers tightly together to keep from reaching out to touch my fire. My eyes move back to Vesta, and I flash a shit-eating grin.

To my surprise, I see her hide a smile. "Do you see, class? How the color of his fire marks his Dark bloodline? Now, you try it."

One by one, the Light students produce white and silver flames. All except Goldilocks. She fidgets in her chair and frowns, unease in her eyes as she stares at her palm. Vesta gives her a kind smile and produces a gold flame—like it literally looks like liquid gold—pushing it toward Luna until it hovers in front of her face. Luna flinches back and studies it, her full lips flattened in a straight line. Her discomfort is palpable. Sympathy flashes through me as I see how new and batshit crazy this must all seem to her.

"To be a Light is to serve," Vesta tells her. "To please the Creator until we can Ascend. Find that tranquil part of yourself and let it warm you, and you'll find your fire."

I resist the urge to projectile vomit. Servitude sounds fun. Not. Plus, none of these little angel wannabes are pure, kind, or particularly humble in their "service." Their treatment of Luna proves that.

Goldilocks focuses on Vesta's words but nothing happens. A few snickers ripple across the room, and she shrinks into herself. Dark flame crowns my head and I snarl, eyes searching for the laughing little fuckers. Shock descends upon the crowd as the Lights observe my skill with fire.

Vesta says in a calm voice, "Class, Caleb is very advanced. One day, you will all be able to have his control. Very nice, Caleb. You can put the fire away now."

I raise a sardonic brow at my teacher, and she inclines her head. I extinguish the flames and turn to regard Luna.

"I-I'm afraid," Luna admits, and I want to hug her.

"If you're afraid your fire is volatile, it will comfort you to know servitude to the Creator will give you the ability to control your powers. You have a higher purpose—"

I give a derisive snort. "Fire isn't tranquility," I counter, my eyes meeting Luna's fearful ones. "It's powerful and destructive and life-saving, at times. But it's *your* power, Luna, not the Creator's. A force you can master and bend to your will. Think of that first moment you felt a connection to your Nephilim nature. That's where you'll find your fire. And when you find it, take control of it. It's yours to wield as you will. Don't be afraid of it."

Luna swallows hard but obeys, brows dipped in concentration.

For the first time, Vesta frowns at me in disapproval. "Caleb, that may be how a Dark connects—"

A startled squeal escapes Luna as fire bursts above her palm, hovering in the air. My jaw falls open as I stare at her flame, and a collective gasp echoes throughout the room. Her fire is ruby red. Blood red. I have never seen anything like it, and judging from Vesta's stunned expression, neither has she.

Holy shit. What exactly is Luna?

eleven

LUNA

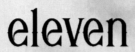

MY HEART POUNDS IN my ears as a surge of blood rushes straight to my head, making me dizzy. Everyone is staring at me, even Caleb. His eyes betray the shock his face is trying to mask, his lips set in a tight, thin line. No one else bothers to try to hide theirs.

I peer down at the flame hovering over my palm, red just like the fire that changed my life the fateful day of my first incident. My past has chased me for as long as I can remember, the tormenting reminder of this willful evil inside me always lingering at the edge of my thoughts. Yet, like when I resurrected the moth in the library, I'm somehow in control of it at this moment. It's not lashing out on its own—it's been summoned, proving that I *do* have power. That I'm a Nephilim, and I belong here as much as the other students, despite how much they torment me for being different. It's proof that Caleb and I…that there's a greater power beyond explanation we share in common, regardless of the divide between the Lights and the Darks. Above all, it's proof that the horrors of my past—the incidents that led to my time in the hospital—really were accidents beyond my comprehension. I didn't *want* to hurt anyone. Fear was always my catalyst, my panicked reactions the puppeteer pulling my strings. But now, thanks to Caleb, I've taken the first step in conquering that weakness, in reclaiming dominance of myself. Like he said, it's *my* power, and only I can choose to wield it the way it was intended. Maybe, if I do learn how to fully control it, I'll never hurt anyone again.

And yet…something about my flame isn't right. I can tell as much by the way everyone is looking at me, especially Vesta. She gapes at my fire, as if I've somehow offended her.

"Enough!" she shouts.

I startle at the booming sound of her voice, and the flame dangling over my hand disappears.

"Class is over," she announces to the other students, her wary gaze never once leaving my face. A sharp breath catches in my chest when she crosses the room and slams a hand down on the table in front of me. "You. Come with me, *right now.*"

I shift my gaze to Caleb, desperate to understand what I did wrong, but he looks as stunned as I feel. Vesta is normally so calm and collected—the perfect picture of control. Right now, her aura is anything but, as it trembles around her in a furious spasm, sizzling across her skin like an egg in a frying pan, the white light burning molten gold.

I don't understand her reaction. How could I, an inexperienced Nephilim, rattle someone as ancient as Vesta? Someone who was perceived as so *other*, so powerful by mortals who didn't know what she really was that they thought only to call her a goddess?

Swallowing, I push back my chair and hang my head to avoid the questioning stares of my classmates. I don't even spare Caleb a second glance as I follow Vesta out of the room.

As we step into the corridor, I expect my classmates to flock to the door to watch as I'm carted off to who knows where, but when I peek over my shoulder, the doorway to *Nephilim Powers* is empty. The other students don't dare to leave the room after us, despite Vesta dismissing them for the day.

My classmates' reactions are burnt into my head. They were terrified—but not of Vesta, even though her uncharacteristic outburst clearly unsettled them all. No, the fear in their eyes was for me. I recognize it, having seen that same expression on the faces of the people around me whenever I had one of my incidents. Considering what I did…well, I understand why my foster families were so afraid. Hell, I was afraid of me, too, until Alaric told me what I am.

But this? Why would a first generation Nephilim like Vesta have any need to fear an untrained student's flame?

Vesta quickens her pace through the hallway, her high heels clip-clopping along the long stretch of white marble like hooves. Her lab coat swishes around her knees.

"W-Where are we going?" I stammer, racing to keep up.

A lock of her burnt orange hair falls free from the neat twist of her updo. Nostrils flaring, she brushes it back into place. "To see the headmistress."

At the mention of Gabriel, my breath hitches and my thundering heart bangs into my ribcage. Seriously? I'm being sent to the principal's office? Sure, my fire looked a bit different when compared to the other Lights' flames—less like starlight and a lot more like blood, which yeah, I can see how that might be unnerving to a group of people who thrive on uniformity. But what do the teachers at this place expect from me? I'm new to this, and I'm trying my best. With time and practice, I'm sure my flame will be just as bright and pure as everyone else's.

Unless there's something wrong with me.

I shake off that thought and focus on the back of Vesta's white coat as she leads me down the corridor to the office. I haven't seen Gabriel since the day Alaric brought me here, but the memory of what I felt when we met is fresh, as if our encounter only just happened. I remember the awe consuming me in her presence…the way my heart seemed to seize at the sight of her…the terror when she fixed her hawk-like eyes on my face…

I'm not sure I'm ready to go through that volatile wave of emotions again so soon.

My breaths constrict as the office draws closer, and sweat forms on my palms as I clench and unclench my hands. Vesta doesn't seem to notice the anxiety radiating from my body like heat—if she does, she fails to show any remorse for her part in causing my growing distress. I've never been one to play the blame game, unless the person I'm blaming for something is me, but surely Vesta must be aware that her cryptic silence is pushing me toward an unstable precipice. I already live my life on the brink. Considering where Alaric found me, I suppose I hoped the teachers at this academy would make it a point to pull me back whenever I get too close to that edge.

Vesta peers at me over her shoulder then pushes open one of the glass office doors. Evangeline sits at her desk in reception, blinking once...twice...three times in surprise. Her large cobalt eyes drift back and forth between Vesta and an ornate grandfather clock positioned in front of the opposite wall.

"Vesta," she drawls in a condescending tone, "aren't you supposed to be teaching right now?"

With a delicate sniff, the goddess of fire plants her hands on her hips and jerks her chin toward Gabriel's door. "Is she busy?"

Tension ripples in the air, almost tangible, as I glance between the two Nephilim. It doesn't take a genius to surmise they don't get along.

As I wonder why, Evangeline's face contorts into a mocking, apologetic smile. "I'm afraid Gabriel's rather tied up at the moment—"

The aura of light around Vesta burns white hot and shivers with impatience. "This is important."

Grabbing my arm, she tugs me toward the closed black door in the corner, ignoring Evangeline's protests. Her hold on me is firm, her hand scorching through my shirt, as if the fire she's known for is leaping off her skin, intent on burning me.

Is this what it was like for the unknowing mortals unlucky enough to be around me during one of my incidents? Vesta is the epitome of control, but thanks to my display in class, she's on the verge of absolutely losing her shit. If she, of all people, is struggling to rein herself in, then no wonder I couldn't prevent all the terrible things I did before coming here. I didn't even know I had powers, let alone how the hell to restrain them.

Vesta throws open Gabriel's door without knocking then flashes a warning glare at me that freezes my steps on the other side of the threshold.

"Headmistress."

Gabriel looks up from an antique jeweled tome splayed open across her desk. "Vesta?" she says, scrunching her brow. Her eyes flash to mine, and her face immediately darkens. "Luna. What's the meaning of this?"

"Sit." Vesta signals for me to enter the room and gestures toward the chair intended for visitors facing Gabriel's desk.

Gabriel's narrowing gaze sweeps between us. "I'd like one of you to answer me. *Now.*"

Vesta steps forward obediently, arms pinned to her sides. "In my class just now, she produced a red flame. *Red*, Gabriel!" she shrieks. Her eyes are wild as she shakes her head vehemently. "Having her here has clearly displeased the Creator. It isn't natur—"

"Lower your voice," the Archangel snaps, "and be very careful what else you say." Her dark eyes flash with warning and threat.

Vesta flinches and lowers her gaze as she shuffles backward, cowering in the corner like a puppy who's been kicked by its owner. I wasn't the one Gabriel scolded, and yet, I'm mortified by the Archangel's anger. The displeasure of a greater power is almost painful to behold—like sharpened claws scratching into my soul. I'd hate to actually bear the brunt of her wrath.

If I feel this way about upsetting an angel, then I can only imagine how the Faithful must've mourned disobeying the Creator when He called them back to Heaven for mating with humans. Right now, I'd give anything to quell Gabriel's rage, so who knows what the Nephilim here are willing to do to get in the Creator's good graces.

No wonder they're all so desperate to Ascend. Ascension, to them, must mean forgiveness for their ancestors' misdeeds.

That thought doesn't sit well with me—the notion that everyone at this school was a product of someone else's bad judgment. Does that mean the Faithful viewed their Nephilim children as mistakes or just regretted the choices that led to them?

Do they resent our existence?

Gabriel adjusts the cuffs of her blue, button-up blouse and carefully closes the time-worn book. Folding her hands on top of the leather-bound cover, she fixes her gaze on my face. "Luna, why don't you tell me what happened?"

My chest tightens, and I hear Vesta's shrill voice in my head again. Except this time, I hear the rest of what she didn't get to finish saying before. The partially spoken sentiment wraps around my thoughts like a snake trapping me in its coil. *"It isn't natural."*

I'm not natural.

Something is very wrong with me.

"Am I in trouble?" I manage in a meek voice.

Gabriel smiles, and a weight lifts off my lungs, but it returns the instant I realize she didn't say that I *wasn't* in trouble. My stomach turns. "Just tell us exactly what happened in class. What was on your mind when you conjured your flame?"

"W-Well…" I hesitate, thinking back to that moment. "I tried what Vesta instructed but it didn't work. So, I-I did what Caleb suggested," I stammer.

"Which was?" Her lips twitch at the corners.

I look down at her hands. The knuckles are white from the strain of her fingers lacing together.

A lump rises in my throat, but I force myself to swallow it and keep talking. "He told me fire is a force I can bend to my will and to think…" I swallow again. "To think of the first moment I really felt like a Nephilim. When I did—"

"You produced a red flame," Gabriel finishes. "Tell me, Luna…" She rises from her chair and walks over to the window overlooking the colorful garden beyond. In the glass, I can just about make out her reflection in the bright morning light. "What moment came to mind?"

"I…"

Something feels wrong about this—like Gabriel's invading my privacy by asking. Why does it matter what I was thinking about? They should just be thankful I was able to conjure a flame without setting the building on fire.

The silence stretches on for too long, and I realize any answer I give now will likely seem manufactured. Suspicion ignites in Gabriel's eyes as she turns to face me, although that reassuring smile is still firmly in place.

"It's okay," she urges. "I'm here to help you."

My thoughts drift to Caleb. What would he do?

Based on what he thought of me when we met, I've gathered he's not a big fan of dishonesty. So, I'm going to take a leaf from his book. I'll be honest, if only to get out of this office and away from the Archangel's leering stare. And because I think Gabriel will know if I lie.

"The other day in the library, I…resurrected one of the moths in the exhibit room."

Vesta emits a screeching sound that reminds me of a dinosaur movie I saw with my last foster family a few months before I was committed. The pterodactyls in it made similar noises.

"Blasphemy!" she hisses, her face crimson with rage.

"*Vesta.*" Shadows drown the room as if the sheer boom of Gabriel's voice has sucked all the light out of the world. I shudder in my chair as Vesta presses her back to the wall.

Clearing her throat, Gabriel crosses the room toward me and

perches herself on the edge of her desk.

"Luna, allow me to be frank with you. There are certain forces that we, as Lights, have no business playing with. Those are for the Creator alone to control. Life and death are two such forces."

Her reprimand sinks into my skin, striking me like the thrash of a belt on naked flesh. Tears spring into my eyes, blurring the room.

"I...I'm sorry. I didn't know—"

She holds up a slender hand, silencing me. My voice cuts off with a tiny whimper.

"I think, for your own well-being and the safety of the other students at this academy, it would be best if I put you on academic probation for now. You are to continue attending your classes but you are also to report here every Saturday morning. We will discuss any further developments as they arise."

A frown weighs heavily on my lips. I've been placed on academic probation before, although that's usually meant suspension from classes rather than whatever this is. One of my incidents even got me expelled, and yet, somehow, this seems so much worse. Maybe it's the way Gabriel says it, or maybe it's because I'm convinced I haven't done anything wrong. For once, I was actually in control of my emotions, and now I'm being punished for it.

As if reading my mind, Gabriel adds, "I want to reiterate that this is not a punishment, Luna. I'm doing this for your own well-being."

There's that word again. *Well-being.*

I bite back the temptation to scowl.

Standing, Gabriel skirts around the large wooden desk and gracefully sinks back into the seat behind it. Her long, deft fingers open the book to resume whatever research we interrupted.

"Gabriel—" Vesta pleads, pushing away from the wall.

Gabriel points at the door, which I suddenly realize has been wide open throughout our conversation. Evangeline sits at her desk at the other end of the office, looking just about everywhere else but at us, pretending she hasn't been listening. The heaving of her chest gives her away.

"But—" Vesta protests.

Gabriel's voice is a threatening snarl. "My decision is final."

Vesta shepherds me out of my seat and through the door, having the good sense to close it behind us before the Archangel can dole out any more reprimands. Neither one of us utters a sound as we step into the sanctuary of the reception area of the office. Even Evangeline remains silent.

The shame of disappointing Gabriel is an assault on my senses. I can barely see or breathe past its weight on my heart, and beside me, surprisingly, Vesta seems just as afflicted— the goddess of fire sniffling into her sleeve like a child, once confident but now knocked down by fear. Considering how long she's been alive and how deeply entrenched she is in this world, her reaction stuns me even if I think she deserves it.

After all, she's the one who acted like I did something wrong and decided to bring me to Gabriel. Neither of us would be feeling this way if she had just left me alone.

That thought circles through my head as I finally risk a glance at my teacher's face. Glistening lines of moisture carve over her cheekbones as she steers me toward the closed doors to the hallway, and beyond the tears, I note something in her bereft gaze that makes me feel sick to my stomach. It's the same emotion I saw in the eyes of every other student in class today, including Caleb. I think I might've even glimpsed it in Gabriel's face when Vesta said I produced a red flame.

My chest constricts. No matter what I do or where I go…

Fear will always follow.

twelve

CALEB

I PACE BACK AND forth in the corridor, waiting for Luna. She's still in the office, and she's been in there for a while now. I glance down the length of the hallway, but the doors remain closed.

Frowning, I think back to class. Luna's flame was blood *red*. What does that mean? Nothing about Goldilocks quite adds up. First the resurrection and now this. I don't know what she is. Yes, she displays Dark characteristics, but I can't swear she's wholly Dark, either. Can a Nephilim be somewhere in the middle? I was told that was impossible. I mean, even if Ishtar and Gilgamesh took a roll in the sheets, I doubt they'd be stupid enough to have a kid come out of their affair.

I have a strong suspicion both Lights and Darks—despite their hatred—go slumming sometimes, just for the rush and the secret bragging rights, but a kid? One that was both Dark and Light would be thought of as an abomination and a total admission of forbidden sexing. Thanks to the schools, I know humans don't kill Nephilim children anymore—these days, they don't even know we exist—but a child born from both factions might be in serious danger from our kind. The Creator sure as shit wouldn't approve, and that might lead to the Lights eliminating the threat on His behalf. Hell, the Darks could go murderous, too, to ensure the divide.

But it's another thing I can't be entirely sure of, which brings me back to my Goldilocks.

Luna is an anomaly—and a dangerous distraction. So far, I've had nothing to report back to Ishtar about Alexander. It's true I haven't been here that long, but impatience trickles into my gut like acid, a constant burning. The student population has proven to be utterly useless, at least on the surface.

It's time to start planting suggestions and spies, but if I don't get it just right, I will raise all kinds of suspicions. And let's be honest, the only person who'd be interested in Alexander's whereabouts in this school is yours truly. I can't have that. I can't be sent back to the Tower before I find my grandfather.

One of the glass doors swings open, grabbing my attention as a distraught Luna spills out into the corridor. Vesta is beside her, and the ancient Nephilim's face is streaked with tears, shocking the hell out of me. Vesta says something to Goldilocks then heads off in the opposite direction. When I see Luna's face, I forget all about my mission for a moment. She looks terrified, and her eyes are haunted. What the hell did Gabriel say to her?

Anger rushes through my veins, but I keep my face calm as Luna's eyes find mine. She stumbles down the hallway toward me, and I resist the urge to hurry to her and take her into my arms. Ever since I rescued her, I've been careful not to touch her too much. I can't afford to get too attached, and she's someone I could easily get attached to. I genuinely like her and that's a problem.

She reaches me, and I notice she's trembling. Shit.

"What happened?" I ask gently, clenching my fists at my side, so I don't reach for her.

"I shouldn't be here," Luna says, anguish coloring her voice. "I don't belong with the Lights. I don't belong anywhere."

Oh, fuck it. I clasp her icy hands, trying to warm them. "What the hell are you talking about? Of course, you belong here. You're a Nephilim. That makes you special."

Shaking her head, she tries to pull away from me, but I won't let her. I'm pissed that Gabriel has made her feel this way.

"I'm a freak. I'll always be a freak," she insists, tears springing from her eyes and trailing down her cheeks. "And Gabriel..." She shudders from head to toe.

"Is that what Gabriel told you? That's such bullshit." I sneer. "Please, Goldilocks, tell me exactly what happened."

She takes great, gulping breaths, trying to calm down, and I pull her into a nearby cluster of shadows, allowing her a little privacy to get it together. "She's..." She hesitates, swallowing hard. "She's putting me on academic probation. I have to report to her once a week."

The gears in my head whir. "Oh-kay, that doesn't sound so horrible," I say cautiously, not wanting to upset her further. And I'm a little ashamed to admit that the calculating part of my brain is on red alert, pointing out this is an ideal opportunity to spy on the headmistress.

Luna gazes up at me, and her devastated expression feels like a punch to the crotch. "You don't understand. My powers—they aren't right. There's something wrong with me. That's why she wants to watch me. She and Vesta…they're worried about what I might do. Even here, everyone is afraid of me."

The bleakness in her voice shreds my heart, and I get into her face, forcing her to meet my fierce gaze. "That's the problem with these Light assholes," I say. "Anything that doesn't fit in their cookie-cutter mold is *wrong*. There ain't nothing wrong with you, Luna. I promise you that. Dark Nephilim celebrate our differences. We thrive on them. Fuck Gabriel. Fuck this entire place." Luna flinches at the venom in my voice. I take a deep breath and soften my tone, so I don't scare her. "Let me help you."

Hope creeps into her expression. "You think you can?"

I nod. "Look, our skill sets aren't identical, but we share basic things in common—all Nephilim do. I can help you get better and figure out what you can do. And we can practice away from judgmental eyes."

And in the meantime, I can figure out what she is. I know she's holding back on me, and I need her to trust me if she's going to open up. The awful, dragging anchor of guilt wraps around me, whispering I'm no better than the abusive Lights. At least they're honest in their cruelty. They're not trying to use her to get to Gabriel.

She blinks those big, hazel eyes at me and gifts me with a heartbreaking smile, and I feel like the biggest piece of shit on the planet. "Thank you, Caleb."

Her sincerity makes me want to lash out at her, to tell her not to be so trusting, so soft, but I bite back the words. Clearing my throat, I say, "You're welcome. Let's get out of here."

As I steer her toward the dorms, I stamp down my anger, reasoning that I'm not setting out to hurt her. That I can be her friend and use her to spy on Gabriel. I *like* Luna. I'm honestly outraged at how the other Lights treat her. My offer to help her was an honest one and she needs help. I can help Luna and find Alexander. What she doesn't know won't hurt her. I can do this. I can walk this tightrope.

And I won't fall.

thirteen

LUNA

I DON'T KNOW WHAT I would do without Caleb. Ever since that awful day in Vesta's class a few weeks ago, he's barely left my side. In many ways, he's become my lifeline—the one person keeping me afloat in the waters of sanity when everything else here seems determined to drown me. Without him, I'm not sure I would be able to weather the constant looks and whispers that echo what Vesta said to Gabriel when she brought me to the Archangel's office—that my being here has somehow displeased the Creator. I've been the target of cruel rumors before, but something about what the Lights are saying is worse.

Without Caleb, I'm also not sure I would have the strength to survive my required interactions with Gabriel. Every session, she interrogates me, prompting me with bewildering questions to divulge every single little thing I did that week, right down to how I felt when I woke up that morning. As I talk, I expect her to interrupt and finally explain what these meetings are for—meetings that feel an awful lot like my mandatory therapy sessions back when I was committed—but instead, she just sits at her desk like a statue, staring at me with those predatory eyes. I can never tell what she's thinking. To be honest, I'm not sure I want to know.

I haven't mentioned any of this to Alaric—only that I've made a friend, which he seemed pleased about, even if I was sparse on the details. While he doesn't strike me as the bigoted type, I don't want to risk finding out that he is and lose all trust in and liking I have for the only adult who's ever been in my corner. Maybe that's why I didn't inform him about my academic probation either. Our conversations are a welcome reprieve from the tension of living among the Lights, and I don't want him to blame himself for putting me in this situation...or end up afraid of me like everyone else seems to be since I revealed my flame. I'd rather pretend everything is okay than sabotage one of the only good relationships I've ever had.

Thankfully, I have Caleb to confide in, not that I ever say a whole lot about my meetings with Gabriel since mentioning the headmistress tends to sour my mood, and I don't want to put a damper on the time we spend together, which has doubled over the last three weeks. On top of the few classes we share, we've been meeting after curfew every night—in a tucked away nook in the library, far from any potential prying eyes and ears. More than anything, the Lights value order, and their innate need to please has served us well, since no one is ever roaming the halls after lights out, which makes sneaking off in the darkness of night that much easier. Even the teachers don't bother to check if anyone is out of their rooms when they shouldn't be. They know the teen Lights will follow the rules rather than risk losing any points they've possibly earned toward Ascension. The students here are obedient—except, of course, when it comes to harassing me, although in their twisted minds, I'm sure they believe their actions are justified. Hell, for all I know, they've convinced themselves they're doing the Creator's bidding.

I haven't told Gabriel about how the other Lights treat me. I guess I fail to see the point. With my luck, she'd just turn it all back on me and somehow make their behavior my fault. If she knew more trouble was brewing with me at its center, I'd only be giving her another reason to view me as a blight on this school—the first reason being my friendship with Caleb, not that she's ever used those words, or any words at all, to express her displeasure. While she's never said it, I can tell she doesn't approve, which is why, although I don't hide my public outings with him, I don't dare tell her about our meet-ups after hours. I fill those blanks in my schedule with lies. She doesn't need to know he's been helping me with basic things that every Nephilim our age should be able to do, from how to twist my flame into different shapes to simple techniques like the best way to focus. I even managed to restore a dying plant the other day. Not for long—the leaves quickly wilted again—but it was a good start, although I failed to see the difference between that and what I did with the moth. Caleb explained that restoration is a Light gift and on a separate, more acceptable level to resurrection, but it's all the same to me. All I care about is that I'm finally starting to really feel in touch with my Nephilim nature, and the progress I've made is all thanks to Caleb. Considering it was his advice and not Vesta's that helped me conjure my flame at will, I'm more inclined to listen to him than I am to anyone else—even a terrifying Archangel like Gabriel. Caleb is accepting of the strange nature of my abilities while the Lights here all see me as defective. Even our teachers seem wary of me now and have sidelined me from participating in further class demonstrations. Possibly only out of fear of what I might do, although it's more likely Gabriel gave the order to forbid my inclusion after Vesta acted as if having a red flame was somehow heresy against the Creator.

Their reactions that day still plague my thoughts. It's as if being a Light means we have to all be the same. No one is allowed to be unique—we must all be as uniform as the matching clothes we wear, symbolizing our place at this school. I don't know how I feel about that. I've obviously had my fair share of standing out from the crowd, but that doesn't mean I want to be invisible, either.

Still, despite my frustration with classes and how the other Lights continue to ostracize me, I have zero desire to leave the Serapeum. Mostly because of Caleb, but also because, for the first time in my life, the events of my past are beginning to make some semblance of sense and have an explanation beyond some invisible demons pulling at the strings in my head, as if I'm an unwilling marionette. Whether I'm eventually expelled or I depart this academy of my own volition, I don't want to leave until I more fully understand this mystifying power inside me.

For years, I was branded as a danger to myself and others. Broken. Criminally insane. Unredeemable. Looking back, I can't blame the mortals for feeling that way. I thought it, too, and most days, even now—despite knowing what I know—I still do. Guilt is a tough habit to break, and the horrors I've caused will always find a way to haunt me. But lately, I've found myself wondering how much of what I actually did was my fault, and how much was the fault of the parents who discarded me to suffer through those horrors alone? What did they think would happen to a Nephilim child isolated in a human world? My powers were bound to manifest in some way, with or without someone in the know to guide me. It just so happened the way they came out unfortunately hurt so many people.

Ever since my first day of classes when Gilgamesh talked about our ancestors in relation to the Fall, I kept the notion of my own heritage at a safe distance. I could embrace the thought of a relative who lived thousands of years ago—our only link our connection through blood. But if I dared to draw the line between that past and my birth, I'd be forced to face the questions I've been avoiding ever since I learned I'm a Nephilim.

Who were my parents? Which one had angelic blood? What

generation am I? Are they still alive? But above all, why…

Why didn't they want me?

If they hadn't abandoned me—if they had just taken the time to at least leave me with people who knew what I was—then maybe all the pain I've inflicted could have been avoided. Maybe then I wouldn't be this anomaly with powers no one else can seem to make sense of. Maybe then I wouldn't be left with this aching hole in my chest from so many years without someone to love me.

I hug my books close to my chest and lean my back against the stone wall next to my dorm room door. Caleb always meets me here, his knock a welcome interruption to sleep, which I haven't been doing a whole lot of lately. Despite the progress we've made, our midnight meetings and constant attempts to unearth the full extent of my powers are taking their toll on me—I have the bags under my eyes to prove it. I'm exhausted so sleep should come easy, and yet, I could barely sleep a wink last night, or the night before that, or the night before that, my head dizzy with a flurry of thoughts.

Last week, I realized we're halfway through the term, which means it won't be long until Caleb is forced to abandon the Serapeum and return to the Tower of Babel. He's only here for one year, and our time together is moving too quickly. When he leaves, I'll be without an ally in a school full of people who despise me. When he leaves, I'll be alone again.

Just like I always am.

My stomach clenches at the echo of footsteps, drawing my gaze to the nearby corner of the dimly lit hallway where the path diverts, continuing to the right in another long corridor—the only natural light seeping in through a stained glass window embedded in the wall facing me, which illuminates the tall figure standing in front of it. A crooked smile tugs at Caleb's cheeks when he sees me.

"Morning, Goldilocks. You're up early."

"Couldn't sleep." I shrug. No need to tell him my fear of him leaving me to go back to his own kind was the underlying cause of my insomnia.

"Bad dream?" he asks, taking my books from my hands. He piles them on top of his own, holding the load easily in the crook of his left elbow. The Lights can say what they want about the Darks, but Caleb has better manners than they do.

"Something like that."

A flirtatious smirk crosses his lips. "Well, you're still smokin' hot to me, dark circles and all."

Warmth spreads across my face when he winks.

We walk, side by side, ignoring the usual probing gazes of the other students, as we make our way to *History of the Fall*. Although he tries to hide it, I can sense Caleb's disdain for this class. I see it in the way his aura quivers when we step into the classroom, the darkness striking out in every direction like hundreds of tiny whips in search of bare flesh to cut into. They continue to flail, even as we take our usual seats in the back of the room.

"Good morning, class." Gilgamesh bows in greeting and gestures to the whiteboard with a wide sweep of his arm where "Dark" and "Light" are scrawled in large letters, separated by a bold, black line. "Today, I want to dive into the separation existing between the Darks and the Lights, why that divide was born, and why it continues to thrive to this day, thousands of years after the Fall."

Caleb lets out a soft groan beside me. I glance at him out of the corner of my eye, noting the way his mouth is pinched at the corners, as if he's holding back some choice words on the subject. It must be hard for him—being the only Dark in this school. I'm a Light, and it's hard for *me* to listen to all the reasons why we're different. Or rather, why we're supposed to be different.

In reality, I seem to have more in common with Caleb than I'm sure I ever will with the Lights. Although she hasn't said it, I know that's part of the reason why Gabriel insisted on our weekly meetings. I glimpsed the unease in her eyes when I explained how Caleb helped me with my flame that day in *Nephilim Powers*. She doesn't like that he's succeeded where all the Lights have failed to guide me.

Gilgamesh's deep, soothing voice pulls my gaze back to the front of the classroom.

"At the dawn of time, Darks and Lights were the same. They were all angels under the rule of the Creator, but that changed when Lucifer Morningstar sparked the rebellion that led to the Great Battle of Heaven. As a result, a divide was born with

Lucifer's followers on one side and those who resisted him on the other."

Gilgamesh peers down the aisle, his eyes flicking between my desk and Caleb's. Maybe I'm imagining things—it wouldn't be the first time—but I could've sworn that last sentence was directed at us. As if he's trying to tell us our friendship is dangerous. That we need to stay on our separate sides, as dictated by our bloodlines. To respect the divide.

As if to warn us Darks and Lights have no business mixing.

I look over at Caleb again to see if he noticed it, but he's doodling instead of paying attention to the lesson. He's hunched over in his seat, focusing on a caricature of Gilgamesh he's drawn across the top right corner of his desk. Once that doodle is perfected, he moves onto another—this one of a beautiful woman shooting lightning bolts straight into Gilgamesh's ass.

"The angels who fell alongside Lucifer believed in his fight for free will while those who remained loyal to Heaven believed solely in their duty to the Creator. Over the millennia, these views haven't changed. The Lights continue to swear their fealty to the only being truly worthy of our love while the Darks indulge in the freedoms on Earth that were never meant to be theirs. To this day, they're as blinded by their lust for a 'human experience' as the angels who followed Lucifer were by his betrayal. This is why Light Nephilim are encouraged to only reproduce with other Lights, although we aren't bound by the same rules as the angels in regards to our relations with humans.

Still, in the eyes of the Creator, a union between Lights is the only way to slow down dilution and keep our bloodlines as close to their pure, Ascension-ready forms as possible. Meanwhile, Darks carry on their transgressions with mortals—"

Gilgamesh stops speaking when I thrust my hand in the air, a question forming in the crease of his brow. I wouldn't normally interrupt a lesson, but everything he's saying feels weighted to one side, like he's only telling us half of the truth. There are always two sides to every story—I would know. I don't think I'm a bad person, but I've done terrible things. I'm a Light, and yet, I empathize with the Darks.

If a Light can be filled with such darkness, then surely, a Dark can also reach for the light.

"Yes, Luna?" Gilgamesh asks, his tone cautious.

Caleb looks up at the sound of my name and meets my gaze across the aisle.

I draw in a breath. "Has a Dark ever Ascended?"

A collective gasp swamps the room as the auras of the Lights all flicker and twitch with disgust. Lisbeth and Ellie shoot dirty glares back at me, whispering behind their hands to each other. Even Caleb looks stunned by my question.

"I, uh…" Gilgamesh lets out a shaky laugh and runs a hand over his closely cropped hair. Clearing his throat, he rocks back on his heels. "That's impossible."

"Why?" I press, my own tone edging on forceful.

Gilgamesh stares at me for a moment then turns toward the

board and erases the words written there, replacing them with a new one.

Ascension

"If you'll recall from past lessons, I explained how when the Nephilim were created, part of the angels' punishment for their procreation with humans was that their children would remain here on Earth. The gates of Heaven were closed to us, but the Creator, in His eternal benevolence, offered us the chance to join our Faithful ancestors. Ascension is how we gain entry to Heaven, but to Ascend is to give every part of yourself to the Creator. To pledge your love and devotion to Him. To swear fealty and seek forgiveness for any wrongdoings you might have committed on Earth, which includes relations with humans, an action expressly forbidden for any who are chosen to reside in Heaven. Lights understand that our love for the Creator outweighs all else, even our love for each other. By contrast, Darks are, by nature, incapable of seeking forgiveness or of loving anyone or anything more than they love themselves. That is why they will never Ascend."

Anger burns along my skin. Doesn't Gilgamesh realize Caleb is sitting *right there* while he says these awful things about Darks? The old Luna wouldn't dare talk back to a teacher or to anyone for that matter. The old Luna wouldn't have the nerve to.

But in this moment, I feel reborn in my rage.

"You assume that because of an event that took place hundreds of thousands of years ago?" I scoff. "Isn't the Creator supposed to be merciful?"

The other Light students all shift in their seats, moving as far away from me as the confines of their desks allow. From the looks on their faces, you would think I just threatened them all with the bubonic plague. Beside me, Caleb is eerily still.

Gilgamesh knits his hands behind his back and offers me a condescending smile. There's a sense of pity in the deep pools of his eyes, as if he's thinking, *"Oh, look at this poor orphan girl who is so uninformed about our world."*

"Despite our shared goal of avoiding exposing our kind to the humans, the Darks have been known to torment the very mortals they envy in their desperation to prove they no longer have any loyalty or emotional ties to Heaven," he says in a way that suggests this is a widely known fact. "This is a terrible sin in the eyes of the Creator who put angels on Earth to protect and guide the humans, not to mate with them or torture them for their own personal amusement. This sin is not worthy of His forgiveness."

Torture?

My eyes dart to Caleb, searching his face for a monster, but all I see is my friend.

He wouldn't do that...would he? I wonder.

As if sensing my uncertainty, Caleb snorts, laughing under his breath. "This is such bullshit."

"Caleb, do you have something you wish to share with the class?" Gilgamesh crosses his arms over his broad chest, his gruff voice rife with annoyance, matching the vexed expression on his face.

As I glance between them, I sink into my seat, wishing I could disappear.

"I said"—Caleb sneers, his hands curling into fists on his desk—"this is *bullshit.*"

"Which part, exactly?" Gilgamesh asks through a sigh.

"All of it!" Caleb shouts. "You preach tolerance and forgiveness and act as if you Lights are above reproach when your ancestors were just as much a part of that war as the Darks. It takes two to tango, dick."

Gilgamesh's golden skin flushes red. "The Lights fought for the honor of the Creator—"

"No," Caleb cuts in, jumping to his feet, "they fought to keep us enslaved. That was the real betrayal. All Lucifer wanted was to set us all free—"

Our teacher holds up a hand. "That is the mindset of your lineage. The Darks crave free will, but that is not part of our role in this world. Wanting for something the Creator hasn't allowed you is blasphemy."

A taunting grin sweeps along Caleb's lips. "And I'm guessing *that* viewpoint is why your relationship with Ishtar is such a dumpster fire."

Gilgamesh's face contorts. Clearly, Caleb struck a nerve.

"That is none of your business—"

The older Nephilim takes a heated step forward, and for a moment, I think he might attack Caleb. I move to the edge of my seat, my heart racing.

This is my fault. If I had just kept my ignorant comments to myself, Gilgamesh wouldn't have said those awful things, which in turn incited Caleb to anger. Why am I always the cause of so much pain and destruction?

"Let me guess," Caleb snarks, his voice intentionally cruel. "Being with Ishtar made you feel selfish and maybe even a little bit like a Dark. Wouldn't want you empathizing with the wrong side, G. Is that why you haven't Ascended yet? Assuming that's not some lie you tell your little Lights to get them to behave."

Gilgamesh stalls in his tracks, his eyes wandering over the other desks, suddenly aware of their silent audience. Everyone in the class is staring at him, although a few students cast curious looks over their shoulders at Caleb, as if they aren't sure who, between them, is telling the truth. This is probably the first time their views have been challenged.

Clenching his teeth, Gilgamesh fixes his gaze back on Caleb. "Ascension is very real. You would know that if Darks gave a damn about anything other than their own selfish desires."

My heart trips on that word. *Selfish.*

Gilgamesh doesn't know Caleb like I do. Selfish is the furthest thing from what he is.

"Wanting freedom and love isn't selfish," Caleb retorts. "It's natural. The most natural thing in the world."

"Nothing about you *demons* is natural," Gilgamesh snaps, spitting the words. "That's why the separation exists!"

"Fuck this." Caleb scoops his books off his desk and storms down the aisle, charging straight for the door.

My fingernails dig into my thighs as I stare at his back, watching him storm off in a fury. Part of me wants to run after him while another part considers if he'd want me to. After all, it was my question that led to this mess.

Gilgamesh wags a long finger in warning. "If you walk through that door—"

Caleb spins on his heel. "I'm not going to sit here and listen to your bullshit when you *perfect* Lights are just as bad if not worse than us Darks. At least we're honest about who we are. If being faithful to the Creator means being an asshole, you can count me out. I want no part of it."

Caleb throws the door open with such force it slams into the wall with a bang, and the glass in the top half of the wooden frame shatters, making a few girls sitting in the front row squeal and jump back. The glass shards littering the floor mimic my own scattered nerves.

As Caleb stomps into the corridor, I push to my feet, drawn to his every move like a planet caught in the gravitational pull of the sun. At this moment, I know that wherever he goes, I will follow—to hell with this segregation born from choices made thousands of years ago by ancestors I don't even know. This divide is theirs.

Not mine.

Gilgamesh's eyes narrow on me as I bend down to retrieve my books from under my chair. "Luna, please return to your seat." The threatening edge to his voice makes me flinch.

I drop my head and swallow, searching for the courage to speak. I don't want to cause any more problems, but I also can't bear to hear another word. Right now, I need to know that Caleb's okay. Caleb is my friend. My *only* friend, excluding Alaric, but that friendship is different, hindered by age and distance. In this lonely and isolating place, Caleb is all I have.

We need to stick together.

"No, thanks." I lift my chin and force myself to meet the older Nephilim's gaze. "With all due respect, I think I've heard enough, too."

My heartbeat thrums in my ears as I hurry from the classroom, away from who I'm meant to be, and toward the one person who accepts what I actually am.

I race toward Caleb without looking back.

fourteen

CALEB

RAGE BLINDS ME TO my surroundings. I storm through the halls with no destination in mind. I only know I have to get away from Gilgamesh and his lies. Jesus, no wonder all the Lights hate us if this is the steaming pile of horse shit they're fed. I mean, technically, I know this is what they're taught. Dark Nephilim don't exactly sing the Lights' praises, either. But to experience the one-sided story firsthand feels different somehow, more hurtful, which is ridiculous. Maybe because for the first time, it's hammered home that we're all Nephilim, Light or Dark. Why are we such dicks to each other? We look down on humans for their petty grievances and grudges, but from where I stand, we're no better. We're just gifted with a lot more power that can cause maximum damage.

But the fact that Gilgamesh is the one who said it makes me angrier. He didn't seem like as much of an asshole as some of the other teachers, but I guess I was wrong. Is this why he and Ishtar never worked? He thought she was just some half-demoness and beneath him? The ironic thing is the Morningstar wears his Archdemon label with pride now, as do the other Archdemons. The "demon" label certainly doesn't bother him, and most days, it doesn't bother me, either. But the way it was used here… My blood boils.

I hear a voice in the background, but it takes a moment to penetrate the angry haze. I whirl around, itching for a fight, but I don't see an enemy. I see Luna. Lovely Goldilocks has followed me. She hesitates, and I realize I'm scowling like a psychopath. I relax my features. Managing a smile is beyond me right now, but at least I no longer resemble a serial killer. I hope.

The wariness still clinging to her makes me doubt I look any less scary or pissed off, so I tease, "You stalking me now, Goldilocks? What will all the little Lights say? Such a scandal in these hallowed, sacred halls." Okay, so I don't quite keep the biting mockery out of that last sentence, but I'm still rewarded with Luna's smile.

She shrugs. "They already talk about us. Nothing new there." She manages an eye-roll, and her sass lightens my heavy heart a bit. Usually, she's too shy to be sassy.

My smile is genuine this time. "We'll give them something to talk about for years. Their bullshit, fake truce might actually have worked. A Light and Dark can be friends. Now, they're in the shit. We might start a trend."

Luna's expression darkens. "That would be nice. If only…"

She bites her lip.

I heave a big sigh. "I'm afraid you're right, Goldilocks. If this is what you're taught about the Fall, Lights and Darks are doomed."

I don't know why this bothers me so much. It's not like I've ever been interested in being friends with a Light before—that is until I met Luna. But again, I've never been exposed to this level of prejudice. Or been expected to swallow it like it's normal and right.

Taking a step closer to me, she reaches out a hand, her fingers hovering mere centimeters from my arm. I wait for her to touch me, but her uncertainty overcomes her, and she drops her hand. Disappointment washes over me briefly. I hoped she'd be braver.

Shoving my hands in my pockets, I start walking again and she keeps pace. We duck into one of the many open courtyards, but this one features tall growing fruit trees, offering shade and a bit of camouflage from watching eyes. I sink down on a carved stone bench, heart still pounding in anger.

"What is it that you're taught?" Luna whispers. "I want to know." Her voice is firmer this time.

My brows arch in surprise and pleasure, but I guess I shouldn't be surprised. Luna has always been different. I need to start believing it. It's me who keeps hiding things from her. I rest my back against the trunk of a grapefruit tree, measuring my words.

"Look," I begin, "we don't like the Lights any more than they like us, but it's not because we're immoral demons who are completely selfish and like to torture mankind. The Lights like to think they're better than us, but they're not—they're so not." I groan, shaking my head, knowing I'm making a mess of this explanation. I glance at Luna, but she's just listening, face intent on my words, eyes rapt. I can't help but grin at her. She's gorgeous, my Goldilocks.

Her lips curve up, her smile sweet. "From what I've seen, they're worse."

I chuckle. "They've never been nice to me," I admit. "You have to understand, Luna, the Darks, we're all about free will. Choice. The Fall for Lucifer, for his followers, was about having a choice. They saw humans and their emotions and their capacity to love...and they wanted that. They wanted more than blind devotion and servitude. They wanted it so badly they went to war over it." Sighing, I shake my head again. "Maybe that's selfish. Maybe wanting more is selfish. I don't know. The Lights want to Ascend to Heaven and return to the Creator, but we're just happy to be here on Earth. Living how we want. Loving how we want. I've never tortured a human in my life. I'm a mama's boy, for Christ's sake."

Luna's face grows serious. "You know your parents?"

I study her. I've heard rumors she's an orphan, although I haven't asked her about it. "I know my mom," I say. "My dad is a classic deadbeat. He spreads his Nephilim seed and never sticks around to help raise his kids. Classy guy."

"So your mom...she's not a Nephilim?"

"No, but she knew my dad was. She did her best by me—she's amazing. I'll always be grateful to her."

A wistful expression clouds her eyes. "You miss her."

My chest clenches a little. I hate that Mom lives alone. She needs a boyfriend or girlfriend to look after her. I think my dad did a real number on her. "Yeah, I miss her. I visited her shortly before coming here."

Luna wraps her arms around herself. "You're lucky," she murmurs. "I don't know who my parents are."

Sympathy stabs my chest. "You don't remember them at all?"

Her jaw clenches. "No. For as long as I can remember, I've been tossed around from one foster home to another. There have been so many I've lost count." Her voice brims with bitterness and pain.

I squeeze my fists hard at the sound of it. "I'm sorry, Luna. That sucks." I mean it. I'm starting to gather the pieces of Luna's past, and the picture I'm forming in my head isn't a pretty one.

Luna glances up at me, curiosity replacing the pain. "So torturing humans isn't one of your pastimes?"

"No," I say, shrugging, suppressing a laugh at her unexpected joking tone. "I won't pretend I haven't mind surfed—it's fun—but I've never forced mortals to do anything. Well, okay, so I've heard some bad thoughts before, people planning to hurt someone else, and I...took them off that path."

Her gaze narrows, all traces of amusement gone. "Like the way you took Ellie and Lisbeth and their friends off the path of beating me up?"

I grin. "Something like that. I didn't hold back with those assholes the way I do with humans." Seeing her worried expression, I add, "Luna, they deserved what they got. They were going to hurt you for being different, no other reason."

"And the bad humans? Did they deserve it?"

I raise my brows at the censure in her voice. "I've stopped murderers and rapists, Goldilocks. So, yeah, they deserved it," I say quietly.

She blanches, glancing away. "Sorry," she says. Then her eyes dart to my face. "And me? Do you ever…?" A blush sweeps over her cheeks, flushing her skin with color.

"No, I haven't." Not for lack of trying. "Your thoughts are safe from me." Which is a shame because I might be able to figure out what she is. But with her utter lack of knowledge about Nephilim, maybe not. Sigh.

Relief floods Luna's face. "Do all Darks have the ability to read minds?"

I pick at my stupid tie, trying to decide how many of our secrets to reveal, although I don't think Luna will tell. "Not all of us, but most do. All the Archdemons can tear your mind open if they want to." I shoot her a sardonic look. "And don't think for a second that Gabriel can't, either. She can. That's why I don't want her to know about my tricks. I don't need her poking inside my head, although it's forbidden for her, so technically she's not allowed to." I snort. "Not that I trust a Light not to be a hypocrite." And I have that extra special dagger hidden away if Gabriel comes after me.

A shiver ripples over Luna, pebbling her skin in the heat. "She seems like someone who thinks rules are very important."

"She's a rigid prick, you mean?" I tease.

Shocked laughter escapes her lips, and she glances around, as if afraid someone overheard my remark. "She's terrifying," she whispers.

I frown, thinking back to Luna's meeting with the exalted headmistress the day she first produced her flame, and how she's seemed after every meeting since then. She's never really had much to say about them until now. "Did Gabriel hurt you?" I growl.

"No—no, she didn't," Luna assures me, eyes impossibly wide. "But…the thought of disappointing her, of having her angry with me…" Confusion furrows her brow. "It makes me want to please her, although I can't explain why. Does that make sense?"

I nod. "Yes, angels are beautiful and terrible and can make even the most badass first generation Nephilim shit their pants in a heartbeat. But you don't have to please her, Luna. You don't have to dance to her tune like a puppet."

She laughs, a thready sound lacking humor. "I do if I want to stay at this academy."

She has a point, but I say, "Don't let them change you into some obedient robot. Just go along with their rules enough that they think you're falling in line without losing yourself, okay?"

"Doesn't the head of your school demand obedience?"

I chuckle. "To a point, but then it's go out and do you." At her questioning look, I expand. "All of us—Light and Dark— have to follow certain rules. First and foremost is that mortals can't be aware of us. We can't go flashing our powers around or taking over the world. That's the deal. Sometimes, we fuck up, but since we don't make a habit of killing our own, the only option is to discourage any humans who discover our secret from blabbing about it. Mom wasn't supposed to know what Dad was, but he had a big mouth, and she kept the Nephilim secret or she'd be dead. It's not that unusual for mortal parents to be involved with their kids these days—they just have to keep quiet. And the threat of death hanging over your head like the sword of Damocles is usually a good motivator."

Luna blinks at me, stunned. "*Dead?* So secrecy above all?"

"Yeah, it's the first rule. My teachers expect me to learn how to control my powers, and they expect me to be responsible. And if I step out of line and embarrass them by being blatantly stupid, Asmodeus would strip my hide. She doesn't suffer fools."

"Asmodeus?"

"Archdemon and headmistress of Babel. Someone not to be messed with. Just as scary as Gabriel."

Luna's mouth drops. "And she *whips* you?"

Laughing, I say, "I'm a Nephilim. I'll heal. Besides, if there's ever a time when Asmodeus whips me, then trust me, I deserve it. These rules are in place for our safety, as well as to protect the mortals. But we Darks, we're not encouraged to be little copies of each other, looking and sounding alike. Hell, we don't wear uniforms. This is stupid." I pluck at my tie again, irritated.

A strange expression falls over Luna, and she presses her lips together, her eyes searching my face. "Have you ever met Lucifer?"

Her question catches me off guard, but I guess I shouldn't be surprised. We were just talking about the Fall. "Yeah, I've met him. He comes around to all the academies at least once a year."

"What's he like?" she asks, eagerness in her voice.

I laugh. "A legend. Like all the angels and demons, scary as hell. I never want him pissed at me. Sometimes he's funny. Larger than life. His presence is this big." I expand my arms as far as they go, stretching one behind her and the other one in the opposite direction before letting them fall to my side. "And…sad, I think." I clamp my lips together. I've never mentioned that aloud before, and it feels like a secret I shouldn't be sharing, but I don't know why.

Luna's brow puckers. "Sad? How?"

I glance away. "I don't think he regrets his actions…but he has to miss home, right? I mean, I don't think he wants to go crawling back and beg for forgiveness. He loves Earth and his freedom, but he was banished from his home and the Creator. Losing a parent sucks no matter how it happens, don't you think?"

Her face falls. "I wouldn't know."

I kick myself but point out, "Yes, you do. You might not have known your parents, but you feel their loss, right?"

She gives me a thoughtful nod. "I never thought of it that way. Is it weird to miss something you've never had?"

"Not weird at all," I assure her, resisting the urge to tuck an errant strand of hair behind her ear.

Reaching out, she takes my hand, sliding my fingers between hers until our hands are entwined. I almost yank away in surprise—she's never touched me on her own, though I know she's wanted to. Luna squeezes my hand.

"I wish this—you being here—was a real truce and not just temporary. I wish I could go to the Tower of Babel with you and learn from the Darks as well as the Lights. See it all from both sides." Her eyes drop and she whispers, "I've never had a real friend before you. I don't want them to ever tear us apart."

With a hesitant hand, I tilt up her chin. She gazes at me with silvered eyes, and I want to kiss her tears away, make her gasp until she forgets her pain and sadness. She glances at my lips and I swallow. Shit, I'm in trouble. Instead, I say, "They can't take me away from you. I'll always be your friend, no matter what. You can't get rid of me that easily, Goldilocks."

She gifts me with a watery smile and wedges her head between my chin and shoulder, hiding her face. I snake an arm around her waist and pull her close, and she snuggles against me. My heart thunders in my chest, and I hope I can get through this without breaking her heart. Or mine.

fifteen

LUNA

I PRESS MY FACE against Caleb's chest, breathing in the welcoming smell of him. I never thought I'd meet anyone who would dare get this close to me. I never thought I would *want* someone this close.

His arm around my waist is so warm, so comforting—what I imagine it would be like to be wrapped in the embrace of a parent, only a thousand times better. His other hand sits in his lap in a fist, as if he's not sure what to do with it. Or as if he's restraining himself.

Encouraged by urges I don't understand, I reach out and trail a finger over that hand, tracing the path of his skin up his exposed forearm—his black uniform shirt rolled up to his elbows like always—relishing the way his aura dances and readjusts to my wandering, careful caress. Caleb sucks in a sharp breath at my touch, and although I know I should be embarrassed about what I'm doing, I'm not. I can't help myself.

I just want to feel his encompassing shadows wash over my hand and never let go of this closeness.

An unrecognizable sensation ties my stomach in knots, and I pull away just enough to look up at him. His dark eyes flick down to mine as he swallows.

"Luna?"

I lean in, drawn close to him by his unsteady breaths grazing my cheeks, every last one like the life-saving gasp of air needed to save me from drowning. I don't know what I'm doing. I don't know what I'm feeling. I just need to be closer to him, no matter what that means.

"Go on," a familiar voice says in my ear.

A soft breath fills my throat, and I hesitate with only inches separating our faces. I haven't heard that strange whisper of a voice since that day in the library—at the time, I brushed it off as a figment of my imagination, and with everything that happened right after and since then, I honestly forgot all about it. After all, I've done far crazier things in my life than manifest a voice in my head. Besides, the voice wasn't important—it was what I accomplished as a result of its encouragement that mattered. The voice itself wasn't worth a second thought.

But now, as it croons in my ear, I can't help wondering if some deeper part of myself, long buried and ignored, is trying to speak to me. Perhaps it's the suppressed part of my angelic existence rising to the surface or some carnal desire attempting to make itself known. Or maybe my inability to fully connect with my

Nephilim nature has caused me to develop Dissociative Identity Disorder—my human side at odds with the immortal. At least that would explain why the voice sounds nothing like me, since it's not unheard of to develop an alternate personality in another gender. Or so I overhead once during my time in the hospital.

Regardless of what the voice is or where it's coming from, if I listen to it, then maybe I can finally pluck up the courage to do the one thing I've wanted to do since the first moment I laid eyes on Caleb. It guided me once before and I did something great—or at least, I thought I did before Gabriel and Vesta acted like I had set a litter of puppies on fire. But neither of them are here now to stomp on my confidence, and surely, the voice can guide me again.

Spurred on by its urging, I release Caleb's hand and lift my fingers to his face, cupping his right cheek against my palm. The corner of his mouth twitches, and he licks his lips, the tip of his tongue attracting my gaze, pulling me even closer.

Our breaths collide as the distance between our lips vanishes in the space of a single heartbeat. When we meet, his grip tightens around my waist, his nails biting into my flesh through my shirt with a heady mix of desperation and hunger. That ravenous need rushes through me as well, and even though I don't know if I'm doing this right, I knot my fingers into his sable hair and deepen the kiss until it's impossible to see where his darkness ends and my light begins.

His free hand slides across the side of my neck, sending a

pleasurable shiver rocketing through me, and as he kisses me, I picture a world that makes sense. A world where prejudice and outside influence wouldn't pose a threat to whatever this is growing between us. A world where being Dark or Light wouldn't matter.

"You will change the world," the voice says. *"You have the power to change everything."*

A moan rumbles in Caleb's chest as he pulls me firmly against him, one hand running up my back, making me gasp against his lips, as the other forms a tight fist in my hair. His warmth, the taste of him, it's an explosion of ecstasy. I've never felt anything like it. I never want it to stop.

How? I whisper back in my head, a sense of urgency drawing my free hand to Caleb's shirt where I cling to him with frantic fingers, too afraid to let go.

When the voice answers, I hear the smile behind every word. *"Let me show you."*

Heat spreads through me, wild and fierce—a raging inferno that ignites behind my closed eyes and sears a hole in the idyllic world I lost myself in only a moment before. Everything around me is devoured in a sea of red fire. Buildings I've never seen before tumble to the ground in a swathe of smoke, and as they collapse, my vision pans to the Serapeum, which burns much like the Library of Alexandria must've burned thousands of years ago.

And in the center of it all, I see Caleb. Flames that could only have come from me lick across his bubbling flesh as he reaches out a shaking hand, his lips soundlessly shaping my name.

"No!" I shriek, jerking free of the arms wrapped around me. Sweat beads along my brow as I hunch over, trembling, despite the heat still burning under my skin.

"What's wrong?" Caleb's voice suddenly seems a hundred miles away. I shake my head without looking up at him.

The fire I saw just now in my head was a warning, a reflection of what I'm capable of. Lately, I've been ignoring the lessons of my past and what I just witnessed is a stark reminder of what will inevitably happen if *this*—this sense of comfort I've found with Caleb—is allowed to carry on any longer. Because eventually fear will find a way to slip in. It's *already* sinking its claws into me whenever I think about him leaving this school. And the longer I ignore it, the longer I try to push it back, the stronger that fear will become until I won't be able to stop myself from lashing out.

I should've known getting close to Caleb was stupid. Whenever I've let anyone get close before, I only ended up hurting them. Even just physical proximity to me puts him in danger. All that ever awaits anyone near me is pain.

It was foolish of me to think I could be happy.

Tears slip from between my clenched eyelids and streak down my face as I drag in a strangled breath.

"Hey…" Caleb presses a tentative hand to my back. "Goldilocks, you all right?"

173

"I…"

I raise my chin and fix my bleary gaze on a patch of ivory flowers blooming by my right foot in the seemingly eternal summer of Alexandria, despite it being late October. In the middle of this one tiny patch, a dark purple flower tinged with blue at the edges is wilting, untouched by the celestial magic keeping the rest of the garden alive and intact. That flower is the same shade as Caleb's aura, of his darkness which I find so beautiful…

And I know, if this thing between us goes any further, death will come to claim him, too.

"I have to go," I blurt, launching myself off the bench.

Caleb's protests trail after me, following my steps as I race along the stone path out of the enclosed garden and into the escape of the nearest building. As I run, cracks form along the edges of my heart and work inward, breaking me.

Pressing a hand to my mouth to stifle my cries, I thrust myself through the first door I come across, slamming it shut behind me before sinking to the floor, my knees buckling under my weight. To my relief, I've trapped myself in a small storage closet—no one will think to look for me here. The shadows of the cramped room wrap around me like arms attempting to console me in my grief.

My fingernails bite into my palms, leaving crescent moon marks in my skin, when I repeat to myself what Caleb said to me when we first met.

Best stick to your own kind.

A fresh sob catches in my throat at the thought. But he was right. We never should've walked down this road. Our friendship has painted a target on his back, and keeping my distance from this point on is the only way to ensure his safety from the twisted evil responsible for my many crimes, since clearly nothing at this school can tame it. Because that's what the voice is, I see that now, even though, until recently, it's always been silent. Everyone in the mortal world, from the doctors to the social workers, were right about me all along.

A sinister demonic presence resides inside me.

And if the past is anything to go by, I am too weak to resist it.

sixteen

CALEB

WITH CAREFUL HANDS, I carve the torso of the terracotta figure, adding details to the female warrior's armor. I thought it fitting to create a miniature of Ishtar in her glory days to spy on Gilgamesh. Two more figures lay on the table, already completed. Gabriel and Vesta will be getting their visitors later, albeit generic male ones that might bear a passing resemblance to Hammurabi.

The large art room is empty except for me, my sculpting knife providing the only sound in the cavernous space. I've moved on to phase two of my plan after getting zero info from the student body. They are as naive as they are prejudiced. Luna has provided plenty of information, just not the kind I need.

At the thought of Goldilocks, I dig a little too hard into the clay, gouging it. Cursing, I quickly smooth the surface out. Luna has been dodging me this past week, and I don't like it. Understatement. I *hate* it. After confessing I'm the only friend she's ever had, she snuggled against me, laid a smoking hot kiss on me, then fled the scene like I was an ax murderer. Which under the circumstances, I don't deserve the cold shoulder she's been throwing my way. And I'm a good kisser, dammit, so it can't be that.

Luna avoids me in class and in the hallways, and I refuse to go to her dorm. I don't want to come off like some creepster, and yeah, I have my pride. But I'm…hurt. Despite my intentions and better judgment, I've grown attached to Luna, even though I know that's not a good idea. Because eventually I'm going to leave, and she'll be on her own. I can't be her savior. My grandfather has to come first, not a blonde bombshell. No matter how sweet she is or how much I like her.

Still, her rejection stings. I'm not used to being rejected. And I miss her. She, too, is my only friend in this gilded cage. I almost resent her for that. I expected solitude here, and she was an unexpected gift of companionship, and now she's gone. At least I wish I knew what I did to freak her out. I try to tell myself that she reached for me first and kissed me but it's little comfort. I sigh. Before Luna, I had no problems with women.

Finishing up the miniature of Ishtar, I stand all three figures in front of me and reach for my powers. Wisps of purplish black smoke curl around my wrists and then wrap around the figures. As one, their tiny chests heave, and their painted eyes focus on me. Blinking, I slide into their primitive minds and gaze out of their eyes, seeing myself staring back at them.

"Turn around," I command and they obey, turning their backs to me, and my vision shifts with theirs. Yep, it all seems to be working. If I need to find them at any time, I'll be able to. "Attention back to me."

Like puppets on a string, they pivot, slaves to my will. I smile. "Damn, I'm good," I murmur, crossing my arms over my chest. I show them in my mind what I want from them. I nod at the replica of Ishtar. "You, follow Gilgamesh." I point at the other two. "You, tail Gabriel, and you, Vesta. If you hear anything about Alexander, report back to me immediately. Actually, if you hear anything about Luna, let me know, too." Even if she isn't speaking to me at the moment, Goldilocks is still another enigma worth solving. "And remember, don't get caught."

The three of them nod and salute like the good little soldiers they are then they climb down the table legs. They scurry across the room, keeping to the shadows. They are creepy as hell, and I couldn't be prouder. I grin, rubbing my hands together with glee like a cartoon villain, only I'm not the villain in this piece. The Lights are for imprisoning my grandfather for thousands of years.

I rise, stretching. I've been in here for hours, and it's time to make a public appearance before anyone gets suspicious that the evil Dark transfer is plotting their demise. I head into the corridor, closing the art studio's door softly behind me. No one needs to know I sculpt like a Renaissance master or that I animate my creations. Gabriel will kick me right back to Babel, if she doesn't punish me first for daring to give life to anything.

I don't want that bitch in my head. That could start a war.

I make my way to the dorms, eager to get back to my room, so I can have some quiet time to watch my spies and make sure they're in place. My room is pretty sweet and in a hallway by itself, as I guess they didn't want to upset the delicate Lights by having a big, scary Dark near them. Such bullshit. But it does provide privacy from prying eyes and ears. That's always a bonus.

I take a sharp turn and enter the hallway for the dormitory wing, with a wide, ornate staircase leading up and branching off into the girls' and boys' dorms. As it's the weekend, there aren't as many students around since they're allowed a bit of freedom into Alexandria and anywhere else they want to go. I'm not quite sure how the Lights travel, but I know they have a version of the Shadow Road. And snotty little pricks or not, they're teens with powers who probably want to explore the world and party before leaving it all behind to Ascend. I can relate—not to the Ascension part—although I'd only ever admit that under torture.

As my feet hit the first step, I flick through the thoughts of the kids around me out of habit, catching two that make my pulse pound.

Lights aren't friends with Darks…

She doesn't have her Dark boyfriend around to protect her this time…

Luna. I pinpoint the thoughts leading me to two girls and a guy, threatening her outside her room. For Lucifer's sake, you'd think word would've gotten around about the first beating I dished out. These Light pieces of shit never learn.

Fear makes my feet fly up the steps where I hook a left onto the nearest spiraling stairs leading up to Luna's floor. I sprint down the corridor. I take a turn into another endless hallway—no matter how often I pick Luna up here, this place reminds of a prettier, more luxurious version of the Overlook Hotel—and then I find them. The guy has Luna's arms behind her back, and one of the girls—a freckled redhead—digs her nails viciously into Luna's cheek.

"We know all about you, Luna. Even Nephilim have the internet, psycho. And rumors stretch far. You're a *murderer*. And if that wasn't bad enough, you're a Dark lover. You don't belong here," the redhead snarls in Goldilocks's face. Despite the pressure of Queen Bitch's talons, Luna doesn't bleed, but I can see she's terrified.

Hot anger floods me, and my power reacts to my rage, coiled and ready to spring at my command. But I never get a chance to attack.

Ruby-red flame bursts into life, lighting up Luna's attackers. I skid to a stop, jaw hanging open, as I take in the blazing Nephilim. Their screams snap me out of my stupor. Luna has pulled herself up and hugs the wall, her face averted from the chaos. Taking a deep breath, I reach for the fire, sucking it away from the wailing attackers. Their skin is blackened, and they resemble dolls who've been held to flames. Despite their sorry state, I can't bring myself to feel bad for them. They brought this on themselves, and they deserve every burn, every burst of agony. Besides, they're Nephilim. They'll heal good as new. Eventually.

Luna sobs and my heart cracks. I stare at her attackers, who are in a state of shock. "Get the hell out of here," I growl, "and keep your mouths shut, or I'll come for you and finish what she started."

The boy grabs one of the second girl's hands, pulling her off the floor, and they limp away with the redhead trailing after them. She glances back at me, half her hair gone and fear widening her eyes. I stare her down, and she scurries from me like the rat she is.

Spinning around, I look at Luna. Her body trembles, and her hands are clenched in her hair, tugging at her scalp. Fuck. A cry escapes her, full of unbearable pain, and I shudder in response. Behind me, a rose-shaped, stained glass window casts light on her, illuminating the gold in her hair.

Luna looks up at me, but she doesn't see me. It's like she's peering right through me. Her eyes are blank, vacant, as if she's no longer present in her body. Like a switch flipping, the emptiness is replaced with rage, burning hot. I take a step back, suddenly afraid of Luna. And afraid for her.

"Get out of my head!" she screams, a horrific sound that curdles my blood, and I still. She continues screaming, the sound rising to a crescendo, and the stained glass window shatters.

Shards of glass fly outwards, and I shield my head with my

arms, but slivers slice my hands and back like tiny knives. I grimace as pain stabs me. When I lower my hands, I regard Luna. As I walk toward her, I realize she has no cuts on her skin; it remains smooth and unblemished. I stumble to a halt and hold out my palms. My skin is pushing out the glass and sealing the wounds. In mere seconds, it'll be like it never happened—Nephilim healing powers at work—but I did get cut. I mean, nothing major, the equivalent of an annoying paper cut, but the glass was traveling hard and fast, so I bled.

But Luna did not. What the hell does that mean?

Her eyes meet mine, and my fear melts away at her utterly lost and devastated expression. I reach her in four long strides, and she plasters herself to me as I circle her slim body in my arms. She's trembling like she's in shock, and I hold her even tighter. Her fingernails dig into my waist.

"I'm sorry, I'm sorry," she repeats over and over, and I shush her, smoothing a hand down her back.

"Don't worry about it, Goldilocks, I'm here," I say, but I *am* worried. What in Lucifer's name just happened? I have to find out, and not just because of my mission. Luna needs help. "Come on, I'll take you to my room. No one will bother us there, and we can talk, okay?"

I feel her nod against my chest. Bending, I slide one hand underneath her knees and the other across her back. She gasps in surprise as I scoop her up in my arms. Glancing around the still empty hallway, I hurry to the boys' dorm and to my room.

seventeen

LUNA

MY SURROUNDINGS ARE A tear-streaked blur as Caleb carries me into the boys' dormitory. What little I can focus on through my sobs looks pretty much the same as the wing of the building sectioned off for the girls—dimly lit corridors of beige and cream stone interrupted by wooden doors numbered in gold. A stained glass window—always a different color and image—marks the end of every hallway on each separate floor.

Caleb's arms are warm around my trembling body. He cradles me against his chest as if I weigh nothing, his movements unburdened, as his feet lead us up a spiraling staircase to what must be the top floor of the dorm. While the other floors were squared off at every possible angle, the ceiling here is slanted and marked with windowed recesses overlooking Alexandria and the Mediterranean Sea. The sudden onslaught of light flooding in through the glass is hot against my skin but does little to comfort my nerves.

183

With every step Caleb takes, my tears lighten a little until the moisture on my cheeks is dry, and my breaths are tiny, shuddering hiccups instead of hysterical gulps of air. His thumbs move across my thigh and arm where they touch me—a reassuring caress that seems to say, *Everything will be okay.*

Even though I know it won't.

The hallway is ominously silent as Caleb stops in front of the last door on the right side of the passage and shifts my weight to free one of his hands. My ear grazes his chest when I lift my head, and even in my declining state of mind, I'm aware of the way his heart races beneath my wandering fingertips. They brush across his shirt, my nails gripping the black fabric, as if he is the one thing holding me to Earth.

He lets out a slightly strained breath at my touch, his heart rate quickening when I look up at him, blinking away the remaining film coating my eyes. If I wasn't on the verge of a mental breakdown, I would linger on the fact that he seems on edge.

And Caleb—cool, collected Caleb—is never on edge.

Clearing his throat, he tenses his arm and turns his wrist, unlocking the door. The room we step into is identical to mine apart from a few glaring details. Like the photographs hung up on the walls of people I'm guessing must be Caleb's family and friends. I suspected he was well-liked at the Tower of Babel, but seeing how full his life was before coming to the Serapeum is a bit hard to swallow. The stark contrast between what I glimpse in the pictures and the recognition of my own lonely existence leads me to wonder what he could possibly see in me. By comparison, the walls in my room are blank.

Grimacing, I avert my gaze from the smiling faces as Caleb sets me down on the bed. Without saying a word, he plops onto the mattress beside me but keeps a comfortable distance, as if he's not sure whether he should come any closer. My frown deepens as I consider if he's staying away for my benefit. Or his.

Is he afraid of me?

If he isn't, he should be.

Shivering, I wrap my arms around my torso and force myself off the bed. "I shouldn't be here—"

"Hey, hold on a minute." Caleb's voice is frantic as he cuts off my dash for the door, positioning himself between me and my one route to escape. I tell myself not to look at him—to pin my eyes to the floor—but my attempts to ignore his gaze come too late.

His dark eyes lock me to him, brimming with worry.

"This is the first time you've spoken to me in a week, and I…" He trails off, and his bronze cheeks flush a deep shade of red, taking me by surprise. I don't think I've ever witnessed Caleb as anything less than the perfect picture of confidence, let alone seen him blush. "Well, I've missed you, all right?" he says in a huff.

My heart catches at those words. He's missed me. *Me.* The monstrous abomination who just set three people on fire.

A lump builds in my throat as a fresh onslaught of emotion

rises up from the black hole of my soul to consume me. When Caleb was tutoring me, I allowed myself to believe I was getting the hang of my abilities and learning a modicum of control, and yet, what just happened has proved I was wrong. So very, very wrong. What if next time, he's the one I hurt?

My teeth sink into my lower lip as I try and fail to fight back fresh tears. "If you know what's good for you, you'll stay away from me."

"What the hell is that supposed to mean?" His eyes drift downward, framed by long, delicate lashes, which flutter like butterfly wings when he blinks. "Did I…" He hesitates, rubbing a hand across the back of his neck. "Did I do something to freak you out when we—"

I cut him off before he can finish that thought. The last thing I want is for him to think my behavior is in any way his fault. "You aren't the problem, Caleb. It's me."

The problem is always me.

A curt, humorless laugh fills the silence between us. "Don't give me that bullshit line."

My eyes widen at the biting edge to his tone and the sudden tension creasing his face. The shadows slithering over his skin abruptly cease their usual lively movements and flatten, as if submitting to some darker emotion I can't bear to name.

This isn't what I wanted to happen. I never wanted to cause Caleb pain. I only wanted to protect him from me. From what I am.

From what I might do.

"I'm serious. I…" My feet stumble backward. There's nowhere to go. I'm trapped in this room with Caleb and all the feelings building between us I'm far too afraid to acknowledge. "I'm dangerous. I tried to control this power, like you taught me to, but I can't. It's too strong." Volatile was the word Vesta had used that day in her class when I failed to conjure my flame. Even now—*especially* now—I'm terrified of what I'm capable of, and until I learn to conquer that fear, I will never know the luxury of real control. "It's best for us both if we aren't friends anymore."

Caleb winces as if I've just slapped him, and the look on his face stirs a pain in my chest that's like a thousand knives sinking into my heart. I immediately wish I could take those words back.

Drawing in a deep breath through his nose, he takes a careful step toward me, backing me into the corner of his room like a predator closing in on its prey. The only difference is that I *want* to run into his arms, to feel the safety of his embrace, but I can't. Every moment we spend together only pushes him closer to imminent danger.

"Okay, you're beginning to worry me. What's going on, Luna?" His brow furrows, etching serious lines into his forehead as he crosses his arms, awaiting an answer.

Why can't he see that I only want to protect him and that to do that I have to push him away? Why can't he see how bad I am for him?

Why can't he just let me go like everyone else in my life

always has?

"Do you know where I was before I came to this school?" The question parts my lips in a whisper as I press my back to the wall and slide down along the stone until I'm slumped on the floor. My hands wrap around my knees, hugging them close to my chest.

My heart hammers against my ribcage as the seconds tick by without either of us speaking. I don't dare look up at him, unnerved by his silence.

Of course, he knows. How could he not when everyone has been gossiping about my past since the day I stepped through the doors to this school? How could he not when all it would take is one quick internet search to find out exactly what I've done? I might be a minor, but my crimes were awful enough I was tried in court as an adult, so my name was all over the news across the whole of New England. And probably social media, not that I ever used it or had access to the sites to check. Hell, if my mental state hadn't come under such heavy scrutiny, I imagine I would've gone to prison. There's no way Caleb doesn't know about that.

Not when the Lights who keep tormenting me do.

"You're a murderer."

Swallowing another rising sob, I squeeze my eyes shut. A few stray tears push through my closed lids and track down my cheeks, but Caleb's fingers catch them on their way to my chin, wiping the wetness from my face.

A quavering breath racks my lungs when I open my eyes to find him squatting in front of me, his gaze burning with so many different emotions I struggle to recognize or process them all. In the dark russet-tinged depths of his eyes, I glimpse understanding, concern, and something else…

Something like love, I find myself hoping.

I immediately push that thought away.

"Do you know why I was committed?" I ask. "I *hurt* people. I…I'm not safe to be around."

"I refuse to believe that," he murmurs, cupping my left cheek in the palm of his hand.

For a fleeting moment, I lean into his touch before coming to my senses and turning away with a sigh. My skin feels so much colder without the comforting stroke of his fingers to warm me.

I lower my gaze and shake my head. "It started when I was little at the group home I lived at. Some of the older children were harassing me, and the next thing I knew, the room we were in was on fire."

It was then, as red flames swallowed everything, I realized something was unnatural about me.

I remember that day with such clarity, despite being so young at the time. The police wrote it off as a tragic accident since there was never any evidence as to what caused the inferno, and they blamed the color of the flames on the fumes coming up off the burning mattresses and metal bed frames, even though everyone knew that was a lie. They just didn't have any other explanation and needed one to close the case and help make sense of what happened for the victims. But *I* knew where the flames came from and so did those children in the few seconds before their bodies were forever disfigured.

We all knew the fire was coming from me, although none of us could explain how.

From that day on, the other children in the home made it a point to keep their distance from me and even the adults seemed uneasy in my presence, as if they could sense what I was capable of. I'd never felt so alone in my life as I did then—only six years old and without a single friend in the world. The isolation got to my head, and as a result, further incidents like the fire kept happening. They grew more frequent—I could break glass with a scream or cause someone to lose all their hair if I didn't like how they looked at me—until I was no longer allowed in the group home or around other children except for at school where I was placed under constant supervision. Not that it helped. The incidents were unavoidable—destined to follow me forever and determined to repeat themselves. Eventually, I wasn't even allowed there, and homeschooling became the only option.

Tears burn my eyes at the barrage of memories.

"After the fire, I was tossed around from one foster family to another, usually taken in by do-gooders who had a soft spot for damaged children or by religious nutjobs who thought they could beat the evil out of me. Or exorcise it. Let's just say, they all quickly learned how evil I am and just as quickly gave me up."

Caleb's upper lip curls back with disgust, and he lets out a seething breath through his teeth. "You aren't evil, Luna. You just didn't know what you are. No Nephilim child is capable of control. That's why these schools exist. Hell, it's why our human parents know about us, for those of us who have them. Because, until we learn control, it's damn near impossible to hide what we are."

And yet, no one in this hidden magical world knew about me until Alaric. If only he had found me sooner, then maybe everything would be different.

"Yeah, well, I've hurt a lot of people and even killed the last foster parents I had. Not on purpose," I add, stumbling over the words, "but that part never seems to matter. They were nice people. They didn't deserve what I did. I was actually kind of happy with them, but I..." Grief swallows the rest of that sentence.

The couple who took me in were older and gentle, with no children of their own. In their eyes, I was like a small, abused puppy in desperate need of love and affection. For a while, having that connection to someone else worked. The incidents ceased, and I thought I was freed from my demons until my world was torn apart again in the blink of an eye.

What I did to them was so much worse than what happened to those poor children in the fire or to the others I've harmed throughout my life. I didn't *want* to hurt them; I was just so mad. I woke up one morning to find the social worker sitting in the living room, talking to my foster parents. I knew without having to ask why she was there. They were giving me up. I'd been through such disappointment—or relief depending on my temporary guardian—enough times to recognize the signs of when my fostering placement with that particular person or family was ending. It was inevitable. They always grew tired of me, of having to deal with my issues, of the responsibility of having to educate and care for someone as badly damaged as I am. If I did have any doubts about what was transpiring, the looks on their faces when I walked into the room all but wiped them away.

The next thing I knew, all three of them were seizing on the hardwood floor, and there was blood everywhere. When their bodies stopped twitching, their still open eyes stared up at the ceiling, frozen in fear, even in death. The police didn't write this one off as an accident. How could they? And while they never figured out the method I used, my presence at the crime scene and violent history were all the evidence they needed to declare me the culprit responsible for their deaths. During the court hearings that followed, the full extent of my troubled past was unearthed, and shortly after—after being deemed not guilty by reason of insanity—I was committed to the hospital in Maine where I stayed for a year until Alaric found me.

With a wavering breath, I force myself to look at Caleb—the only other person I've ever been truly happy around. The one person I'm terrified of hurting. The vision I saw of his body devoured by flames haunts my every waking thought.

"All I know is that everyone who's ever been close to me…"
I trail off, unable to say it aloud. The drawn expression on his
face tells me he's filled in the blanks without me needing to.

"Is that why you've been avoiding me? I'm not some fragile
mortal, you know. You don't have to worry about hurting me."

As if to prove his point, Caleb grabs hold of my hand and
carefully weaves his fingers through mine. I can feel his strength
vibrating under his skin, but Nephilim or not, there's still a part
of him that's weak. That's mortal. That can *die*.

That's the part of him I'm afraid for.

I rip my hand away. "I saw it. I saw what would happen
if I let you get any closer. Whatever's wrong with me, I can't
control it—"

"There's nothing wrong with you," Caleb insists, taking my
hand again and holding it between both of his. "You're still
new to all this. It's going to take more than a few months to
get acquainted with your powers and figure out what you can
do. Do you know how many things I destroyed trying to get a
handle on mine?"

"You don't understand," I protest, flinching when that now
familiar voice whispers again in my ears. I run the fingers of
my free hand through my hair, dragging them roughly over my
scalp, trying to claw the sound out of my skull. "You haven't
seen what it wants me to do. Even now, it won't stop talking."
I clench my teeth, biting back a scream of frustration. "I just

want it to go away."

Caleb's pupils blow wide as his grasp on me tightens. "What won't stop talking?" he asks. I hear his panic behind every word.

"The demon." I jab a fingertip into the side of my temple. "He keeps speaking to me, but I want him to stop. It's so hard to hear or think over the noise."

Silence falls between us, the air heavy with the unspoken thought dying on Caleb's lips in a hiss. I glance up at him, half hoping and half petrified that this will be the thing that finally scares him away. As much as I want to, *need* to, protect him, I don't want him to look at me like everyone else always has. Like I'm crazy. Like I should be feared.

To my relief and horror, my admission only brings him closer.

"Luna…" He says my name slowly, as if it's a glass balancing on the tip of his tongue, and repositions his hands on my shoulders. His fingers are firm where they press into my skin. "I need you to listen to me very closely. When was the first time you heard this voice?"

I blink, taken aback by the edge in his tone and the urgent way his eyes search my face. He isn't looking at me like I'm crazy. No, his piercing gaze says only one thing.

He thinks I'm in danger. But from what? From myself?

Confusion rips through me, and I reel back a few inches until I no longer feel his ragged breaths on my face. I might be insane but I'm not suicidal.

Regardless, I find myself answering his question, if only to prove my point that he's the one at risk here, not me.

"In the library…when I resurrected the moth. Then, I heard it again when we—" I bite my lower lip, afraid that if I say it, I'll only want to do it again. And I can't.

Not without endangering him.

Clearing my throat, I drop my gaze to the floor. "And now, it's always there in my head. I'm afraid of what it wants me to do… Of what I might end up doing to you."

Caleb sucks in a sharp breath at my words, and I recoil at the sound, drawing my legs tighter into my chest until my body is curled into a ball. The emotions searing through me rival the isolation that consumed my daily life at the hospital. This paranoia, this fear, this certainty that there is something very, *very* wrong with me…

I will never escape it.

"You see?" I gasp, my voice breaking. "I really am as crazy as everyone thinks."

"Hey, come here." Caleb's hands shift from my shoulders, wrapping around my back and pulling me close until my chest is flush with his, encasing me in their warmth. My face presses into his shirt, and I breathe in deeply, relishing his scent.

Although I've never had one to know, I can't escape the thought that he smells like home.

"You aren't crazy, okay?" His voice is low in my ear as his fingers graze along the full length of my back. "I'm going to help you figure this out. Remember what I said to you last week in the courtyard?"

I peek up at him through a fresh haze of tears, my brows knitting together, as I shake my head. A smile hitches up the corners of his mouth, and for a long moment, he holds my gaze before leaning in and planting a careful kiss on my forehead.

His words hold the weight of the world as he murmurs, "You can't get rid of me that easily, Goldilocks."

eighteen

CALEB

A COUPLE DAYS AFTER my talk with Luna, I exit one of the few senior classes the exalted Gabriel has allowed humble me to attend. I excel at *Nephilim Combat*, despite every Light gunning for me. Being in this shit hole and worrying about the voice plaguing Luna has caused me to store up all kinds of aggression, which I get to release on some Light's face. One of the faster girls here managed to get a good shot at me—and she conveniently forgot to take off a giant-ass diamond ring—but the gash above my eyes has sealed shut. And I did send her a few nightmare images as payback. I grin at the memory of her screams. No one was too suspicious, as a lot of people scream during that class.

Goldilocks and I are speaking again, and I kicked the crap out of some Lights, so I'm feeling pretty good until I think about my grandfather. Shoving my hands in my pockets, I resist the urge to growl in frustration. I've had nadda to report to Ishtar about

Alexander. Zilch. And I'm afraid to keep her waiting too much longer. She's expecting results from her star student, and so far I'm coming up with a big, fat zero. My little spies have yet to report anything of interest—well, unless you count Gilgamesh having a secret stash of Ishtar memorabilia that he likes to look at, his face all tormented and guilty. Hell, it's no wonder he never noticed her golem watching his every move. Loser.

Guilt creeps over me because I know my relationship with Goldilocks serves as my main distraction from my mission. I'm just as determined to solve the mystery of Luna as I am to find my grandfather, and I know that's messed up. He's my family. My *blood*.

But I can't stop thinking about Luna, and not just because I want to kiss her again, which I hope will eventually lead to us spending several hours naked together. It would be a pleasure to seduce Luna, and after what she told me about her past, it's clear there's been very little pleasure in her life. I'd love to change that. But first, I need to know who the hell is talking to her and messing with her head. There aren't any demons the way Luna thinks of them, cruel spirits floating around, waiting to possess someone. There are only bored Darks who like to mess with people. The Lights do it, too—they just don't admit to it, as it would ruin their perfect image. I know Luna is genuinely terrified she's losing her mind, and she's going to hurt me, but I don't buy that. She's not crazy. There is something else going on here. Something…sinister and it worries me.

Luna's whole childhood has been one big nightmare, and if someone is screwing with her intentionally to hurt her, I'll rip through them like tissue paper. Goldilocks might not be a Dark, but she's an honorary part of my tribe now, and we look out for our own. I won't let anything happen to her if I can help it, but I'm not going to lie. Nothing adds up when it comes to Luna—her fire, the moth, the fact that the shattered glass didn't cut her, and now this voice. She's a Light—I know she is—and yet, I swear she has Dark qualities, too. But that's impossible, right?

Glancing up, I slow as I see the headmistress headed toward me, a thundercloud practically surrounding her stern, beautiful face. I don't like Gabriel but she *is* stunning, like a master sculptor chiseled her from marble. Her eyes pin me down, and I see the angelic power rolling behind them. I resist the urge to take a step back from her. Instead, I continue toward her, my gait casual, until we meet in the middle of the corridor. Orange rings her dark gaze, emphasizing how other she is—if the scary amount of power cloaking her didn't manage to clue you in.

Luna told me once that Gabriel's power made her want to obey the Archangel, but it has the opposite effect on me. It makes me want to flee, knowing I'm in the presence of a bigger predator. One who would gladly eat me if she thought I stepped out of line. I'm dangerous in my own right, but she plays in another league, which is why I've made it a point to avoid her as much as I can while I'm here. But I can't avoid what's directly in front of me and if I've learned one thing in this world, it's not to show your underbelly if you don't want it ripped open, so I hold my ground and paste a pleasant smile on my face.

I give a shallow, mocking bow. "Headmistress," I drawl, "to what do I owe this honor?"

Her brows form a vee over her eyes, her mouth twisting into a scowl. "Some rather alarming rumors have reached my ears, so it seems you and I need to have a chat. Come with me. *Now*."

A shiver of fear ripples over me, but I just nod and follow her as she makes her way back to her office. We cross into the outer office first, which is suspiciously empty of the foxy gatekeeper who is usually there, vigilant at her desk. Gabriel opens the ridiculous door of the inner office with the silver crest and wings and steps in first, ushering me to sit down. She closes the door with a click behind me.

I feel trapped, but I sink down into the guest chair as she settles behind her desk, eyes blazing with anger as she focuses on me. My mind races, trying to figure out why she's pulled me into her office. I'm pretty sure she's still clueless about my mission to find Alexander.

Slight movement under the desk catches my attention, and I see my little golem warrior give me a wave. Despite my unease, I have to bite the inside of my cheek to keep from grinning. He's a cheeky little bastard. He must take after me.

Gabriel shapes her fingers into a steeple, staring at me over the tips. Resisting the urge to squirm, I arch an eyebrow. We lock eyes for what feels like hours, but despite the sweat beading on the back of my neck, I refuse to speak.

An irritated sigh blows past her lips. "Caleb, you're an intelligent young Nephilim. Don't play games with me. You know why you're here."

I shrug. "I've got no idea why I'm here. I've been a very good little Dark ever since I got to this school, despite being treated like shit by your saintly Lights." Anger fills her face at my blunt words. "I'm disappointed. I thought you'd teach them better manners."

She leans forward, her glare sharp enough to stab. "I know you've been starting fights," she hisses, eyes brimming with fury. "Need I remind you that you're here on a diplomatic mission, not to practice your Fallen arts on my students?"

Rage smothers my fear. "I never started any fights. I just finished them." If we're being technical, I finished one. Luna had no problem finishing the other all on her own, not that I would ever tell Gabriel that. "I hate bullies, and your precious, moral Lights decided it was okay to attack Luna in a pack. And where I come from, that doesn't fly. So yeah, I handed them their asses, and I would do it again in a heartbeat."

Gabriel's spine stiffens. "I assure you, we don't condone that sort of behavior at this academy."

"And yet, it happened. Twice. But maybe you looked the other way because it was Luna and she's different. And if there's one thing I'm sure of, you Lights *hate* anything different. I guess it doesn't really matter if someone kicks the shit out of her, right?

Way to take care of your students." The moment the words leave my mouth I know I pushed the mighty Archangel too far.

Her stony facade cracks, her mouth twisting into a ferocious snarl. With the flick of one wrist, the desk between us jerks to the left and careens into the wall, cracking. My heart threatens to pound from my chest as she leans over me, trapping me against the chair. Gabriel's power is palpable, and I resist the urge to piss my pants. Instead, I meet her glowing eyes boldly.

"The safety of my students is paramount to me," Gabriel says. "And if I had known Luna was being put in danger, I would have punished those involved. But instead of coming to me, you chose the Dark way, jumping into battle and not trusting that a higher authority would take care of it." Her eyes narrow as she realizes she's caging me in, and she takes a deep breath, easing back from me. A brush of pink stains her pale skin as she takes in the scene and her loss of control.

I glare at her, my chuckle derisive. "If I hadn't 'jumped into battle,' Luna would have been seriously hurt. There was no time to get you or anyone else," I argue, keeping the little detail to myself about the glass not cutting Goldilocks.

The Archangel clenches her fists and then crosses her arms over her chest to hide her reaction. "I concede you have a point, but you could have reported the first incident afterward, so I was aware of the situation and the hostility Luna faces," Gabriel says, her voice calm once more. "And perhaps then, the second incident wouldn't have occurred."

Rolling my eyes, I say, "Yeah, right. Like you would've believed me. I can see how that meeting would've gone. Your precious Lights would have denied it, and you would've taken their side because I'm a Dark, so I must be a liar, right? At least that's what you teach them." Bitterness edges my every word, and her eyes smolder with anger once more.

"I would've believed Luna," she says coldly. "It's a shame she didn't feel she could confide in me. And you're mistaken. I don't think Darks are liars. I think you're selfish and impulsive. I think your jealousy of humanity's free will is destined to be your undoing. You allow your emotions to rule your decisions, instead of seeing the larger picture and recognizing your true place in this world."

I shiver but not in fear. Her icy facade gives me the chills. In this moment, she is a beautiful and unfeeling statue. I don't like that Luna is in her care because I have serious doubts about Gabriel's ability to care for someone like Goldilocks. Someone fragile and terrified.

Weighing my words, I say, "I'm sorry I didn't report what happened to you, but I'm not sorry for defending Luna. I'm not sorry for caring about someone and being willing to defend them. And I won't apologize for liking humans and loving being a part of this world. I deserve that as much as anyone else."

Gabriel studies me. "You remind me of someone. He thought he deserved the world, too. And now, he can never go home."

I hold her gaze. "Maybe he is home."

She spins on her heel and presents her back to me. "No more fighting, Caleb, or I'll send you back to Babel before you can blink. Do you understand?"

"Yeah, I got it," I say, wondering what she's thinking. I know I hit a nerve, but I'm not quite sure how.

"Then you're dismissed," Gabriel says. "Leave."

Jumping up from the chair, I flee her office and don't look back.

nineteen

LUNA

TERRIFYING IMAGES FLASH BEHIND my closed eyes, and I startle awake, gasping, covered in sweat. I haven't been sleeping well for a while now and even less since that day in the courtyard with Caleb, when the demonic presence living in my head re-emerged for the first time since I resurrected that moth, its voice rising from the depths of my subconscious like a wave building at the start of a storm. I've barely had a moment's reprieve from its unwelcome return a few weeks ago, and with every gruesome vision it forces upon me, I wonder how I could've ever convinced myself it's here to do anything other than drive me deeper into the clutches of madness.

Caleb doesn't think I'm crazy, but he also hasn't given me cause to think otherwise. He just keeps saying he'll "figure it out," as if there's some logical explanation for my derangement. As if it's a problem that can somehow be solved. I know he's only trying to help, but I don't like the idea of him thinking

I'm broken and in need of fixing like everyone else always has.

In the meantime, to avoid another incident and ensure I don't accidentally maim one of our classmates again, Caleb has only left my side when our varying schedules have forced us apart. He suggested restarting our one on one practice sessions— which were on hiatus due to me avoiding him after our kiss— to try to help me with restraint, but I shot that idea down the instant he aired it. I don't want to so much as spark an ember until I know that I can keep my fire and any other powers I may have in check.

Although I'm still wary of having him near me—the fear of what I might do to him like a constant itch burning under my skin—it's a relief to be talking again. That one week without him felt more like a year, and I don't think I can relive that separation, regardless of the potential danger. As much as I want to protect him, I can't overcome whatever is happening to me alone and I have no one else to turn to. Despite our camaraderie, I don't feel comfortable telling Alaric about what's been going on, and have been making it a point to dodge his texts and calls so I don't accidentally slip and give him any reason to worry. We might be friendly, but he's also a doctor, and my declining mental state could be all the reason he needs to intervene in my placement here and take me somewhere far away from whatever he perceives to be my triggers…and from Caleb. I won't allow that, even with the risks surrounding our friendship. I guess I'll just have to trust Caleb when says he can take care of himself.

His face flashes through my head as I sit up and push the heels of my hands into my eyes, which ache with relentless exhaustion. Behind my closed lids, the image warps, switching back and forth between the Caleb I know and the version of him now constantly haunting my thoughts. I see him just like I saw him that day in the courtyard—standing in the middle of a crumbling world with hungry flames devouring every inch of his skin.

Groaning, I rake a trembling hand through my sweat-matted hair. "Stop it," I breathe. "I don't want to see that."

A low chuckle reverberates deep in my ears. *"You only see what you are afraid of. Embrace your power, and the visions will stop."*

Will they, though? Or will I just open a door to further destruction that I won't be able to close?

Despite practicing with Caleb, despite reminding myself what he told me about how to manipulate and master my powers, none of it mattered once I was cornered and my senses registered the impending danger—in the moments when having these abilities counted. Fear pushed his guidance out of my brain and cut loose what little hold I had on control.

I'd rather not have any powers at all than risk a repeat of what I did to those Nephilim.

Frustration rips from my lips in a scream. "I don't want to!"

I jump at the volume of my own voice and grip the duvet crumpled around my waist, squeezing the soft, velvety fabric, until I manage to get a hold of myself. As if taunting me, the vision reappears in my head.

Straining my jaw, I grind out through clenched teeth, "Not if it means hurting Caleb."

"You only see what you are afraid of. Embrace your power, and the visions will stop," the voice repeats.

"So, what?" I scoff, pinning my eyes on a spot in the room where the darkness is thickest, as if doing so will force the voice to manifest there and step out of the shadows to face me. "So I can burn the world like you want?"

"Not the world, but the evil and hatred that consumes it. With my help, you can banish the divide between the Light and the Dark, so we can all become one again."

Flickers of the Serapeum tear through my mind followed by disjointed images of thirteen other locations. Every last one is engulfed in red fire. Judging by the way my stomach twists at the sight of them, I gather these places must be the other academies for the Nephilim.

The vision ends just as all the others have before it, with Caleb standing among the flames, reaching out to me, his beautiful face contorted in agony. My name is a tormented hiss on his lips.

I shake my head, cowering into my mattress at the terrible thought of such needless destruction and death. I don't understand it. I don't understand *any* of this.

How would destroying a bunch of schools get rid of a divide

that's been around for millennia? The only motivation I would even have for such an atrocious act is my desire to ensure no one—be they human, Nephilim, or immortal—ever comes between Caleb and me. Is that why the voice keeps telling me to do it? So Caleb and I can be together without any obstacles in our path?

But…in every vision, Caleb dies. I'd rather bite my tongue and silently rage against a system determined to keep us apart than risk everything and lose him in the process.

"If I do that, Caleb will die." My voice breaks, and I sink my teeth into the inside of my cheek to hold back tears.

"Casualties are inevitable in war," the voice says. *"Unless…"*

Unless? I blink back my terror, straining my ears. "Unless what?" I breathe, desperation leaching into my tone.

A shudder rolls over my skin when the demon answers. *"You conquer the control that eludes you. Take possession of your powers and Caleb will live. If you refuse, he will die. You must choose: control or chaos. Take control of your fate or it will control you. Either way, your role in this world is inescapable."*

My role?

I cling to that last word. *Inescapable.* If someone had asked me a few months ago if I believed in destiny, I would've said no. Of course, that was before I found out I have celestial blood and discovered angels are real and that famous mythological and historical figures are alive and teaching at my school.

Now, I don't know what to believe.

All I *do* know is that if the voice in my head is right, then what I've seen will eventually happen, and more innocent people will die at my hand. My powers will continue to grow out of control and attack everything in their path, including Caleb, unless I find a way to not only rein in my madness…but somehow overcome it.

If that's the case, I'm a ticking time bomb.

Panic claws its way through my skin like worms wriggling out of loose soil. I can't even manifest a normal Light flame, let alone get a handle on powers I only just learned I had barely three months ago. If the world is relying on that, we're all doomed.

"I can't. I've tried! I…" My tone quivers with dread and I swallow, trying to steady my voice. "I always end up hurting someone. I don't know how to stop that from happening."

Silence spreads through the room like an icy mist, sending a shudder through my body, as the hairs on the back of my neck all stand on end. Goosebumps rise along my bare arms and continue under my T-shirt, which clings to my skin, damp with sweat.

When the demon speaks again, its every word is a tantalizing hum in my ear. *"Then allow me to teach you."*

This suggestion pulls at something inside me, and without thought, I rip back my duvet and swing my legs over the side of the bed on auto-pilot, drawn to my feet by a siren-like call in the distance. As if sleepwalking, I cross the room to the door and step out into the empty hallway. The stone floor is freezing against my bare feet, but I'm too entranced to notice the cold.

The sound calling me reaches into the depths of my soul, like the lasting reverberations of a tuning fork tapping against my bones. The sensation guides me, as if my body is metal being drawn to a magnet somewhere else in the school.

I glide through the corridors of the Serapeum without any clear idea of where I'm going. The call leads me down several spiraling staircases into the underground belly of the ancient building where the white marble, wood, and gold-lined decor give way to unending darkness and a moisture in the air that sends a chill through my bloodstream.

A half-formed thought tells me I shouldn't be down here, but I ignore it and trudge on ahead through the shadows. My fingertips dance along the walls, tracing the puckered dips in the stone as I follow the narrowing path. The call gets louder with every step, encouraging me forward, until I'm running, my heart pounding with anticipation of what I'll find at the end of this path.

A sharp breath catches in my chest, and my steps slow as confusion barrels through me like a punch to the gut. My head swings left and right, my eyes focusing on the walls on each side of the passage, every detail in the stone visible despite the complete lack of light. My vision sharpens, and there's no mistaking the truth of what I've been racing toward. What this corridor has been leading me to.

It's a dead end.

The siren call ceases, its sudden absence throwing my body off balance. Vertigo washes over me, and I sway on my feet, lightheaded.

My vision blurs as I snap out of my daze and glance around, bewildered by my surroundings. *Where am I? What the hell am I doing?* As if hearing a voice that keeps telling me to embrace my pyromaniac tendencies isn't bad enough, I've mindlessly wandered into a gloomy underground corridor that looks like the setting for a Europe-based slasher or Gothic horror movie. I almost expect Dracula to step out of the shadows and ask politely to feast on my blood.

Squatting, I comb my fingers through my tangled tresses and grip my scalp, letting out a deep breath. "This is insane. I'm losing my mind."

Laughter echoes down the length of the passage, and when the voice speaks, it's like an air horn in my ear—loud and clear, unlike its usual whispers. *"You've lost nothing. You are precisely where you're meant to be."*

I clamber to my feet as a silver light cuts through the murk, forming carvings on the broad stretch of wall marking the end of the corridor, as if some unseen hand is guiding an invisible pen. It slices through the stone in a montage of intricate symbols—twenty in total, split into two rows of ten, each one an elegant swoop of curved lines and sharp angles.

"Wh-what is this?" I stammer. A building apprehension ties my stomach in knots as my gaze sweeps over the script.

Whatever this is written on the wall, it's not in any language I've ever seen.

"This"—the symbols brighten, glowing the same white as the core of the hottest blue flame—*"is how you set me free. Only then can I teach you control and give you the liberation you desire."*

Free? My eyes widen at the thought.

Up until this moment, I had believed the voice was the manifestation of a suppressed part of my mind, of *me*, that this place had somehow dragged to the surface. I may have called it a demon, an evil presence, but, deep down, I always knew the demon was me—that the terrible thoughts I've been having were the doing of my own unhinged psyche. But upon hearing these words, I can't help questioning whether the voice is actually part of me like I thought, or if maybe it's something else altogether.

As my eyes once again crawl over the symbols, I feel the truth in the shiver creeping over my skin. What I'm seeing…what I'm hearing…this is something outside of me.

Something fear tells me I have no business messing with.

My legs quake, threatening to give out beneath me as I'm reminded of that day in Gabriel's office when she warned me about the forces in this world that we Lights are forbidden from attempting to exploit.

As much as I want to believe Caleb was right and that he'll find a way to rid my head of this voice, I'm starting to think this is a lot bigger than either of us anticipated. This isn't something two Nephilim students can figure out on our own. This is a problem for someone else. This is a problem for—

Gabriel, I realize.

This is her school, so if someone is trapped down here, locked away behind this stone wall, she'll be the first to know what to do.

Unless she's the one who put them here.

I shudder at the thought. If whomever the voice belongs to was trapped down here on purpose, then there's no telling what they're capable of or what other terrible acts they might ask of me. I have to go to Gabriel. I need to tell her what's going on before I inadvertently do something I regret.

My hair whips around me in a frenzy as I retrace my steps through the passage, sprinting toward the series of winding stairs leading back up to the first floor. Although my lungs burn with the effort, I don't stop running until I've reached the eastern annex of the dormitory where the teachers reside. Students aren't allowed in this part of the academy unless there's an emergency.

To hell with that. If this doesn't qualify as an emergency, I don't know what does.

I spot an arched door at the end of the hall with an elaborate insignia branded into the surface that's identical to the monogram marking the entrance to Gabriel's office. Panting, I tiptoe down the length of the corridor, pinching the hem of my T-shirt between my fidgeting fingers.

My knees knock together as I rap my knuckles three times

against the embellished, carved wood. A dim light appears through the crack underneath, seeping onto the stone like spilled milk and inching toward the exposed skin of my toes. I curl them under, shrinking into myself, my breaths coming in rapid bursts when the door creaks open.

Gabriel, surrounded by her usual golden glow, appears in the entryway, a red silk robe wrapped around her lean body and her face twisted into a mask of surprise and suspicion.

"Luna?" Her dark eyes narrow, alert. "What's wrong? It's the middle of the night—"

"I'm sorry," I gasp, my voice hoarse and palms slick as I repeatedly clench and unclench my hands. "I should've come to you sooner, but I was scared—"

She reaches out, wrapping an arm around my shoulders, and steers me quickly into the room. "Come in," she murmurs, closing the door and gesturing toward a plush armchair in the far right corner. The cream-colored fabric is soft against my hand and embroidered with flourishes in glittering gold, which are repeated on the blankets strewn across an impressive four-poster bed and again in the sculpted wooden beams lining the walls.

Unlike her sparse office, this space is extravagant. Murals are splashed across the high ceiling and the panels of wall visible between vertical beams, depicting scenes in a surreal landscape I imagine can only be Heaven. I waver next to the chair, holding onto the arm for support, and stare at the paintings surrounding me in wonder.

"Sit down," Gabriel prompts, perching on the end of the bed. It never occurred to me until now as my eyes dart from her face to the bedspread that angels might have the same need for sleep that Nephilim and humans do. Either that or they just do it to have something to break up the endless days of their eternal lives. I guess I assumed they were unencumbered by such basic mortal needs. Just goes to show how little I know.

I file that thought away for later to ask Caleb about sometime.

"Now, speak plainly," the Archangel instructs. "What is this about?"

My tongue seems to swell to twice its normal size, and my throat is thick with a rising, dry lump determined to choke me into silence.

Gabriel's brow hooks upward impatiently, and I gulp, pushing aside my fear.

"I…keep hearing a voice," I manage. "I've been hearing it since that day in the library when I…when I resurrected the moth."

The Archangel's expression remains unchanged. "And this voice says what, exactly?" she asks.

"I don't always know. Sometimes, it speaks in a different language. Greek, I think. Or something else. Something older. Other times…it tells me to do things."

This admission seems to get Gabriel's attention. She leans forward, her unblinking eyes sweeping over my face. "Like what?"

Oh, you know. Like burn down all the Nephilim academies and destroy the divide.

I swallow. "The moth…" I force out the words between unsteady breaths. "The voice told me what to do to bring it to life."

Gabriel's robe shifts as she crosses her long legs and taps a slender finger against her chin. She considers me for a moment, those hawkish eyes piercing. "Has this voice instructed you to do anything else?"

Yes.

"No," I lie. As much as I want to unburden myself of the truth and tell her everything, I'm terrified of what will happen to me if she finds out I've been keeping this secret from her for so long. The desire to not disappoint her runs deep. "Nothing I can really understand, but…I think it's trying to lead me to something. I…" Hesitation distorts my voice as tears trail over the curve of my cheekbones. "I'm afraid, Headmistress."

The Archangel rises from the edge of the bed and walks toward me, placing a careful hand on my shoulder. A shudder races up my spine at the cool touch of her fingertips. "Stress can do remarkable things to our brains, even those of us who live outside the confines of mortality."

My eyebrows draw together in confusion. What is she trying to say?

"I'm not imagining it—" I begin to protest, but her stern voice cuts me off.

"You had a difficult childhood—more challenging than most,

I dare say—and you came to an academy far later in life than is typical for your kind. Your struggle to adjust has been noted."

A deflated breath parts my lips. "So, you think this is all in my head," I whisper. It isn't a question.

"I *think* you are not doing yourself any favors by spending so much time with a Dark," she counters, her tone brusque as she withdraws her hand from my shoulder.

I reel back and blink up at the angel. "Caleb? What does he have to do with this?"

A shadow crosses Gabriel's face as she scowls. "The divide exists for a reason, Luna. Darks have a talent for burrowing themselves inside our heads and twisting our thoughts until they feel like our own. It wouldn't surprise me to learn your friend Caleb is responsible for the voices you're hearing."

Voice. Singular. And you're wrong.

"He would never do that to me," I snap.

My teeth press together as a sudden blaze flares to life in the pit of my stomach, stoking my anger and disappointment that I could've been so wrong about the Archangel. What does she know? She's just as prejudiced as the rest of them, too lost in her own moral superiority to realize the Darks aren't any different from us.

Us. Even thinking the word leaves a sour taste on my tongue.

"Perhaps not," Gabriel concedes. "But such proximity to him is bound to have an adverse effect on your already fragile mental state. You should focus on spending more time with your own kind."

I shake my head as a hysterical laugh escapes me, coaxing a curious look from the Archangel. If being a Light means thinking the worst of the Darks, then I'd rather not be a Nephilim at all.

"You're the one who invited him here," I point out.

Her lips press into a tight, thin line. "To keep the peace with the Archdemons, yes. Not because I believe having a Dark in this school is in anyone's best interests. Especially yours. You want my advice? Keep your distance from that one. You may find you have a clearer head without all that darkness around to smother your light."

"His darkness is beautiful," I snarl under my breath.

Gabriel frowns at my comment but takes my hand and pulls me to my feet. As she leads me to the door, she presses a hand to my back, tearing my soul in two separate, conflicting directions. On one side, lives my desperation to please her. To heed my Faithful angelic blood and do whatever the Archangel commands of me and, in turn, show my allegiance to the Creator. On the other side, live my feelings for Caleb.

And I know, without a doubt, which one is stronger.

"It's late," Gabriel says. "You'll see this all more clearly in the morning after you've had some sleep. I think, given everything, perhaps it would be best if you'd come by my office first thing tomorrow. Then we can discuss this matter further."

I drop my eyes to the floor and nod, although I know I won't feel any differently by then. I'll still be terrified of what I've heard and of what lives deep underneath this school, calling to me. I'll still believe Caleb would never do the awful things that Gabriel has suggested he would. And I'll still live in fear of what I might do to him if I can't convince the Archangel to help me.

But, maybe by tomorrow, Gabriel will realize how unfair she's being and actually listen to my concerns.

At this point, that outcome is all I can hope for.

twenty

CALEB

A VISION BURSTS ACROSS my brain of Gabriel in her office, her desk repaired and standing in its usual place. The Archangel paces back and forth, a scowl turning down her soft mouth. The lines of her muscles are rigid as she moves, her usual grace absent. I shift to my side and bury my face in the pillow, trying to dispel the vision. But her image persists, and her agitation pulls me from the darkness once again. Shit, why am I having dreams about a pissed off Gabriel? Can't I get peace in this place even in my dreams? Or if I do have dreams, I'd rather they be of Luna, not a terrifying Archangel. I jerk fully awake as if someone slaps my face. What the hell?

Blinking, I notice my vision is different. Dimmer. And it's not the darkness in my room. Nephilim can see like cats in the night. Wait, that wasn't a dream. My golem is trying to talk to me. I sit up in bed, alert. Through my little buddy's eyes, I see figures pop into Gabriel's office. Archangels and...

Archdemons? This looks like a gathering of the Council—the angels and demons in charge of the academies—which from what little I know of them doesn't happen often. So why are they meeting now, in the middle of the night? What in Lucifer's name is going on?

My heartbeat thunders in my throat as I watch the spacious office become increasingly crowded. Asmodeus and Mammon are there—the latter a tall, glowering male presence who radiates aggression. I recognize Raphael and Uriel—from pictures in class at Babel, and they're literally in all the depictions of the Fall—as they make their way to Gabriel's side. Flames wrap around Uriel's arms like living vambraces, and his hard eyes settle on the two Archdemons, his fingers on the hilt of a large sword.

Asmodeus tosses her long, crimson hair and offers Uriel a snarky grin. "You've come to fight, Brother?" she asks.

A scowl mars Uriel's deep brown skin. "If need be," he says, his voice like rumbling thunder.

To my surprise, Gabriel actually rolls her eyes in impatience. "Enough! We don't have time for posturing or petty grievances."

Mammon raises a dark blond brow. "Really? I thought that was what our relationship has been reduced to, but I'm delighted to hear we can move past that."

Raphael shoots Mammon a bland look. "I don't know if we'll ever move beyond it, but if Gabriel called us here, it must be important. Certainly worth putting past hurts away." She shrugs a slender shoulder, her long-legged figure gamine.

Asmodeus snorts. "Yes, war is an easy thing to just put away. Do carry on, Gabriel," she says, giving a mocking bow. Then an almost gleeful expression crosses her face, but it's not one of joy, but malice. "By the way, he sends his regrets."

Gabriel stills, her hawk eyes narrowing on Asmodeus with predatory focus. The Archdemon meets her eyes in challenge, as if daring Gabriel to bring it. There's a sudden tension I don't understand permeating the room. I mean, they're all immortal beings who've lived for hundreds of thousands of years, so I guess there are lots of things here I don't understand.

Gabriel relaxes. "So, is it just us then?"

Mammon nods. "Yes, we'll pass on your message to the others—if we deem it worthy."

Disgust fills me as I listen to their banter. No wonder the Dark and Light Nephilim can't get along. Our leaders are just as petty as their students. But I do admire Gabriel as the Archangel refuses to rise to the bait.

"We have a possible Alexander situation on our hands," she says, her voice grave.

My ears perk up at my grandfather's name as the room goes painfully silent. I straighten, heart pounding in my chest, mouth suddenly dry.

They glance at each other, faces wary and worried.

"He can't have escaped," Asmodeus says, "otherwise our brands would have warned us. You were tasked with watching over him. We trust you to keep him contained, Messenger."

Her accusatory tone shocks me. "This is your responsibility."

"Yes, he's a danger to us all," Mammon rumbles. "That's why we helped you entomb him."

"Calm yourselves. Of course, Alexander remains in his tomb, where he belongs," Gabriel says, hands on her hips.

My mind spins, my breath coming too fast. Asmodeus and Mammon knew Alexander was here this whole time? The Fallen knew, and they left him here to rot. Anger boils in my gut. How is this possible? I mean, Ishtar couldn't have known, or she wouldn't have sent me here to free him. I've been told my whole life it was the Lights who had taken away my grandfather. Now to find out the Archdemons had a part in it? Betrayal stings my chest. Nothing makes sense. Why would the Fallen work with the Archangels to imprison one of their own?

Raphael flips her short hair behind an ear. "Then why are we here, Gabriel?" she huffs.

"Because I believe we have another Gray in our midst," Gabriel says, and that catches everyone's attention, although I have no idea what a "Gray" is. "A new student here has shown qualities of both the Light and the Dark."

"How long have you known about this?" Uriel demands harshly.

"Yes, how long have you known?" Asmodeus says.

Gabriel crosses her arms over her chest. "Not long. I had to be sure before I alerted everyone."

Mammon holds up a hand. "Wait a moment. Tell us of these

'qualities,' so we can judge if this student is, indeed, a Gray."

Gabriel looks like she wants to punch Mammon in his smug face. "The girl, Luna, has blood-red flame. She managed to bring a moth back to life"—Gabriel talks over Asmodeus's skeptical snort—"but most damning is that Alexander has been speaking to her. And *only* her."

Shock rolls over me at her statement. Gramps is the one who's been talking to Luna? That's the voice she's been hearing? What the hell's going on?

Raphael gasps. "What has he been saying?"

"I believe he's been leading Luna to him," Gabriel says, and for the first time, I hear a hint of fear in her voice. What is she so damned afraid of? "I don't know what he wants from her, and I certainly don't like the fact that he's speaking to her at all."

Uriel's severe face is somber. "If Alexander is leading someone to him, he must believe they can set him free. How is this possible? How could we have missed another Gray?"

Asmodeus snarls, "Well, we certainly haven't been hiding one."

Raphael shoots her an impatient look. "No one is accusing you of that, Sister. Neither the Faithful nor the Fallen are foolish enough to be concealing a Gray."

Gabriel stills for a moment and then nods. "Certainly not. Let's not waste our time on needless accusations."

I almost direct my golem to scream, "What the hell is a Gray?" But I keep myself in check. Barely. Sweat mists my skin, and I know I'm witnessing something that a mere Nephilim was never meant to see or hear.

"We're not asking the obvious question," Raphael says. "Whose child is it?" She shoots the two Archdemons suspicious looks.

Mammon balks. "It's not mine."

"Or mine," Asmodeus growls. She treats Raphael with a venomous glare. "We might be rebels, but I don't yearn to bring about the End of Days."

"Besides," Uriel says to Raphael, "a Light would have to participate as well." The censorship in his tone makes her flush.

"Only a child born of both the Dark and the Light can bring about the prophecy," Asmodeus adds. "So someone has been very naughty."

"I thought after Alexander nearly destroyed the world, this wouldn't happen again," Mammon mutters, pacing.

Stunned, I try to make sense of what they're saying. I always assumed Alexander had one immortal parent and one human, like most of the other first generations. But for him to be of both the Dark and the Light, that would mean one of his parents was an angel or demon and the other a Nephilim—a pairing I struggle to envision considering the divide. For one, the Faithful are all up in Heaven, and I doubt any of the Archangels would ever go near a Dark Nephilim, let alone fuck one. I suppose one of the Fallen could've seduced a Light Nephilim, although that doesn't really jive either, despite being the only possibility that works. It's pointless trying to figure it out, though. Nobody knows who his birth parents were since he was abandoned on Earth and raised by mortals—royal mortals, no less—but if what I'm hearing is true, I think it's safe to assume why exactly they ditched him.

I shake my head. Even if a Light and Dark were stupid enough to have a kid together, considering how much our factions hate each other, how would that bring about the apocalypse? And I know Alexander wanted to rule the world but *destroy* it?

And this probably means…Luna is a Gray. Which makes a whole lot of sense, actually. She has both traits, like Gabriel said. And she's an orphan, likely cast away like trash for the same reason my grandfather was. But if she *is* a Gray and Alexander is speaking to her… I don't care what Gabriel says, if Alexander has sought Luna out, it's for a good reason. I might have had the key to his freedom right next to me this whole time. I don't want to use her like that, but I don't know if I have another choice.

My mouth falls open as another thought smacks my already frazzled brain. If Alexander is a Gray, does that mean I am, too? But I'm not like Luna. I've only displayed Dark powers. I practically live in shadow. God, does this mean at any moment I could shoot rainbows out of my ass or something? What the hell is happening?

"We should imprison the girl," Raphael says, and all eyes flash to her.

At the thought of them imprisoning Luna, I want to take out

my special angel-killing dagger and stab Raphael through her treacherous heart.

"No," Gabriel retorts, a firm finality in her voice. "That's not necessary. I have the girl well in hand. She's confessed to me what has occurred and I'm watching her. She's desperate to fit in, to belong. I'll use that to keep her in line."

Her callous words freeze my blood. Luna deserves better than this. Then I think about my plans for her and I wince, sick to my stomach.

"But she might be able to pass through the wards," Raphael points out, scowling. "We never planned for another Gray to come waltzing in. How can you be sure Alexander won't lead her right to him?"

"I said I'll keep her in line. Besides, she has no way of reaching the wards, and even if she managed to get that far, she still couldn't release him," Gabriel counters.

"You will let us know the moment she steps out of line," Uriel says. "I understand she's just a girl, but she's a danger to us all. We can never forget that."

"She's just a girl who can barely tap into her powers. She's no Alexander," Gabriel says through gritted teeth.

Asmodeus glares at Uriel and Raphael. "Always with the imprisoning." She sneers. "I agree with Gabriel. Leave the girl alone as long as she obeys the rules. She need never know what she is, and if she doesn't find out, she won't be a problem."

Mammon nods. "Keep us informed, Messenger."

Gabriel gives a brief bow of her head. The remaining Archdemons and Archangels vanish from the room, with the exception of Raphael. She gives Gabriel a long, cold stare.

"I hope you know what you're doing, Messenger," she says. "Or the next thing you'll herald will be our doom."

Gabriel's stare is equally cold. In fact, I'm surprised I don't see frost on her skin. "Get out."

Her words stun me. Here, I thought all the Faithful were lovey-dovey with each other and skipped through tulips holding hands or some shit.

Raphael just smirks and fades from the room, leaving Gabriel alone. It's time I make my exit, too. Blinking hard, I'm back in my dorm room. I stand on shaky legs, still unable to wrap my head around what I just heard. I need to speak with Ishtar. She needs to know what's going on, and how the Fallen—our own people—have been lying to us.

twenty-one

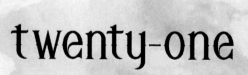

LUNA

MY EYES BURN AS I glare at the glowing red lines forming numbers across the face of my alarm clock, counting down the minutes until the grating beeping begins. Despite the exhaustion pressing down on my body, I didn't sleep a wink after my conversation with Gabriel. Nothing new there. The voice continued its assault on my mind through all hours of the night as it has for so many days now, depriving me of rest, and when I wasn't focusing on ignoring its attempts to lure me back under the school, I was mulling over what Gabriel said to me in the confines of her bedroom. Her dismissal still rings in my ears— the slanderous words she spoke against Caleb like an iron brand searing into my flesh. Even now, hours later, I'm consumed by the pain of them. They feed my anger like oxygen feeds a flame.

Since I got back to my room, I've been debating whether I should bother going to her office this morning. Part of me believes the endeavor is pointless. Surely, she'll just brush me off again, or worse, continue her vain attempts to turn me against the only person here who's ever been on my side. Another part of me knows I don't really have a choice in the matter. It wasn't a request—it was a politely phrased demand—and if I don't go, the punishment for disobeying could be worse than not getting her help at all. Caleb once told me the headmistress at Babel whips students who dare to break the rules. Would Gabriel do the same to me? Or worse…whatever worse may be? I can't imagine what sort of discipline she's capable of, and the not knowing chills me to the darkest depths of my soul.

The clock ticks over to seven and unleashes a shrill assault on my senses. My palm slams down on the button protruding from the top of the black plastic casing, shutting off the alarm, as my legs kick off the blanket, sending the duvet tumbling to the floor.

My skin is still sticky with sweat, and my hair is a poofy mess, but I lack the strength to care how I look or how badly I might smell at the moment. I don't even bother to get changed out of the T-shirt and shorts I wore to bed or brush my teeth before throwing open the door to my room. Standing at the threshold, I shove my feet into a fresh pair of white sneakers—one of a handful of new articles of clothing Evangeline gave me along with my uniform when I began classes at the Serapeum—then draw in a breath and storm into the hallway.

The school is eerily quiet as I begrudgingly make my way toward Gabriel's office. It's early—classes don't begin until eight—but I still find it strange there isn't a single Nephilim, student or teacher alike, either in the hallways or outside in the courtyards, which are already drenched in the warm morning light, tempting me through every window I pass. The only presence in the silence is the voice, now my constant companion, even if the identity of its owner eludes me. Its call lingers in my ears like white noise, a ceaseless rush of sound I've had to learn to hear over. At this moment, it's like an ebbing wave in the ocean. It recedes, slinking to the back of my mind.

I press on into the academic building and continue past the empty classrooms until the ornately carved pillars marking my destination slide into view. Through the broad panes of glass looking into the administration office, I spot the closed black door emblazoned with Gabriel's silver insignia.

Swallowing, I push the glass doors open and step into the air-conditioned reception area of the outer office. To my right, the seat where I expect to find Evangeline is empty. Strange. I don't think I've ever *not* seen the friendly Nephilim at her desk.

Raised voices draw my gaze to Gabriel's office, and with all thoughts of Evangeline's absence forgotten, I inch closer to the imposing door, ignoring the unease building in the pit of my stomach that's telling me to turn around and walk away before I overhear something I shouldn't.

"All the more reason to listen," the voice encourages, every word it speaks growing in volume as its presence flows back to the forefront of my thoughts.

Although I want to ignore such reckless guidance, I find myself doing exactly what it says against my better judgment. Driven by my unbridled curiosity and desire to better understand the Archangel, I tentatively press an ear to the wood.

"Did you know?" I hear Gabriel growl.

"How could I have known?"

I immediately recognize the male voice that answers, having heard it over the phone at least a dozen times throughout the last three months I've been here. That strange accent that almost seems to be from everywhere at once, not that dissimilar to Gabriel's, sends a shudder of familiarity racing through me.

"Don't toy with me, Alaric," the Archangel retorts. "You know as well as I why you were assigned this task. Your own father, may the Creator watch over his soul, was the one who sensed the truth about Alexander before he was so brutally slain. We both know that skill has passed on through Michael's bloodline to you. Do you deny it?"

"No." Alaric's tone is level, and yet, I can sense the tension behind that one word like it's a physical force pounding on the other side of the door.

The faint click of high heels on solid ground brings the angel closer to where I stand, my shoulders hunched over and trembling, my heart racing as I eavesdrop on a conversation I don't comprehend. Why is Alaric here? Has he come to check up on me because I've been avoiding his calls? And what task has he been given by Gabriel?

Whatever it is, he doesn't seem too happy about it.

"So, you admit that you knew?" Gabriel's accusation is a venomous hiss.

"I didn't say that," Alaric bites back. "These things aren't always easy to see, although…"

My brow furrows when the silence swallows the rest of whatever he was going to say. *Although what?* I test the limits of my hearing, straining, searching for the end of his sentence.

"Although?" Gabriel presses with the same impatient eagerness coursing through my veins.

Alaric clears his throat. "I might've had my suspicions."

"And you chose to say *nothing*?" The Archangel's fury booms through the office like the bone-chilling roar of a lion, sending me stumbling back a few steps until I'm cowering against the nearest wall in crippling terror. Her displeasure is like claws digging lines into my skin. Every second that passes without her placated is another scratch drawing my blood to the surface.

I can only imagine how Alaric must be feeling right now bearing the full brunt of Gabriel's rage.

It takes several deep breaths and a quick mental pep talk to convince myself to return to the door. Knees knocking together, I push my hands against each side of the frame to hold myself upright and lean in, once again pressing my ear to the wood.

On the other side, Alaric's voice is unflinching. "Maybe I thought I was protecting her. I thought if she was surrounded by Lights—"

"You thought wrong," Gabriel interrupts. "That was not your

call to make. It doesn't help matters that she's chosen to latch herself onto that Dark transfer from Babel."

The disdain in the Archangel's tone is familiar—I stood in the direct path of it only a few hours ago—and at the mention of Babel, I instantly know who she's talking about. The Dark transfer is Caleb, which means the "her" Alaric is talking about can only be me. But if that's the case, what does he think he was protecting me from by bringing me to the Serapeum?

What do he and Gabriel know about me that I don't?

My heart pummels against my ribs at the thought. As if my life wasn't enough of an unending disaster, now I have this new mystery to worry about. A mystery that encases me in a fresh bubble of fear.

Gabriel lets out a long-suffering sigh. "How did we not know about her sooner? How did *you* not know? Finding lost Nephilim is your job." She spits that last word, hurling it like an insult.

Alaric scoffs. "That's easy for you to say. There are nearly eight billion people in the world, Gabriel, any of which could be Nephilim. It doesn't aid matters that the courts disregarded her as just another juvenile offender, and the states never helped, tossing her from one foster family to another with little regard for her safety or mental well-being. She never stayed in any one place longer than a year, and as a minor, her records were sealed except to those directly involved with her case. I didn't even catch wind of Luna or her situation until she was committed, when news of the conviction was leaked to the media." There's a long, agonizing pause, and when Alaric speaks again, he sounds tired—not in the human way but in his soul. "I might have an advantage against these mortal doctors, but I'm still only one man. The numbers don't exactly work in my favor. Plus, Luna's scent wasn't nearly as potent as it should be," he mutters, his tone suddenly thoughtful. "It was barely discernible, actually, which made it far more difficult to track her than I expected. And even once I did manage to hunt her down, modern laws make it increasingly challenging to extract children tangled up in their system without drawing too much attention or suspicion." He lets out a frustrated sigh. "I'm doing the best I can."

When Gabriel says nothing, I'm overcome by the urge to crack open the door and peek inside just to catch a glimpse of the Archangel's beautiful face for some idea of what she must be thinking. I can all too easily imagine her almost tangible anger and disappointment, remembering when Vesta dragged me into this very same office, and we both suffered Gabriel's temper. I just hope Alaric isn't afflicted with an even greater discomfort being in such close proximity to her.

"Does anyone else know?" he asks after a moment, breaking the dreadful silence.

"Vesta, along with an entire class of Nephilim, witnessed her flame," Gabriel says, her tone grim, "and she knows about the resurrection, but I've banned Luna from future class participation, which should buy us some time. As far as Vesta is concerned, you needn't worry. She's a zealot, as always, and believes this to be some sign of disapproval from the Creator, but she doesn't know the truth. I can't say the same for the other teachers or students, but they have no reason to suspect differently."

It takes everything in me to remember to breathe. Buy them time? For what?

"Buy *us* some time?" Alaric echoes. "What is it you want me to do, Gabriel?" I'm taken aback by the contempt in his voice. The ire behind every word he utters is like a hot poker pushing into my skin. A shudder rips up my spine, and for a moment, I'm torn between sharing those feelings and wanting to slap him across the face for his blatant lack of respect.

I draw in a breath then let it out, calming myself. This whole ingrained allegiance thing toward the Archangel is really starting to get old.

"Your job as a physician," Gabriel snaps. "Talk to the girl. Assess her mental state. Then report your diagnosis to me. Your *real* diagnosis, Alaric. Not those ignorant human medical reports you provided before. I need to be certain this won't be a problem."

"And if I do as you ask, how are you planning on using that information?"

A long moment passes before Gabriel answers. "I don't know yet. But if I fail to act, there are others who may intervene, and they will not show the same mercy that I would."

My heart drops into my stomach, like a weight attempting to drag me down to the floor. What are they talking about?

Who might intervene if Gabriel doesn't act...whatever the hell that means?

What have I gotten myself tangled up in?

"You told the Council about this? Creator's sake, she's only a child!" Alaric shouts.

Council? Familiarity tickles my senses and I rack my brain, trying to recall where I heard this before. To my frustration, the answer escapes me.

"As was Alexander once," Gabriel ripostes. "And look what he grew into."

"A legend," the voice whispers in my ear.

Annoyed by its interjection, I scowl and swat the voice away. After weeks of having it in my head at all times, I've found ways to suppress it. I can't tune it out entirely, but if I really focus, I can push it to the back of my mind until it's nothing more than a low hum, like a television chattering in the background of a conversation, ignored. Whatever I'm listening in on is more important than anything it could have to say right now.

A sigh fills the fraught silence between Alaric and Gabriel, the sound heavy with exasperation and...something else. Something my heart tells me might be grief.

"Do we at least know who her parents are?" Alaric asks, the words soft.

A gasp tumbles into my mouth, and I have to press a hand across my lips to smother the sharp breath that threatens to expose me. As the seconds roll over one into the next, my body goes to war with itself—my legs aching with the desire to run as far and as fast as I can before the Archangel discovers me here while my racing heart holds me flush to the door, my limbs paralyzed by the realization that I'm close to finally getting answers. Answers I've wanted for as long as I can remember.

Answers I'm terrified of.

But more than terror, I'm enveloped in the scorching hot embrace of rage. If Gabriel knows who my parents are, why hasn't she had the decency to tell me? She has no right to keep that information from me. I deserve to know.

I *want* to know.

My breaths are shallow and burn my throat as I await her response. A year seems to pass in the space of ten seconds.

"Even if I knew, do you think I could tell you?"

Alaric snorts. "Fine. Keep your secrets behind lock and key. But I won't be a party to your plans if they in any way replicate what the Council did to Alexander. You forget, not all of his friends were Darks."

The door rattles with the impact of something large and solid slamming into the other side of the wood. I bite back a yelp of surprise, keeping my ear where it is, even as my whole body trembles. Although faint, I can hear what sounds like someone—probably Alaric—wheezing.

"Threats don't suit you," Gabriel seethes, her words muddled as if she's speaking through clenched teeth. "Don't make me question your allegiance."

Through the crack under the door, shadows of movement spill into the space where I stand, quaking like a leaf in the wind. Another thud. Alaric says nothing as he drags in several loud gulps of air.

"Luna?"

I whip around at the sound of my name, my blood turning ice-cold at the sight of Evangeline standing next to her desk.

"H-Hi," I manage, casting a wary glance at Gabriel's office, which has gone unnervingly silent.

"What are you doing here?" Evangeline's brow hooks upward as her bright eyes flick between my face and the closed door behind me then back to me, taking in my scruffy appearance.

Answer quickly, I chide myself. Straightening, I lock my hands behind my back, so Evangeline won't see that they're shaking. "The headmistress asked me to come see her this morning. Is she in?"

Before she can answer, the black door swings open, the gentle creak of the hinges sending a prickle of goosebumps over my skin. I peer over my shoulder, meeting Gabriel's gaze, which scans my face with an intensity that turns my stomach.

"Luna." She rolls my name off her tongue as if it's laced in acid. "I trust you haven't been here long."

It isn't a question. She's testing me. She wants to make sure I haven't been listening.

I swallow. "N-No, Headmistress," I manage.

Her brows pinch together as her razor-sharp eyes search my

face, as if she's staring straight into my soul. After a second, her gaze falters and her lips part, her expression somewhat stunned, although I can't comprehend why. In the time it takes for me to blink, her face settles back into its usual mask of stone.

"Good." She sweeps her arm into her office, gesturing toward Alaric who steps into view with an impossible poise considering it sounded like he was being choked by the Archangel only a few moments ago. "You remember Dr. Walsh?"

Alaric's dark hair falls in front of his amber eyes as he offers me an amiable wave. If he's upset with me for ignoring his calls, his expression doesn't show it. "Hi, Luna."

"Hi," I whisper.

A gentle smile spreads across his kind face, but I hesitate to return it given what I just overheard between him and Gabriel. When he brought me here, he left me with the hope I could trust him and our interactions over the last few months only reinforced that.

Now, I don't know what to think.

He must notice my reluctance because the smile slips from his lips, and the golden glow vibrating across his skin tenses, pressing flat around his body.

Beside him, Gabriel nods, her piercing gaze never shifting away from my face. "I'll leave you two to get reacquainted." She then brushes past me, only looking back once to shoot a warning glance at Alaric as she makes for the glass doors leading into the hallway. His warm honey eyes trail her retreating figure, and when she reaches the office threshold, she snaps her fingers for Evangeline to follow. The startled Nephilim chases her steps like a dog heeding the call of its master.

Once we're alone, my posture relaxes, my shoulders sagging forward a little. The air in the room is somehow lighter now that the Archangel has left. Biting my lip, I peek up at Alaric. The soft exhalation escaping him tells me I'm not the only one affected by Gabriel's absence.

"Fancy a walk?" he asks, tilting his head to one side.

I shrug, unsure what to say and not entirely convinced I have a choice.

He grins. "I'll take that as a yes."

I allow Alaric to lead me out of the office, tracing his lithe movements through the corridors in silence until we reach the entrance hall to the school. My eyes move between the statues on each side of the path as I wonder why he brought me here of all places.

"It's good to see you," he says, turning to face me. "How have you been since we last spoke?" He cocks a curious eyebrow at me, and I finally glimpse it in his gaze—the question as to why I've been avoiding him.

A defensive chill runs over my skin. To hell with answering his questions when he's been keeping secrets from me. A frown tugs at the corners of my mouth. Is this why he's been so kind to me and humored me with his phone calls and texts? Why he's seemed so determined to position himself in my life as a friend rather than yet another adult trying to diagnose me? If he's as chummy with Gabriel as I suspect—enough so for them to discuss matters openly—it's not only likely but guaranteed he knows about everything that's been going on. Everything the Archangel is aware of, at least. I can only assume the reason he hasn't brought any of it up is to avoid me thinking he discusses my mental state behind my back.

To get me to trust him, I realize.

Trust Gabriel now wants him to use against me.

My stomach sours at the thought.

Jaw tensing, I grind out, "I know why you're here, Alaric. Gabriel wants you to find out if I'm crazy, like she and everyone else in the world seem to think."

At least, that's part of why he's here. There's so much to unpack from what I heard, and that's just from the half of their conversation I actually understood.

Alaric is silent for a moment, and as my nerves go wild waiting for him to speak, it occurs to me that if he tells Gabriel I *am* insane and that everything I'm hearing is all in my head, not only does that thrust me into uncharted territory—where do they send mentally unstable Nephilim?—but it would also confirm what I'm beginning to fear. That the relationship I have with Alaric...all of it was a lie. A charade. It would mean he *only* pursued being my friend, my confidant, to keep a watchful eye on my mental state, not because he actually cares about me. Maybe that was even the task Gabriel spoke of.

I find comfort in reminding myself that, no matter what happens—even if this conversation puts an end to the relationship I have with the older Nephilim—I'm not alone. I have Caleb. So long as I have him, I don't need anyone else, even if the thought of Alaric deceiving me hurts.

Still, despite the ferocity of this belief, I'm relieved when Alaric responds with a laugh. "Well, we've already established that I don't think you're crazy. Disembodied voices aside."

My heart trips at the mention of the voice, but he doesn't press me about it, which I'm grateful for. Nor does he look at me like I'm crazy like everyone else at this school always does. Like I expect him to.

We're quiet for a moment, but despite my doubts about Alaric, the hush between us is comfortable and easy in a way I've only ever known with Caleb. Although we're more than acquaintances now, given our frequent correspondence, this is still only the second time we've met in person. I anticipated feeling shy around him, or on edge, like I always am around strangers or people I don't know very well. Or let's be honest, everyone except Caleb. But being around Alaric is far easier than I thought it would be, which only serves to heighten my suspicions about his motivations for being my friend.

I sneak a glance at him out of the corner of my eye, wondering if he's doing that thing again, using his special talents to put me at ease. Calm, he called it. The older Nephilim has an unfair advantage. I've still yet to figure out what my talents are and

I'm not trained enough to fight off whatever magic he might try to use on me per Gabriel's bidding. As much as I want to believe he wouldn't do that to me, the fact remains.

I don't really know Alaric at all.

"Who's Alexander?" The question explodes from my mouth before I have the sense to stop it. So much for not letting him know I've been eavesdropping.

A flicker of pain flashes across his fair face. "An old friend." After a moment of hesitation, he adds, "A Nephilim, like you and me."

My breath catches as I remember the last thing Alaric said to Gabriel before I was discovered. *"You forget, not all of his friends were Darks."* Does that mean this Alexander person was a Dark? If so, then Caleb and I aren't the first to try to cross the divide between our two sides. Others before us, Light and Dark, have surpassed their ingrained bigotry and formed friendships.

I find that notion encouraging.

And yet, sorrow, as clear as the sun rising in a cloudless sky, wells in Alaric's eyes like tears. The small glimpse of optimism I felt a moment before is diminished by his now sullen expression.

"Is he dead?" Fear drenches my words.

"Not exactly," Alaric says in a bleak monotone. "But he's not around anymore, either."

The hairs on the back of my neck stand on end. "Why?" My voice is barely a whisper.

The older Nephilim shoves his hands in his pockets and averts his gaze, glancing at the white statues beside us. "Let's just say he got involved with the wrong crowd and made some incredibly foolish and naive decisions. Even angels and demons have a system of punishment, and all born of celestial blood must abide by their rules. What he did… Well, there were consequences."

Alaric lowers his eyes to the floor. It's strange to see him like this—almost insecure in his body when all I've known from him is a natural grace befitting a god. His aura ripples in waves along his skin, agitated and morose.

Whatever happened to Alexander can't have been good. Alaric implied as much when he refused to take part in Gabriel's plot if it in any way resembled what befell his friend. But when he said that, they weren't talking about Alexander… They were talking about me.

Does that mean the Archangel views me as a threat? That I'm going to be punished, too, whatever that entails? But for what? I haven't done anything wrong except "struggle to adapt," as Gabriel so patronizingly put it. Oh, and have the nerve to be friends with a Dark. Yeah, so awful. I deserve to be drawn and quartered for that one.

My hands ball into tight fists at my sides. "Is that why Gabriel doesn't want me to be friends with Caleb?" As I recall the unfair and biased comments she made, a strange sensation thrums through my veins, and I know—based on the rage twisting my stomach in knots—that my power is on the brink of exploding. Still, I can't stop myself from shouting, "She thinks being around a Dark makes you bad?"

"She doesn't think that, she just—"

The truth I've been hiding from Alaric rushes out in a snarl. "He's the only one here who's been nice to me, you know. The Lights all treat me like I'm a monster. Even Vesta practically tried to have me burnt at the stake."

Her voice, along with that of the girl who saw me resurrecting the moth in the library, still rings in my ears, like the lingering echo of a death knell. *"Blasphemy."*

Alaric's eyes widen and pin me in place. "I sincerely hope you're joking."

A tremor crosses my lips as I push out a breath. "If she sent you to talk me out of being friends with Caleb, I'm sorry. I can't do that. I won't."

I will not negotiate on this matter. I refuse to bend to Gabriel's will when it comes to my relationship with Caleb, even if that means suffering the Archangel's wrath.

A soft chuckle floods the space between us, and I jump when Alaric rests a hand on my shoulder. "Haven't I already told you how great I think it is that you've made a friend? If you don't remember, I have the text history to prove it."

I blink. That was not the reaction I expected considering how much I neglected to tell him. "Even though he's a Dark?"

"Especially since he's a Dark." He waves his arm, gesturing vaguely behind us toward the distant doorway leading back into the main halls of the school. "Has anyone else at this academy even attempted to see past their prejudices and get to know him as anything other than a Dark?"

"No," I mutter, recalling all the nasty things I've heard the Light students say about Caleb. They all made up their minds about him the moment they saw him.

"See?" A smile beaming with pride spreads across Alaric's delicate features, warming me to my core. "I stand by what I said when we met. You're special, Luna. And not just because of what you're capable of but because of what's in here." He taps a finger to the top of my chest, just under my collar bone, and the gentle reverberation forms a straight line to my heart.

Bemused, I shake my head. "That's…a bit different to what everybody else seems to think."

Another laugh, harsher this time, springs from his throat. "I like to consider myself to be a bit more open-minded than our Light brethren, no doubt thanks to my relationship with Alexander. It's an enlightening experience getting to know someone so different from yourself. Besides, the world would be a boring place if we painted everyone with the same brush just because of how they were born. Wouldn't you agree?"

I nod, bobbing my head vigorously. Alaric seems to get it, so why doesn't anyone else?

Although I feel momentarily lighter knowing my first impression of Alaric was right, the weight returns to my shoulders when it occurs to me why nothing has changed in all the years since the Fall, and why it probably never will. The

Faithful and Fallen are incapable of letting go of their hatred, born from a disagreement that transpired millennia ago. Until they do, the Lights and Darks will never move forward.

Until they do, the segregation will continue to exist, and Caleb and I will have to fight to be friends.

I exhale through my nose, my nostrils flaring. Life would be so much easier if the divide was my only problem.

"Yeah, well, Gabriel isn't like you, Alaric. She's not open-minded at all. In fact, she seems to have a pretty strong contempt for the Darks or anyone who doesn't tick the right boxes. The way she treats me, I might as well be a Dark."

Alaric's expression softens further at my tone, melting into a pitying smile. "Do you remember when we met, I told you how all Nephilim have a skill they excel at? Well, you have skills that aren't exactly common among the Lights. Gabriel is just concerned about you."

Frustration rips through me, hot and fierce. "I know I'm not normal. Gabriel's already told me I'm messing with forces I have no business messing with. But I'm not *trying* to do it, that's the thing. My powers are just"—I fling my hands in the air and then drop them with an exasperated huff—"coming out that way."

"You'll find your balance, Luna. I truly believe that."

Balance?

My eyes scan Alaric's still face as I mull over his cryptic words. "Can I ask you a personal question?" I say after a moment.

He nods. "Of course."

"Alexander…" I hesitate. I don't want to unearth old wounds, but I have to understand what the connection is between myself and Alaric's old friend. From what I overheard between him and Gabriel and the way Alaric reacted when I pressed him about it, I can only assume one thing. "He did something really bad…didn't he."

Bad enough to be punished severely.

Alaric nods again, and it's a testament to his strength that he doesn't look away from my questioning gaze. "He killed my father."

I stifle a gasp. "And your father, he—"

"Was an Archangel," he says, his expression like stone. "Michael, the Protector."

That would explain why Michael isn't among the Archangels in charge of the seven Light academies. His absence crossed my mind once or twice, given what I learned before coming to the Serapeum about the hierarchy of angels, but I never bothered to ask any of the teachers about it. I didn't want to seem any more ignorant about this world than I already am. So, I just figured he wasn't a real angel, and that the Bible probably got that part wrong. I mean, it wouldn't be the first time. I still remember my shock at learning Gabriel is a woman.

"If he was an Archangel, that means he was in charge of one of the Light schools, right?" I ask.

"Petra," Alaric mutters, almost absentmindedly. "When he

died, responsibility for the academy and its pupils transferred to Serathiel, much to her dismay. She didn't like being second string." A humorless chuckle breaches his lips.

A sudden realization cuts through my chaotic thoughts, forming a link in my head I was too blind to see a moment ago. "If your father was an angel, then you're—"

"A first generation," he finishes. "Yes."

According to my lessons, angels stopped procreating with humans when they realized their actions angered the Creator. All the Lights born nowadays are the product of Nephilim with diluted blood—either from two Lights getting together or from a Light reproducing with a human, although those relations are rare. So, if Alaric is a first generation, that means he's been alive for thousands of years. Maybe even hundreds of thousands, depending on how soon after the Fall he was born.

I stare at him with wide eyes, stricken by awe. I've met other first generations, but there's something so humble about Alaric that isn't shared by my teachers. I guess I assumed he was younger because of it. "I…I had no idea. I'm guessing Walsh isn't your real last name then."

He laughs again, more lightly this time. "Definitely not."

I nod, overwhelmed by the influx of information I'm receiving today. Suddenly, another, darker thought consumes me.

"So angels can die?"

I figured some were killed during the Great Battle of Heaven, but it didn't cross my mind enough to wonder how. It also hasn't been mentioned in lessons, although for all I know that was on the curriculum before I transferred here.

An unreadable expression darkens the Nephilim's gaze, and I can't help wondering if he remembers his father. Surely, he must—if angels retain their memories about the Fall, then Alaric must be able to recall the early days of his existence. Then again, the Creator forbade the Faithful from having any interaction with their Nephilim children...

Maybe Alaric never had the chance to meet his father.

His voice cuts through my thoughts with such unexpected force, it gives me whiplash. "The Faithful and Fallen are immortal, but that doesn't mean they can't be killed. They're incredibly powerful, so their deaths are uncommon though not entirely impossible. Saying that, one would be hard pressed to find the tools required to commit such an unforgiving act. Most wouldn't even dare attempt it. To kill a pure celestial being is the worst sin one could commit, like destroying a piece of the Creator Himself."

And yet, Alexander killed Michael, I muse.

A Nephilim somehow overpowered an angel.

Based on everything I've learned in my classes, I didn't even know that was possible. Nephilim are naturally weaker than our ancestors because of our mortal lineage and the dilution of our celestial blood, so how did Alexander manage to kill not just an angel but an *Archangel*—one of only a few held in the Creator's highest esteem? What power or weapon was at his disposal capable of killing Michael, the sword of God?

Another question shifts to the front of my thoughts, claiming dominance over all the other noise in my head. More than anything else, I wonder why he did it. Alexander and Alaric were friends, and yet, the former murdered the latter's father. Why?

What happened between Michael and Alexander that could've led to such betrayal?

Something tells me Alaric wouldn't answer that particular question if I dared to ask it. Whatever transpired, the way he's spoken about his old friend makes me think there's a lot more to this story than I'll be able to glean from the vague answers he's given me. Surprisingly, his tone hasn't held any blame—only sadness, as if he doesn't resent Alexander. If anything, he seems to mourn his friend far more than he does his Archangel father.

"Maybe Michael's death was justified," the voice says, reading my mind.

I consider that idea for all of ten seconds before my stomach clenches, and all the nerve endings in my body come alive like high-pitched alarm bells signaling danger. If there was a good reason for the Archangel's death, then maybe that means Alexander was acting in self-defense. That would explain why Gabriel's concerned we're the same.

How often have I hurt someone—or worse—to protect myself without meaning to?

If that's the case, then this little heart to heart...is this Alaric's way of trying to trick me or warn me? Maybe he brought me to this part of the school where we wouldn't be seen by the other students or teachers, so he could subdue me before the past is repeated. Why else would Gabriel insist that he talk to me? I heard what she said. Her words were as clear as her intent.

She wants to know if I'm a threat.

A shiver of dread rolls up my spine. "If Gabriel's right and I'm anything like Alexander, why would you *want* to help me?"

I tense, waiting for the inevitable, but Alaric makes no move to harm or restrain me. Instead, a downcast look floods his eyes, and he crosses his arms in front of his chest, as if to hold himself together. As if he might break. I've never seen anyone look so impossibly fragile.

Or utterly determined.

"Because Alexander was my friend and I failed him," he murmurs. "And because, when we met, I promised myself I wouldn't fail you, too."

He reaches out and places his hand on my head as a smile forms along the curve of his lips. I don't know if he's using his Calm or if what I'm feeling right now is a product of my own emotions, but as he tousles my hair, I know one thing for certain. Despite my doubts, and regardless of whatever Gabriel employed Alaric to do…

I believe him.

twenty-two

CALEB

DECEMBER IS GORGEOUS IN Alexandria, and I enjoy the warm breeze as I skip class, sitting at a tiny outdoor cafe, one of many crowding the busy street in a touristy area. The awning blocks most of the sun, and a pair of aviators perched on my nose blocks the rest. The color of the sky is so cerulean it almost hurts to look at it. The *ibrik* containing my Turkish coffee sits on a brass platter next to a delicate coffee cup and saucer. Grasping the handle of the little pot, I pour some coffee into my cup and add two cubes of sugar. I glance at my watch before taking a sip of the steaming liquid. The rich flavor explodes on my tongue and I sigh. Damn, I love a good cup of coffee, and I'm a super snob about it. Sue me.

My shaded eyes wander the street as my fingers tap out an impatient rhythm on the table. Ishtar should be here at any moment. I don't relish the conversation I'm about to have with her. Hell, at this point, I don't even know if I can trust her to be

255

honest with me. So much shady shit is going down that I feel like my entire world is spinning out of control. Archangels and Archdemons working together to imprison Alexander. What the hell is going on here? And did he really try to destroy the world, or did they just lock him away because he was a Gray? Different in a way neither side liked. I always believed it was just the Lights who were intolerant assholes, but maybe I was wrong. But I don't want to be wrong. If I am wrong, this blows my entire world up, and I don't know if I can handle it.

And there's that nagging voice in the back of my mind that keeps asking what I really am. Am I just a Dark or something more? But I have yet to shit rainbows, so I'm pretty confident I haven't turned to the Light side. And if I were a Gray, wouldn't my grandfather be talking to me and not just to Luna? But according to Gabriel, he's singled my Goldilocks out, which kind of tells me everything I need to know.

I spot Ishtar weaving her way through the crowd, her glossy hair hanging in a long braid over one shoulder. She wears loose linen pants and a pink cotton tank top, and despite her understated clothes, people still can't help but stare. Me included. But unlike these fools, I know this desert rose has thorns. Big ones. She pats the head of a dazzled child, pulling a coin from behind the boy's ear, and he giggles, in awe of the goddess before him. I roll my eyes at her antics. She gave that kid a solid gold coin. Show off. Man, will his parents be shocked when he gets home.

Spotting me, the goddess gives a brief wave and sashays to my table. She slides into a chair on the side opposite of me. "Caleb," she purrs, "so good to see you. You said this was urgent, so I assume this means you have good news." Her cat-who-ate-the-canary grin makes me uneasy because I know my news is going to piss her off. And she's not the type of person you want pissed off.

I take off my sunglasses and meet her eyes, my heart pounding in my ears. "I've got news, but it's not good. I don't know who to trust anymore, but I still hope I can trust you."

Her grin slowly melts like ice cream dropped on a sidewalk. "What are you talking about, Caleb? What's happened?"

I scrub a hand across my face, wondering where to begin. "So, I sent my little spies out at the Serapeum, and I got more than I bargained for. I…" Clenching my fists, I stare into my coffee cup trying to find the words to explain the betrayal I witnessed.

Ishtar grips one of my wrists, her touch almost bruising. "Tell me, child. Who can't you trust?"

I meet her dark gaze and I confess, "I saw them, Asmodeus and Mammon in Gabriel's office with Uriel and Raphael. And they were talking about Alexander." At her confused expression, I lean in closer and whisper fiercely, "Don't you get it? The Archdemons *knew* my grandfather was imprisoned here this whole time and they did nothing."

The goddess of love and war jerks away, her jaw dropping in shock. "No, no, you are mistak—"

I shake my head. "I wish to the Morningstar I was but I saw them. They not only knew, Ishtar, they helped entomb him. They helped the Lights." My voice breaks on the last word, and I reach for her hand, clinging to it. "They helped," I repeat. "Why would they help the Archangels leave my grandfather to rot?"

Horror blooms across Ishtar's face, draining her skin of color. "That can't be. Alexander was one of us. I don't understand. You must have heard wrong."

I take a deep breath. "Alexander isn't exactly one of us, I don't think."

Her voice is harsh. "What do you mean, Caleb? Alexander is one of us. He was never a slave to the Creator."

I flinch. "I'm not saying that. When I overheard Gabriel and the others talking, they called my grandfather a...Gray. They implied that he has both bloodlines, Dark and Light."

The words fall between us like a death knell, and she reels back as if I slapped her. "That's not possible," she whispers.

My laugh is bitter. "Well, they seem to think so. It's why they locked him up. They said he would bring about 'the End of Days' or some shit. Do you know what they mean by that? Did Alexander try to destroy the world?"

Ishtar's face shutters. "Alexander wanted to conquer, yes. I won't lie about that, but he didn't want to destroy the world. He didn't want to rule over ruins. He loved humans. He simply felt he was the best person to lead them."

Her words make me uneasy, but I don't believe my grandfather is a monster. I can't. "What about this 'Gray' thing?"

Scowling, she says, "That I'm uncertain of. I have never heard this term mentioned before, but then again, I am not privy to all the Archdemons' secrets. That's apparent." Her own anger and bitterness slips out. Her gaze locks with mine. "Are you sure Asmodeus was part of this?"

She can't quite hide the hurt in her voice. I never thought anything could wound Ishtar. She's so self-assured, so confident of her power and her place in the world. But she and Asmodeus are close, and I know she feels true friendship with the headmistress of Babel. The Archdemon's lies must particularly sting Ishtar.

I don't flinch under her hard stare. "I'm sure. I think they're all in on it. Even…"

"Lucifer," she finishes, skin flushing with rage. Then her eyes pin me in place. "Caleb, why did they call this meeting about Alexander now? What was the catalyst? Do they know about your quest?" Concern coats her last words and my heart sinks.

This is what I've been dreading, where I have to reveal Luna's part in all this. And I know it's my grandfather's freedom at stake here, and I want him free—I do—but I want to protect Luna, too. She doesn't deserve to get wrapped up in any of this.

"Caleb, answer me now," Ishtar commands, and I balk under her authority. She has commanded legions, and she can reduce me to a good little soldier just with a change in her tone, but I don't want to give Luna up. I want her as far from this shit-show as possible.

"Answer me," she snarls, and when I turn my head from her, I feel talons seize my mind. Gasping, I clutch my head against the painful invasion, but Ishtar is merciless in her assault. Her powers dig into my mind, cracking my will. "This is your grandfather's fate you play with. Your blood. Speak!"

"There's another Gray at the academy," I say, the words spilling out in a rush as guilt punches me hard in the gut. "My friend…Luna, I think. Alexander has been talking to her, and it freaked Gabriel and the others out."

Ishtar releases me, and I catch myself from hitting the table. She leans back in her chair, studying me. "What about you, Caleb? You're his blood. He doesn't speak to you?"

I shiver, despite the warm sun caressing my skin. "No. I don't think I'm a…Gray."

"No, you've always been a Dark through and through." Her eyes narrow. "You must care greatly about this Luna, Caleb. And while I understand the need to protect your friends, Alexander is your family. Bloodlines outweigh everything, even friendship. Do you understand?"

Shame weighs on me and I nod, even as guilt continues to twist my insides.

"Alexander has been speaking to Luna, so she must be special then. They were certain she's a Gray?" Ishtar asks.

I give another reluctant nod. "She exhibits powers of both Dark and Light, and apparently Alexander has never spoken to anyone else before. They were freaking out. Raphael wanted her locked up, but Gabriel said she can handle it, and Asmodeus backed her up."

"Such a Light quality, locking up everyone who is different," Ishtar says, ignoring the mention of Asmodeus.

"Well, I guess it's a Dark quality, too," I point out quietly.

Her eyes snap to mine, resentment shining in their black depths. She doesn't like the fact that her worldview has been blown up, either. "It would seem so. I just can't believe... Alexander and this Luna are a product of both the Dark and the Light..."

My chuckle holds no humor. "According to Asmodeus, someone has been naughty. There's a prophecy about it, and everyone is shitting bricks because of it."

Ishtar tosses her braid over her shoulder, bending forward until our faces are only inches apart. "I don't give a damn about their prophecy," she hisses, fury lining her every word. "My friend is rotting because of their cowardice and prejudices. We can't allow that, Caleb. This betrayal cannot stand."

"I want to free my grandfather, too, but they're all watching now. How are we supposed to get him out?" But even as I ask it, I know the answer.

"Why, your friend, Luna, of course," she says with a vicious smile. "We'll undo their schemes with the girl. Oh, and how they'll turn on Gabriel. While they fight amongst themselves like dogs, we'll whisk the Great to safety. He can begin his work again."

"Gabriel was pretty certain Luna can't free Alexander," I counter. "She was more worried about Luna and the prophecy."

Arching a brow, Ishtar gives me a searching look. "And what do you believe, Caleb? Do you think your grandfather would have chosen this girl for no reason? That he's wasting his time blathering to a child to amuse himself? If they're both Grays, he's speaking to her for a reason. You know that."

I steel my spine. "Maybe that's true, but I can't put Luna in danger like that. I don't know what they'll do to her—if they'll throw her in a tomb, too, or worse."

Ishtar grabs my knee, squeezing until I flinch. "Did you hear what I said about bloodlines, boy? They're sacred. You've just met this girl. She doesn't matter. Your grandfather does."

Shaking my head, I bite back, "She does matter. And if she is a Gray like my grandfather, then they'll hurt her. I can't just use her and leave her behind. I *won't.*"

Tilting her head, Ishtar gives me a calculating look. "I never said you'd have to leave her behind," she croons, and my eyebrows raise in surprise. "You're right, if she is a Gray, they will hurt her. Just because the makers of our bloodlines dish out betrayal, doesn't mean we will. Free Alexander, and we will take her with us."

Blinking, I stare at her. Ishtar isn't known for her generosity. I eye her with suspicion. "You'll take a complete stranger with us? Someone who isn't even a Dark."

"Well, according to you, she's half Dark, so she is one of us." Her nails dig into my leg harder and I yelp. "Besides, dear Caleb, if you don't persuade her to free Alexander, I will. And as you know, I won't be nearly as pleasant, nor will I care if she's left behind."

I snort. "How would you even get into the Serapeum?" I ask, calling her bluff.

"You know exactly how," she says, smirking.

God, I hate Gilgamesh. Such a hypocritical bastard.

"It's your choice, dear boy. You convince Luna to help us, or you leave me to persuade her. And we both know how that will turn out."

Icy fear encases my heart, threatening to shatter it. Ishtar doesn't give a shit about Luna, but she'll save her if I cooperate. She's throwing me a tiny bone, but at least it's a bone.

"Fine, I'll convince her, and then we take her with us. Deal?"

She smiles. "Deal." Then her expression darkens. "And unlike our traitorous brethren, you can trust me to keep my word."

I don't like it, but I do believe she'll honor her promise. And maybe, this way, I'll be able to get my grandfather back and also keep Luna.

twenty-three

LUNA

MY CONVERSATION WITH ALARIC concludes mid-sentence with him snapping his head to one side like a bloodhound picking up a scent. He's silent for a moment then clumsily spouts an excuse about a prior engagement, although I can tell by the wary look in his eyes, it's a lie. His parting words are a promise he'll be in touch soon, and then he vanishes through the front doors of the school like a specter fading into a shroud of thick mist. I stand in the entry hall for a long while after he leaves, at a loss for what to do with myself, considering everything I've heard today, and jarred all the more by his sudden departure.

A cacophony of questions thunders in my head. Is Alaric really not worried about the voice I keep hearing, or is he keeping his concerns to himself? Is he trying to deepen the trust between us, hoping I'll open up to him about it in my own time? And then, there's the more daunting fear hanging over me. Is it even safe for me to stay at this school if there's a chance that Gabriel might do to me whatever she did to Alaric's friend, Alexander? The irony isn't lost on me that she's worried about what I might become when, between us, the Archangel is the far bigger threat.

My eyes drift to the row of white statues beside me depicting the headmasters and headmistresses of the seven academies of Light, skirting from face to marble face until I find the one I'm looking for. Even in stone, Gabriel's gaze is intense. She stands beside the towering golden doors leading out into Alexandria, as if to deliver one final warning before departure from the Serapeum—a reminder to all of what happened during the Fall, and why our place is here among our Light brethren.

The look on her face chills me down to my marrow.

"Hey!" a familiar voice calls from behind me.

My head whips toward the sound, and the shiver crossing my skin melts away at the sight of Caleb, his tall figure emerging from the steepled wooden door leading into the adjacent courtyard. His obsidian brows are drawn together, and his lips are pulled down in an uncharacteristic frown.

"I've been looking for you everywhere—"

I cross the space between us before he can finish that thought and slam my chest into his, hugging him tightly. The tension in his shoulders relaxes as his warm arms snake around my back. The unease rippling through my body dissipates at his touch.

His chuckle tickles my ear. "I could get used to a greeting like this," he murmurs before slipping out of my grasp and holding me at arms' length. The molten depths of his eyes scan my face with worry then cast a bewildered glance down at my outfit. "Did you just get out of bed or something? Are you okay?"

A snapshot of the last hour bursts to life in my thoughts like the flash of a camera. My head is still reeling from what I overheard between Gabriel and Alaric and what the Nephilim confessed to me afterward. I can barely wrap my head around everything, let alone work out how to voice it so it'll make sense to Caleb.

"It's...been a weird morning," I settle on then let out a sigh, running a hand through my ratty hair in a vain attempt to flatten it.

After I breathe out, it occurs to me that I haven't brushed my teeth yet today—the events of last night pushed all notion of daily hygiene out the window of my mind in favor of paranoia and fear. With how close Caleb is standing to me, there's no way he hasn't noticed, although his expression gives nothing away.

A flush creeps up the back of my neck as I quickly slap a hand over my mouth. "Sorry," I squeak through my fingers. "I probably have morning breath."

Confusion alights in his eyes as the smile on his lips falters a little. "Actually...no," he says, tilting his head and pinning me under the full force of his stare. "You're all good. You smell great, just like always." As if to reassure me of this, he slings an arm around my shoulders and pulls me into his side. "So, why has it been a weird day?"

I lift my hands in a shrug then drop them, letting my arms fall to my sides like limp noodles. Where to begin? I have a feeling Caleb will be furious if I don't tell him about what I saw in the early hours of this morning under the school. As scared as I am of what I heard in the Archangel's office, Gabriel's vague threats pale in comparison to the possible proof that I'm not really insane. Or, at least, not as insane as I previously thought.

One problem at a time, I decide.

"Gabriel," I mutter with a nonchalant wave of my hand, putting all thought of her on the back-burner. When Caleb's mouth opens to question me further, I cut him off. "Also, I found something."

He glances behind us to make sure we're still alone then leans in until our noses are practically touching. "What?" he asks, voice low and breathy. "What did you find, Goldilocks?"

I shake my head. "It's hard to explain. It'll be easier to show you."

Stepping out from under the comfort of Caleb's warm arm, I grab his hand, pulling him after me. His palm is hot against mine as we make our way from the entrance hall to the dorms, taking the long route around through several side buildings to avoid the main path, which leads straight past the classrooms where I'm sure our absence has been noted by Vesta now that second period is starting, the peal of bells overhead indicating our tardiness. I might be able to use my meeting with the headmistress as an alibi to get me out of trouble for missing first period and now bailing on second, but something tells me Caleb doesn't have an excuse for skipping other than his endearing concern for me.

When we reach the split staircase leading up to the dorms, I sweep my gaze over our bright, gold-encrusted surroundings, trying to recall the path I took to the underbelly of the school the previous night. As if on cue, the siren call that guided my steps hums in my ears again, whispering the way.

Caleb trails my hurried movements without protest or hesitation, although, as we run, I can sense some unspoken emotion in the way his hand squeezes mine. Excitement, perhaps? Curiosity?

No, I realize as my fingers constrict around his. It's fear.

He's afraid to let me go.

"Help me, and I'll ensure he never has to," the voice says in my head.

That promise spins through my thoughts on a loop as I lead Caleb the rest of the way, down spiraling staircase after spiraling staircase, to the underground passage where the glowing symbols continue to burn along the wall in the distance, illuminating the stone in a silver white light. Although still riddled with shadow, the corridor is brighter now that it's daytime, despite being several stories underground, as if the school itself is activated by the sunshine outside. I take comfort in that thought. It somehow makes what I'm about to tell Caleb less terrifying.

My steps slow to a stop as I cast an expectant glance up at him. Meeting my gaze, he waggles his brow.

"You know," he drawls through a devious grin, "if you wanted to whisk me away to a dark corner to ravish me, we could've just gone back to my room."

At the mention of me ravishing him, my skin flushes red and seems to burn hotter than the surface of the sun. Despite everything else I should be worrying about, now all I can think about is that day when we kissed. Something carnal took hold of me at that moment—something that still lingers deep and stirs in my stomach every time I lock eyes with Caleb.

Does he feel it, too? I wonder. The hungry desire crawling under my skin that makes me feel like I'm about to explode?

I don't even realize I'm gawking at him until he grins—no doubt amused by the flustered look on my face. Winking, he moves his thumb back and forth along my hand, caressing the skin and sending my nerve endings into a meltdown. "What made you wander down here, anyway?"

It takes every last bit of self-control I still possess to push out the words. "The voice. It…led me there."

Swallowing, I point to the far end of the passage where the wall marking the dead end is drenched in the light radiating from the glowing symbols. Caleb flicks his eyes in the direction of my outstretched hand then pins his gaze back on me, anger dragging his dark brows into a vee.

"You heard it again? When?" he presses.

I roll my lips inward and look down at the floor. "Last night." *And the night before that, and the night before that. And pretty much all the time now, come to think of it.* Not that I've told Caleb that.

A sigh hisses through his teeth, and out of the corner of my eye, I glimpse him shaking his head. "Why didn't you come wake me up?"

So you could do what, exactly? I'm tempted to ask, but I bury my annoyance and swallow that comment.

Pursing my lips, I pull my hand free of his. "If I woke you up every time I heard it, you'd never get any sleep."

Caleb blinks at the biting tone of my voice, several comebacks warring behind his brown eyes, each one fighting to break free of the silence in his head and find a home on his tongue. The inevitable flirty remark I've come to expect from him wins.

"Hey, you can keep me up anytime you want. There are plenty of ways we can pass the time, all of which require a bed, and none of which actually involve going to sleep."

A smile tugs at the edges of my lips, but I turn my back to him before he can see it. "Come on, Casanova," I mutter.

Caleb weaves his fingers through mine once again as we continue, side by side, to the end of the corridor. The symbols burn brighter with each step we take, as if responding to our presence.

"Welcome back," the voice says with glee.

I peer up at Caleb who meets my gaze with a shrug. "Oh-kay.

It's a dead end. What now?"

My eyes dart from his face to the symbols and back again as comprehension sinks in. "You can't see it, can you?"

His grasp on my hand tightens, his fingers suddenly rigid. "See what?" Alarm seeps into his words.

I wave my free hand at the wall. "The writing! Can you really not see it?"

Caleb's startled expression is all the confirmation I need. So much for hoping I'm not imagining things.

My disappointment trickles out in a deflated breath as I sink to the floor and tuck my head between my knees. Caleb squats beside me, keeping a firm grip on my hand.

"Hey." His voice is a gentle murmur as he brushes a lock of hair behind my ear. "Just because *I* can't see it doesn't mean it isn't there. Why don't you try describing it to me?"

When I peek up at him, his mouth curves into a smile, and he offers a slight but encouraging nod. Nodding back, I allow him to pull me to my feet.

"I-I don't know," I stammer, trailing my gaze along the lit stone, my eyes tracing every shining line and curve. "It's not in any language I've ever seen before. It's symbol-based, like Arabic or Hebrew but more…elegant, somehow? I don't know. It's really hard to describe. It's almost alien."

"It's probably Enochian."

"Enochian?" I cock an eyebrow at Caleb who taps the side of his pointer finger to his full bottom lip.

"The native tongue of the angels and the liturgical language of Heaven," he answers, as if reciting a line from a textbook. "They don't teach it to us lowly Nephilim. And now"—his voice drops to just above a whisper—"I think I know why that is."

As his eyes narrow with contempt at the wall, the tendrils of shadow surrounding him all stand on end like hackles raising on a cat. I stare at him, puzzled by the sudden shift in his mood. The cogs of his spinning thoughts turn behind his stern expression, making me wonder what he's pieced together that I'm failing to see.

Before I can ask him, he squares his shoulders to face me. "Listen, I meant it when I said I don't think you're crazy. This… what you're hearing and seeing…" His voice trails off, and he tsks in frustration, as if searching for the right words. "I don't want to freak you out, but I think someone is trying to talk to you. That voice…it's not in your head. Well, it is, but you're not imagining it. Does that make sense?"

Yes.

I direct my gaze back to the wall. The light from the white symbols seems to pulse, as if to say, *Keep going. You've nearly figured it out.*

"I had the same thought once I saw these markings. Since then, the voice…it keeps asking me to set it free. Caleb—" His name is a tremor on my tongue as the reality of what I'm about to say sinks in. I tried to tell Gabriel, and she didn't believe me—hell, she didn't even let me get this far—but Caleb…

Caleb will. He *has* to. "I think someone's trapped down here."

And for whatever reason, I'm the only one who can hear them.

"Because we're the same," the voice trills in my ear.

The same?

Caleb bristles, gaping at me for an unnerving moment. Then he scoffs, his gaze suddenly flinty. "The Archangels have a habit of trying to bury things they don't understand, so it wouldn't surprise me if there is."

"What do you mean?"

He runs his free hand through his silky black hair and locks his gaze on the dead end before us. As his eyes move over the wall, seeing only stone where I see illuminated script, the normally relaxed features of his face harden.

"I've heard rumors about there being Nephilim who have both traits. Light *and* Dark." He casts an unsettled glance back the way we came, as if to make sure we're still alone, and no one is lurking in the shadows behind us, listening to our every word. He leans in until his lips graze my ear, hesitation dampening his tone. "If that's true, their very existence could pose a threat to the divide. How do you keep the two apart if there are beings who straddle that line?"

Confusion ripples through me. "What are you saying? That these—"

"Grays," he repeats.

"Grays…" I roll the word around on my tongue.

I've known since the day I arrived here that I wasn't like the other Nephilim at this school. I sympathized with the Darks when everything around me was saying I shouldn't. Hell, I even displayed some Dark powers, much to the dismay of my teachers and Gabriel. Knowing there's a deeper reason for those conflicted feelings about who I am versus who I'm supposed to be fills me with an overwhelming relief, like I've been carrying an immense burden on my shoulders, and now it's gone, cast off forever.

Gray. I nod. It makes perfect sense. More than being just a Light ever did.

"Are—" Unease muffles my voice, swallowing the words meant to follow. Clearing my throat and shoving my nerves to one side, I try again. "Are you saying you think whoever's behind this wall was put here because they're…both?"

Caleb answers with a stiff one-shouldered shrug. "I'm *saying* that the Faithful have never taken kindly to anyone who stands against their one-track beliefs. Look what happened with the Fall. Not that the Fallen are guiltless, either."

As he says this, the jumbled pieces in my head slot into place, forming a picture that finally explains everything that's been happening to me. What I overheard this morning…it's not separate from the voice at all.

They're part of the same mystery.

A soft whimper escapes me as I nearly choke on the thought that comes next. "I don't know. I think this is different. If you're right and someone is imprisoned down here, maybe they did something really bad."

Like murder an Archangel, I finish silently, remembering what Alaric told me about his father.

"Or maybe," Caleb says, sneering, unaware of the understanding dawning on me, "they were just too different to shove neatly inside our little Light and Dark boxes."

"The boy is right," the voice interrupts. *"And it won't be long until they discover that you don't fit their perfect molds, either. You can sense it. You know what you truly are. Now, embrace it."*

Tears blur my vision as a sharp pain cuts into my temples, bringing me to my knees. An image fills the chaotic space in my head, revealing a cramped, pitch black space that even the brightest light would fail to penetrate. There's a joylessness to the writhing shadows, and I know at once what I'm seeing is the tomb on the other side of the wall before me. The place reserved for those who don't confine to the boundaries of the Light or the Dark—for Nephilim the Archangels deem to be abominations. A prison for Grays. A cage…

For someone like me.

I gasp through tears, my body trembling, as Caleb drops to the ground beside me. His hand is warm on my back but brings little comfort. "Is this what will happen to me?" I breathe.

Gabriel knows what I am. She *must*, given what I overheard.

"Goldilocks?" There's an uncertain tremor in his voice.

My teeth clamp down on my lower lip, biting back a scream. My lack of control already makes me a danger to others, so what's to stop the Archangels from using that as an excuse to throw me in a tomb just like this one?

Being both Dark and Light only makes me more of a threat.

"I'm both, Caleb. I…I can feel it," I whisper. "You know it, too, don't you?" I risk a glance up at him, both fearing and needing to see the look on his face. To my surprise, what I find is a smile.

"Whatever you are, you're my Goldilocks," he says, cupping my cheek in his hand and brushing away my tears with his thumb. "Dark, Light, or both, I don't care. I will *never* let anyone lay a finger on you. But in the meantime, I think we should address the elephant in the dark, creepy passage."

"Elephant?" I wipe the remaining moisture from my face with the heel of my hand.

Caleb jerks his chin toward the wall. "Our captive friend back there."

I follow his gaze to the illuminated silver script. "Friend…?"

I toss that concept around in my head. For weeks, I thought the voice was a symptom of my eroding sanity—a representation of the many risks I pose to Caleb. Then I saw it as something other. Something dangerous. A monster hiding in the shadows. But could it be something else altogether?

Is the Nephilim trapped behind this wall a friend or a foe?

"Friend," the voice echoes.

"Yeah," Caleb adds, pulling me to my feet for the second time since we got down here. "I mean, whoever's in there is asking for your help, so they must think you're someone they can trust, right? Otherwise, they would've just reached out to someone else."

"Maybe." Unless no one else is able to hear him because our differences have bonded us.

Caleb's voice buzzes in the background of my thoughts. "Has our friend said anything else to you? Do you know who it is?"

"Alexander," I say absentmindedly.

"What?"

I step forward, pulling my hand free of Caleb's, and carefully press my palm to the wall. The symbols burn beneath my touch.

"His name…" I answer, feeling the truth in my bones. "I think it's Alexander."

twenty-four

CALEB

MY HEART POUNDS LIKE a snare drum in my chest as I watch Luna place her hand on the wall, and it takes everything in me to present a calm face to her. My grandfather is somewhere behind these stones in this creepy-ass corridor. She's confirmed it. I'm so close to finally freeing him that my hands shake with fear and anticipation. I fold my fingers into tight fists, not wanting to freak Luna out or make her suspicious. I can't tell her my plan, and I need her to trust me. I sure as hell don't want her tangling with Ishtar.

"So, our mystery man is Alexander," I say. "Nice to have a name to go along with the voice. Look, I know this is a bat-shit crazy situation, and none of it makes sense. Trust me, my mind is blown"—I bring my fists to either side of my head then spread my fingers, making an explosion sound—"but I think we should help him get out of here."

Luna's brows make a grab for her hairline. "How would we

even do that? Like you said, Nephilim aren't taught Enochian, and I…I think you need to be able to read this to release him."

"Okay, I know you don't understand it, and I don't understand it, but can you draw what you see?" I ask, keeping the edge from my voice with great effort. I stare at the blank wall, wishing with all my heart I could see what she sees. God, I wish I could *hear* what she hears, too. Then I could keep her safe and far away from this.

Luna backs away from the smooth stone, her face spooked. "I don't know if that's a good idea. And what good would it do if neither of us can read it?"

Because Ishtar might know someone who can.

I swallow my impatience, saying gently, "If someone is trapped, Goldilocks, it's up to us to help them. Well, up to you, really. I can't hear our friend, but if I could, I sure as hell would try to save him."

She blinks those big eyes at me, fear filling them, and guilt delivers a swift kick to my crotch.

"But what if he's evil, Caleb? What if he's only pretending to be in trouble? What if he's trying to trick me?"

A hint of anger enters my voice. "I doubt he's evil. More like the Lights don't like anyone different, so they shoved him in a tomb like a dirty secret they want to bury." My anger doesn't stem from the Lights' part in this tragedy, but I can't really tell her my own side decided to play ball with the enemy.

Luna takes a step back from me, and I silently curse myself for scaring her even more. Her muscles quiver like a hunted rabbit, as if at any moment, she's ready to bolt. Shit and double shit.

I run a hand through my hair. "I'm sorry. I'm not trying to pressure you or anything. Being here with people who hate me and now this? It's just rough for me. And to think that the Lights have left someone to rot and die in there…" The sorrow in my voice is not feigned. I could have had a relationship with my grandfather, but the Archdemons and Archangels took that away from me. I want it back.

Goldilocks rocks back on her heels, staring at me, uncertainty painted all over her face. "I just… I have to think about this," she says in a shaky voice. "I don't want to put anyone in danger again because of something I've done. Because of what I am. What if this…*Gray*…only talks to me because he knows that, deep down, I'm evil, too?"

At her terrified words, I reach out and grasp her wrists, tugging her close despite her protests. "Baby," I say, and she stills at my endearment, her skin warm and enticing under my fingers. "You don't have an evil bone in your body. There's not a damn thing wrong with what you are, I promise you. And if you need time to think about drawing those symbols for me, take all the time you need." My voice is low and cajoling, and I want to press her against the wall and kiss away all her doubts and fears until she can only see me. But she's not ready for that, and I have to stay on mission to get us both out of here.

Her smile is relieved, and her hands twist, so her fingers grip my forearms. "Thank you, Caleb, for being here. No one has ever been there for me before you."

Her words cause my heart to thump harder. "I'll always be there for you, Goldilocks. Always. Come on, I'll walk you to your room."

I release her with reluctance but stick out my elbow like the gentleman I am. She hesitates for a moment, still afraid if she touches me for too long she'll hurt me, but then links her arm through mine.

After seeing a frazzled Luna safely to her room, I hurry to mine. The curtains are shut, and the dim light soothes my rattled senses. Grabbing my cell phone, I send a quick message to Ishtar, asking to meet. For someone as old as dirt, she's into technology. Then I sit on my bed and wait. It's almost noon now, and she's most likely sending her students off to lunch after putting them through a grueling class on mind control. My phone beeps. I wonder if Ishtar will give me a gold star for getting back to her the same day. I swipe to read the message. She asks to meet in fifteen. Well, she never asks for anything, she demands.

Flicking on an antique brass lamp, I watch a puddle of shadows fill a corner. Stepping into them, I pull them around me and enter the Shadow Road. A few minutes later, I pop into the Hanging Gardens of Babylon, the sun strong in the bright blue sky.

I spot a hooded figure entering the Gardens, making their way to my orange tree. Tracking their movements, I tense for a moment before Ishtar throws back her hood. I roll my eyes at her.

"What's with the cloak and dagger shit? I mean, literally," I say, annoyed. One imperious brow rises, and I hold up my hands. "I didn't mean any disrespect." The last thing I need is to piss Ishtar off, but I'm jumpy as hell.

Ishtar smirks. "Sure you didn't, dear boy. Tell me what's happened."

I glance around, suddenly paranoid. "You don't think—"

This time, Ishtar rolls her eyes. "Caleb, I have more stealth in my little finger than you do in your entire body. No one followed me." She waves with a hand for me to get on with it.

I take a deep, steadying breath, my nerves wrestling with my tongue. Once Ishtar knows where Alexander is, there's no turning back. I have to guarantee Luna's safety.

"Look, I don't want to offend your sense of honor," I begin and her eyes narrow, "and I know you gave your word, but I have to know Luna will be safe. This has turned out to be much more dangerous than I thought it would be. I never thought we'd be up against our own kind."

Ishtar studies me, her dark eyes weighing and judging me, and I try not to squirm under her fiery gaze. Instead, I harden my expression, letting her know I mean business.

"I gave you my word, Caleb, and I always keep my word," she says, her voice dipped in scorn. "If Luna can free Alexander, then she'll live as a Dark, protected and cared for. I'll see to it personally and so will your grandfather." At my skeptical look, she laughs, a harsh sound in the still Gardens. "I thought about it after you and I spoke. If Alexander speaks to Luna, she's important to him. And he repays his debts as do I."

I give a curt nod. "Thank you."

So fast I barely track her movements, she grips my chin. "Don't let this girl make you too vulnerable, Caleb. Let what happened to Achilles be a lesson to you."

Jerking my head back, I growl, "I repay my debts, too. And I owe Luna as will you."

The goddess tilts her head in silent acknowledgment of my words. "Now that all is settled, tell me exactly what happened," she presses, her hands on her hips, revealing her impatience.

"Alexander is leading Luna to him. She took me there after we met this morning," I say, "but the trail leads to a dead end."

"A dead end?"

I nod. "Yeah, Luna took me deep into the Serapeum, straight into a huge wall. I didn't get it at first, but then she told me there's Enochian script written on the stone."

Ishtar's eyes snap to mine. "Enochian script? Did you see it as well?"

Shaking my head, I say, "No, I didn't. I'm guessing she saw it because—"

"—she's a Gray," she finishes, flattening her full lips into a frown. "Can she read it? I wonder if the Archdemons and Archangels are aware a mere Nephilim can see the script. I'm sure that wasn't in their plans."

I snort. "Um, she's known she's a Nephilim for a hot second. No, she can't read it. Besides, we're not taught that."

Ishtar's eyes shoot laser beams at my head and I flinch. "It's not so ridiculous if you think about it. She can see it, after all, when others can't. It's unfortunate she can't magically read it as well."

I shrug, conceding the point. "I asked her to draw it for me."

She taps a foot. "And?"

I cross my arms over my chest. "And she freaked out, okay? She's afraid she's going to release something evil."

Ishtar steps closer to me. "And were you able to persuade her otherwise?" she asks, radiating menace. "I'd rather not do this the hard way, Caleb."

"I calmed her down. I just need a little more time to convince her. I'm this close." I move my index finger and thumb a few centimeters apart.

Ishtar smiles, a savage expression that hammers home that although she may be a seductress, war runs through her veins. "You have two days, Caleb. Two days to convince your lover to free Alexander."

I startle. "She's not my lover." But my protest sounds weak to my own ears, and I hear the longing in my voice. Fuck, that's not something I want Ishtar to know. I've just given her another weapon to wield over me.

"Yet," she says. "I'm fond of you, Caleb. I always have been. That's why I'm giving you two days, no more, no less."

I swallow down my fear and nod. "I understand. But Ishtar… why imprison Alexander? Why not just kill him?" That question has lived in the back of my mind for a while. Why this ruse?

Her brows arch. "Why go for the kill when you can go for the pain, dear boy? They wanted Alexander to suffer for his audacity. Two days," she reminds me.

I nod again.

Slipping her hood over her head, Ishtar turns on her heel and walks back to Babel. I watch her go, heart pounding. I have to convince Luna to draw that script for me. I can't let Ishtar get a hold of my Goldilocks.

twenty-five

LUNA

I TOSS AND TURN, my skin clammy with sweat, as a dream rages in my head behind my closed eyes. It unfolds before me but at a slight distance, like I'm looking in through a window at the workings of my own brain—not a part of the dream, but a spectator.

Two figures emerge as if from thin air, and I immediately recognize one. Alaric. His hair—the same dark shade as the bark of a mahogany tree—is a few inches longer than it was yesterday, the jeans and button-up I last saw him in replaced by brown leather sandals and a white chiton, pinned at his left shoulder with a simple gold fibulae and cinched around his waist with a belt. He looks to be the same age he is now—although that means little considering how long Nephilim can live—but his skin, usually light in complexion, is a few shades darker, tanned from the blazing sun overhead.

When my eyes shift to the other figure, a pang of familiarity

286

rushes through me, even though I've never seen him before. Short tawny blond hair forms a wreath on his head, the locks above his brow brushed into an anastole, and the young man's skin is golden against his own more extravagant tunic, the embroidered cloth topped with a red chlamys positioned over broad, confident shoulders.

A sly smile curls his lips up at the sight of Alaric, and the two step toward each other, longing evident in their matching lustful expressions. The way they look at each other…I recognize it. I glimpsed it in Alaric's wistful gaze when he recounted the vague story of his old friend. Their bodies tangle in an embrace, lips landing on lips in a kiss that leaves me equally embarrassed and envious. And as the realization unfolding inside me takes hold of my sleeping brain, it occurs to me that what I'm seeing now isn't a dream at all but a memory.

A memory of the time when Alaric knew Alexander.

Several more scenes pass in front of my eyes, showing the lovers meeting in what I can only assume must be ancient Greece based on their style of clothing. Their lips move, but I can never hear what they say, although their body language speaks loudly enough. Discomfort rushes through me as I encroach on these moments of obvious intimacy between them.

I'm not sure how long I watch the pair, but I sense the danger that approaches from above before they do—the two young men focused only on each other as they kneel in a patch of high grass, holding hands and muttering words I have no way to hear. Alaric breaks their grasp, moving his fingertips to Alexander's face, cupping his cheeks, and they both close their eyes as the wind rushes by in a fierce funnel around them, as if they're casting some sort of magic spell. A blinding light bursts from Alaric's palms, and mouth parting in a cry, Alexander falls backward into the grass, grabbing his head. As he convulses on the ground, the clouds above part, and an imposing figure descends from the sky, smashing down into the earth with fury, snowy white wings stretching out to the sides. When the angel looks up, a vengeful rage fills his silver-rimmed eyes, which he immediately directs at Alaric.

I know at once this fearsome Archangel is Michael.

Alexander claws at his face, a silent scream on his lips, as Alaric clambers to his feet, cowering before the wrath of his angelic father. Baring his teeth, the Archangel pulls a golden whip from his belt and flays his son's back without mercy, the Nephilim's cries soundless and yet impossibly loud in my ears. Michael's mouth shapes the same words again and again, keeping in time with each lash against his half-mortal son's skin. Although I can't understand what the angel is saying, a recognizable voice stirs in the silence, translating for me: *"What have you done?"*

Why was Michael so angry? I wonder as I gape in horror at the vicious assault, wishing I could intervene, despite knowing I'm several millennia too late to. Because Alaric dared to fall in love with a Gray and the Lights consider anything different a threat? Because that Gray also happened to be a man?

Alexander finally pushes up from the ground, his face contorted in pain from whatever ritual he and Alaric performed moments before. His mismatched eyes—one dark brown, one blue—spring wide as they register Michael's attack, his features skewed into a grimace of loathing as he launches himself at the Archangel. Michael scoffs and raises his free hand to strike down Alexander, but Alaric grabs his arm, delaying his movements by a few fateful seconds. Mouth stretched in a war cry, Alexander collides with the angel's chest before he has the chance to attack then pushes away, leaving behind an ornate dagger plunged to the hilt in Michael's heart.

Alexander stumbles, his knees going weak, and Alaric immediately rushes forward to catch him. With their arms wrapped around each other, the two Nephilim gape at the Archangel in muted horror. As Michael falls, the familiar thrum of the voice—Alexander's voice—expands in my head once more. It reverberates through me, filling every crack and crevice and overpowering every thought I have with one simple statement.

"I only wanted to protect Alaric."

My eyes snap open, but I'm blinded by darkness, and it takes a moment for my vision to adjust to the familiar setting of my dorm room. For my brain to process that I'm awake again and everything I saw just now was only a dream.

No, not a dream, I correct myself. *Memories.*

Alexander's memories.

Sitting upright, I dig the heels of my hands into my tired

eyes and push out a breath. My mind has been torn in two separate directions since showing Caleb the passage with the script yesterday. On the one hand, there's the concern that we don't really know who Alexander is or the whole story behind his imprisonment, meaning there's a good chance he could be dangerous. But on the other hand, I trust Alaric, and the look in his eyes when he spoke of his friend was overwhelming in its sincerity—as was what I just saw of their past. Now that I've witnessed the true extent of what they once were to each other, can I really fault Alexander for what happened? Can I just sit here and do nothing while knowing his punishment was likely a consequence of him falling in love with a Light?

Aren't Caleb and I victims of the same segregation?

Straining my jaw, I throw back the duvet and jump up from my bed, heading straight for the door. Caleb told me I can come to his room anytime, and I doubt I'll be able to fall back asleep, so I figure I should take him up on that offer.

I pad, barefoot, through the hallways until I reach the split staircase, crossing it to the boys' dorm and climbing the three stories it takes to get to where Caleb resides. Glancing at the numbers affixed to the doors, I pass empty room after empty room until I reach the sole occupied space on the floor, remembering which is his from the last time I was here. A gold 623 stares back at me from the last door on the right.

Irritation rips through me, laser focused on Gabriel for her decision to isolate Caleb this way by putting him all alone on the top floor of the dorm—as if he's not good enough to live surrounded by Lights. Then again, it's probably for the best there are no lurking eyes or ears around to notice my visit. We aren't allowed in each others' dorm rooms after curfew, and the last thing I want is to get Caleb in trouble.

Breathing in, I lock my eyes on his door, working up the nerve to knock. My pulse hammers in my ears as my knuckles tap softly against the wood.

A moment later, the handle turns and the hinges creak as the door swings inward, revealing Caleb standing on the other side of the threshold, wearing only boxer shorts. I startle at his state of undress, having never seen a half-naked man before in my life. I have to admit, I don't hate it, and a flush sweeps up my neck and burns my cheeks at the daunting sight of him. His arms are lean and muscular, and his abs are defined, drawing my curious gaze for a moment. Swallowing, I force myself to focus back on his face, suppressing a grin at his disheveled hair and his eyes, which are sleep-soaked and remain at half mast. A yawn erupts from him as he takes me in.

"Luna?"

"Can I—" I swallow, wringing the hem of my T-shirt, pinching the fabric between my trembling fingers. "Can I come in for a while?"

That seems to wake him up. His eyes, which were hazy with sleep just a moment ago, now stare at me, alert.

Nodding, Caleb steps to one side, and I rush past him into

the unlit space, barely containing a sigh of relief. With a quick glance into the corridor, he closes the door and then spins around to face me.

"What's wrong?" he asks, his tone steeped with concern. "Is it the voice? Has it said something else?"

I begin to shake my head but pause, recalling the dream that pulled me from my bed and led me here. To Caleb's room. In the middle of the night. Worrying my lower lip between my teeth, I throw all caution to the wind and hurl myself into his arms. His chest is warm and hard but comforting against my cheek. My pulse skyrockets when it once again occurs to me how little he's wearing.

"Just hold me for a while? Please?" I whisper.

Planting his chin on the top of my head, he wraps his arms around my back. "For as long as you want, Goldilocks."

I melt into his embrace and breathe in, trying to remember this smell—to brand it on my memory like a tattoo, so I can always carry it with me. His hands change position, moving away from my back to trail down the full length of my bare arms, his fingertips feather-light in their caress, making me shiver.

"You know," he breathes in my ear, his voice a low, throaty hum, "we'll be more comfortable on the bed."

I peek up at him, my cheeks burning even hotter at the suggestion. He swallows loudly, as affected by the proximity as I am, and when our eyes meet, I find myself nodding, as if my body has a mind of its own.

My racing heart speeds up to a million miles per hour as he leads me over to the bed. It sags a little under his weight when he sits and flings back the duvet, his eyes finding mine as he tucks his legs under the blanket. An inferno of heat spreads through me, the warmth pooling in my stomach, when he pats the empty space on the mattress, inviting me to join him.

I nod again, barely breathing, as I slide next to him and curl into the welcoming loop of his arm. His hand flattens against my back, pulling me closer until my chest is flush against his side, and my head rests on his shoulder.

We stay this way for a while—wide awake but not speaking, our bodies pressed together on the narrow twin mattress. Caleb's fingers graze up and down my spine, stirring a warmth in the pit of my stomach that's reminiscent of what I felt that day in the courtyard when I let my desire for him overwhelm me. It threatens to take hold of me again now, but this time, I'm not sure I'd be able to stop it. To distract myself, I concentrate on the way the shadows squirm over his skin, twisting and reaching for me as if hungry for my touch when I lay my hand on his chest.

"Your aura really is beautiful, you know. I thought so the first time I saw you."

He shifts a little to look down at me. "My…what?"

I tilt my chin upward to meet his questioning gaze. "Your aura. You know…" My fingers dance across his exposed torso, down his arm, and settle on his hand, lifting it up so he can see the lively coils of shadow.

When my eyes dart to his again, he blinks in confusion. "I… no. I honestly have no clue what you're talking about."

Disappointment consumes me. "Oh." Dropping his hand, I reposition myself in the crook of his arm, pressing my face into his shoulder. "I guess I shouldn't be surprised."

Seeing and hearing things that aren't actually there must be my Nephilim superpower.

A withering sigh breaches my lips and I pout. The one aura I haven't been able to see is my own, and I was really hoping Caleb could tell me about it. Especially now that we both know I'm not fully Light or Dark, but a mixture of both.

A Gray. The term still sounds weird in my head. The more I think about it, my unique heritage must be why the majority of my powers are displaying so differently when compared to the other Light students' abilities. Why my flame is blood red and not white or even purple-toned like Caleb's Dark Nephilim fire. Why I was able to bring that moth in the library to life when resurrection is a power beyond the Lights' grasp. What other abilities do I have that I'm unaware of? What kind of aura would someone like me even possess?

"What's it look like?" Caleb's voice is soft in my ear. Soothing. Pushing away all the questions I have no way to answer right now, I look up at him, grinning.

I move my hand, overly aware of his naked flesh, and trail my fingertips across his bare stomach and chest. Nerves twist my insides to the point I feel nauseated, but I ignore the discomfort as the darkness reacts to my touch, weaving through my fingers like snakes. "Like…a wave of fire hugging the outline of your body. The shadows move like flames, and they react when you do. If you're happy or angry, they show it."

"What are they showing you now?"

"I don't know." I glance down at my fingers. The violet-tinged shadows twirl over my skin, buzzing with an erratic energy. "They seem kind of…agitated."

His warm breath tickles my cheek when he chuckles. "Maybe because you make me nervous."

I wince at the sudden rush of old memories, remembering my life before I came to the Serapeum. Before I knew Caleb. A time I'd rather forget. I hate that word—nervous. I hate it almost as much as I hate the word crazy. I've always associated it with the way people behave around me when they're worried I might implode. When they're worried another incident might be imminent.

Nervous is the last thing I want Caleb to be.

"In a bad way?" I whisper.

He turns onto his side and scoots down the bed a little so we're facing each other. His eyes take me in as he presses a hand to my cheek, and slowly, he brings his face closer to mine until our mouths are mere inches apart. "No," he murmurs, trailing his thumb over my chin. "In a very good way."

My heart nearly bursts from my chest as he pulls me in and brushes a tentative kiss over my lips. That one touch is all it takes to undo me, and before I know it, I'm fisting my hands in his hair, lost in the wild throes of every single desire I've been suppressing for weeks. His tongue slides into my mouth, deepening the kiss as he rolls me onto my back. The delicious heat of his body hovers over my chest, and the warmth racing through me in response is so intense, I fear I might melt into the mattress.

What I'm feeling right now…it devours every inch of my being, spreading from my fingertips down to my toes, and then deeper, into my blood and bones. I've only seen the manifestation of such incredible emotions once before.

In the dream that led me to Caleb's room in the first place.

A gasping breath explodes from my lungs as I rip my lips away from Caleb's. "I want to do it."

His pupils blow wide, and his jaw goes slack for a moment before he seems to recover himself, clearing his throat. "Do what?" he asks, his tone edged with doubt.

Lowering my gaze, I wriggle out from under the heat of his body and push myself into a sitting position. Propping my back against the wooden headboard of his bed, I glance at the door. "Set him free."

Caleb flops onto his back and lets out a strange, strangled laugh. When I glance at him, he runs a hand over his face, his lips pressed together as if he's suppressing a smile. I cock a bewildered brow at him, but he just shakes his head. "Seriously? Are you sure?"

Yes, are you sure? I repeat in my head.

Alexander's promise to teach me how to control my powers in exchange for his freedom rings in my head, loud and clear like a warning bell. Regardless of whether he deserved to be entombed for his actions, I don't know any other way to prevent what happened to separate him and Alaric from repeating itself with me and Caleb. Control or no control, I refuse to let anyone—angel or demon alike—tear us apart.

Nodding, I look down at my hands. "He showed me…well, I think they're memories."

My eyes flick sideways, once again noting the muscles in Caleb's arms as he pushes himself upright.

"Of what?" He stares at me intently, his gaze black in the darkness of the room.

I peer back down at my lap. "Of something he did." The memory of what Alexander showed me surfaces in my head, and I recall the flash of steel as he thrust the gold-hilted dagger into the heart of Alaric's Archangel father. "Something bad."

"That got him imprisoned?"

Good question. The dream ended with Michael's death, so I have no idea what events followed.

"Maybe…" I drag out the word in a slow, drawling breath. "I'm not sure. But…"

Caleb, seeming to sense my reluctance, reaches out and touches my hand. "But what?" There's an eagerness in his voice that tempts my gaze, drawing my eyes back up to his face. And although I'm embarrassed, and it seems insane trying to justify what I saw, I can't help the words that bolt from my lips.

"He only wanted to protect someone he loved, that doesn't make him evil," I say in a rush. "I can understand that desperation. I feel it every single day." *I feel it every time we're together, and I worry if I'm going to hurt you.* "And I just keep thinking…he and I…" I close my eyes and let out a shaky breath. "Maybe we aren't so different."

What Alexander did…it wasn't right. But can I honestly say I would've done any different if I had been in his position? If the choice came down to an Archangel or Caleb, without doubt or hesitation, I will always choose Caleb.

A sigh trickles out of me when Caleb runs a hand up the side of my neck, his fingertips skimming over my cheek with delicate precision like I am a work of art he's admiring. My eyes flutter open to find a mischievous grin tugging up the corners of his lips.

"Are you trying to say you love me, Goldilocks?" His breath is hot on my face as he murmurs these words, his voice a teasing purr that sends a shiver racing over my skin.

I gulp, racked by the nerves of an inexperienced, socially inept virgin, then open my mouth, ready to tell him everything I've been holding in my heart since the very first moment we met. As those thoughts find form, my tongue turns to sandpaper, and I fumble the words.

"I-I…I mean…"

"Easy there." He drops his hand with a half-hearted laugh.

"I'm only joking." Running his fingers through his hair, still messy with sleep, he leans back on one elbow and averts his eyes—possibly to hide the glimmer of disappointment I thought I glimpsed in their depths.

My hands clamp together as my cheeks burn with frustration.

"Okay," he says after a moment.

Confused, I tilt my head and peer hard at his face. "Okay, what?"

Caleb meets my gaze with a crooked smile. "I'm with you. Let's go set him free."

twenty-six

CALEB

BACK IN THE DEAD-END hallway that looks like it's straight out of an *Indiana Jones* movie, I watch as Luna sketches the Enochian script. I still taste her sweetness on my tongue and smell her on my skin. She never ceases to surprise me, my Goldilocks. I sure as hell wasn't expecting her to show up in my room tonight, looking for comfort. And the offer to free my grandfather was a definite sucker punch, but warmth floods my veins because she *did* come to me. Her trust is precious, like a secret you can never share. I hold it close to me and treasure it like the gift it is.

I stare at the blocks of buttery sandstone, straining to see what she sees, but like always, all I see is a rough, blank wall. But I do feel something. I can't describe what exactly, but something feels off here. Like there's a force repelling me and telling me to walk the other way as quickly as I can. You'd think my own blood would call for me, but I'm guessing Gabriel put some powerful wards on this place. Or hell, Lucifer himself could've done it. They're all working together on this cover-up.

"Can you hurry this up? We need to get moving," I urge, noting the careful movements of her pen and wishing she'd just get on with it.

Luna pauses, her brows raised. "I'm just trying to get it right," she says.

"You'll get it right, I have no doubt, but time isn't exactly on our side here."

She frowns, studying me, before giving a brief nod. As Luna's hand flies across the paper, my palms sweat. I pace back and forth, resisting the temptation to chew my nails to the quick. I'm so close to freeing my grandfather I can almost taste victory on my tongue. Finally, Goldilocks finishes her sketching and regards me, eyes brimming with uncertainty. I still. My gaze narrows to the paper she clutches, and it takes everything in me not to grab it from her. My fingers curl into my palms.

"I'm finished," she says shakily as she observes me.

I force a smile. "So I see." I keep my voice as light as I can manage.

My gaze can't stop straying to the paper. There, written in her lovely, sloping handwriting, is the key to Alexander's freedom. As I walk toward her, reaching out a hand, I can't disguise the slight tremor running up my arm. Her eyes narrow at me, picking up on my tension.

"Luna," I murmur, an urgent note creeping into my tone,

"can I have it?"

She stretches out her hand, but just as the edge of the parchment grazes my fingertips, she snatches it back. I raise my eyes to hers in surprise. Two splotches of red paint her pale cheeks.

"Why so grabby, Caleb?" Luna demands in a hard tone. "You're acting weird." She's never spoken to me like that before. Never looked at me with suspicion, like I might be one of the bad guys. It hurts.

"What are you talking about?" I ask, the edge of my own anger peeking out.

Luna shakes her head. "Ever since we got back down here, you've been…agitated. You keep looking at this paper like it's the Holy Grail or something. I know you want to help, but this goes way beyond some moral sense of injustice. I don't really get why you're so invested in this, and I'm not giving you this paper until you tell me the truth. What is *really* going on, Caleb?"

"You calling me a liar, Goldilocks?" I snarl and she flinches, and I feel like the biggest dick on the planet. It's not her fault she doesn't know Ishtar has a timer counting down over our heads.

Her eyes shine, making me feel even lower. I managed to make my girl cry. Tilting her chin up, she says bravely, "Maybe I am. I don't know why you would lie to me after everything, but if you want this paper, you need to tell me why you want to open this tomb so badly. I know you care about me—I do—but I…I'm starting to think there's something you're not telling me." She holds the sheet up with two hands, preparing to rip it apart.

I could stop her if I wanted to. I'm stronger than she is. As soon as that thought crosses my mind, I want to vomit. I would *never* hurt her, not even to save her. I spin on my heel away from Luna, my fingers clenched into tight fists.

"Caleb?" Her voice is wary, fearful.

Of me. My Goldilocks is afraid of me, her best friend. Her… well, whatever else we are to each other. I don't usually roll around half naked with my friends. Don't the Darks always say the truth will set you free? Even though it turns out they're lying pieces of shit, too. But I want to be set free. It's time to come clean. She deserves the truth.

Rubbing my temples, I slowly pivot back toward her. The gold ring around her irises captures my attention—probably because her pupils have pretty much sucked the hazel out like a black hole. She looks terrified, and I hate that I put that fear there.

"My grandfather is in there," I confess, watching her.

Shock wipes the fear clean off her face. "Your—*what*?"

I sigh. "Alexander. He's my grandfather. Alexander the Great, actually. Ever heard of him?"

Her hands sag, bringing the paper to her side. Hysterical laughter bubbles past her luscious lips. "Alexander the Great? As in…*the* Alexander the Great? The voice that's been speaking to me is your grandfather? He's in *there*?" With her free hand, she jabs a finger at the wall.

"Yes." I take a step toward her, and to my relief, she doesn't back away from me. "He's been trapped for thousands of years, and I have to free him."

"*The* Alexander the Great?" she says again. "Like...from history?" At my nod, she throws up her hands, paper rattling. "Well, of course, he'd be a Nephilim. Why am I surprised? I mean, Gilgamesh is our history teacher, and we have an actual Roman goddess teaching us magic. Why not toss Alexander into the mix?"

Her incredulity makes me chuckle. I can't help myself. She's so damn adorable. Luna scowls at my amusement, her accusing glare stifling my laughter.

"You lied to me," she mutters, hurt on her face. "All this time, you knew... Why would you keep that from me?"

"Shit, Goldilocks, I didn't know how to tell you the truth," I say, and it's not a lie. "And I sure as hell didn't want you involved in any of this. I had no idea you'd be the one who could help me. I certainly don't want Gabriel's wrath brought down on you. I knew what I was getting into when I volunteered to come here. I can handle it."

"But you knew I was hearing a voice, and I told you his name was Alexander. Why didn't you tell me the truth then?" she presses, eyes sparking with anger. "If I had known sooner, maybe I wouldn't have thought I was losing my mind!"

I'm sinking in quicksand, and I have no idea how I'm going to climb out. "I didn't know you were hearing *his* voice at first. I thought someone was messing with your head intentionally just to be cruel, and I was going to find that person and kick their ass. It wasn't until you brought me here that I really let myself believe my grandfather was talking to you." When she opens her mouth to speak, I hold up a hand. "I'm not a lone gun in this, Luna. I was deliberately volunteered by my teacher at Babel to be an exchange student here because she suspected the Lights had imprisoned my grandfather just because he was different. Just because he was like you."

"A Gray," she whispers.

Well, that's not technically true. Ishtar didn't know shit about Alexander being a Gray at the time, but Luna doesn't need to know that. Right now, I need to get her onside, and the best way to do that is to make her empathize with my plight.

"Yes, his powers didn't exactly fall into a neat category, either, so they punished him for it. And I guess…they punished him for protecting someone he loved, too. I'm sorry I got you mixed up in this, I am, but you're the only person who can free my grandfather, Luna. I need your help. He's my family."

"Don't you think if I'd known he was your family, I would've wanted to help you? Honestly, knowing that would've made this decision so much easier for me. Did you think I'd turn you into Gabriel?" Tears curve down her cheeks and my heart cracks.

I shake my head, reaching for her, but she shies away. "Of course not, but don't let Gabriel fool you. She can break into your mind just like a Dark and take what she wants from your thoughts. But if you didn't know anything, she couldn't steal anything from you."

She trembles. "What happens after I set him free? Gabriel will know and come after me, come after us both. Then what? Did you think of that? Because I sure as hell didn't. Not until now…" She trails off, the realization sucking almost all the color from her skin.

"Luna," I say, my voice fierce, "of course, I did. I made arrangements for you to come with me to Babel. I have a teacher who will help get us out." Her mouth drops open at my admission. "Light, Dark, Gray, I don't care. You're my friend, you're my…" I pause, not sure how to finish that sentence, before continuing, "And that means I'll always have your back. I'll always protect you."

"You…want to take me to Babel with you?" she asks, hope on her beautiful face.

This time when I go to her, she lets me. I cup her cheek in my hand, running my thumb over her plump bottom lip, pressing down a little, my heart pounding. "Yes. I would never leave you behind."

Crushing her soft lips under mine, my free arm snakes around her waist, pulling her into my body, careful to never touch the paper in her hand. As I coax Luna's lips apart, her breath catches, and I relish the sound and the heat of her body. Was it only an hour ago she was beneath me? It feels like days. My hand shakes as I thread my fingers into her silky hair, tugging her head back. I nip her bottom lip and she gasps, and I swallow the sound, sliding my tongue into her mouth. I feel her small hand dig into the back of my neck, urging me on. I press against her, and suddenly her back hits the wall. My lips move down her chin to caress her throat, her little moans making me crazy. This is how I want my Goldilocks, making those noises that drive me wild while my kisses drug her with pleasure. Tugging her shirt to the side, I bite the sensitive juncture where her neck meets her shoulder.

"Caleb," she gasps, voice thready.

Breath ragged, I raise my head and look at her. Jesus, she's flushed and gorgeous. I want to strip her to her skin and show her exactly how I feel about her. But we're in the middle of a dark underground hallway, trying to rescue my grandfather, and it's not exactly the time or the place to do what I long to. I have shit timing. My body doesn't seem to care. Down, boy.

With gentle hands, I detach myself from her. Her chest heaves, her breathing as shallow as mine. I give her a rueful look, rubbing the back of my neck.

"Sorry, I got a little…excited," I admit. I grin when Goldilocks's eyes dip down, and she flushes apple red.

Glancing away from me, she says, "I want to help you. If he's your grandfather, I want to help set him free. I meant it before I knew the truth, and I mean it even more now." Her face turns back, and her gaze holds mine, sincerity shining there.

Hope spreads through me, dousing my desire. "You trust me, then?"

"I trust you." She holds out the paper to me, the drawings

bold in black ink.

I take the page from her, her trust a beautiful thing. I make a promise to myself to never break her faith in me. "Thank you, Luna. I'll show this to my teacher, and I'll meet you at midnight."

She slides her hand in mine. "Midnight," she agrees.

twenty-seven

LUNA

MY TEETH CLAMP DOWN on the tip of my thumbnail as I pace my room, my fidgeting wearing a path in the wooden floorboards underfoot. Every few seconds, my eyes flick to the clock on my bedside table, counting down the minutes to midnight.

Two to go, I note, tracing the lines of the red numbers with wide eyes, ignoring the tightening knot in my stomach. The time displayed burns painfully into my retinas, but I'm not sure if it's my exhaustion causing the ache that blurs my vision or my apprehension finally getting the better of me. If I had to guess, it's probably a combination of both.

When was the last time I properly slept? It's hard to remember, given how much has happened in the last forty-eight hours. Hopefully, when this is all over and we're safe at Babel just like Caleb promised, I'll be able to rest for what might be the first time in my life. Although, the thought of uninterrupted sleep without a voice buzzing around in my head and freedom—real freedom to be who I am, without shame or guilt—almost seems too good to be true. As such, I'm hesitant to trust it. Not Caleb's intentions—I know those are honest—but the idea that his fellow Darks at Babel will be as welcoming as he is.

Guilt grips me as I glare at the phone on my desk. I'll have to leave it behind—leave Alaric behind—and that's the part that makes me second-guess what we're doing. After departing the Serapeum abruptly yesterday morning, Alaric sent me a single text, the words of which are seared into my memory.

I'm your friend, and you can trust me.

I hope you know that. -A

I consider telling him what I'm planning for all of ten seconds before reminding myself that doing so would only create problems for everyone involved. There's the risk of him intervening to consider, and if he doesn't and Gabriel were to find out he knew what I was up to, I shudder to think what the Archangel might do to punish him for withholding that information.

No. I shake my head, resolved. *The less Alaric knows the better.*

I narrow my eyes at the clock face. 11:59. A shudder rolls up my spine, prompting a wave of goosebumps to erupt on my skin. Any second now—

A soft knock on the door has me whipping around, two simple taps filling me with a dizzying rush of elation and fear. Racing forward, I yank open the door to find Caleb, his normally relaxed expression unnervingly serious.

When our eyes meet, he mutters a single word. "Ready?"

"I think so." Peering over my shoulder, I give my dorm room a quick once-over to see if I've forgotten anything, averting my gaze from the abandoned phone. The small, faded rucksack I brought with me from the hospital is slung on my back, holding my few belongings along with a handful of essentials Evangeline provided me with my first day here when she gave me my uniform, like spare underwear and a fresh toothbrush. Caleb said he'd be able to get me anything I need once we get to Babel, so I'm traveling light. He is, too, from the looks of it—he only has a backpack, nothing else.

My eyes drift down to the outfit I came to this school in: a gray T-shirt and jeans, finished with the new sneakers encasing my still fidgeting feet, which shift my weight from side to side, giving away my hesitation. Although I've made up my mind about releasing Alexander, I can't shake this bad feeling I have. Our mission seems too easy considering how long he's been imprisoned under the school, and it's hard to ignore the doubt festering in the back of my brain that keeps reminding me Caleb only came to the Serapeum to set his grandfather free, not to make friends...or whatever we are to each other. Part of me worries he only got close to me so I could help him achieve that goal, while another part—the louder part—screams in protest that he would never use me that way.

I can only hope the louder part is right.

A warm hand presses against my cheek, instantly calming my frantic nerves.

"Hey." Caleb tilts my chin upward, forcing me to meet his gaze. "It'll be okay."

The lump in my throat makes it too hard to speak, so I just nod and let him lead me by the hand from the room. The fearlessness and certainty of his body language helps to quell the unease rocking me to my core, and for the first time since he mentioned it earlier, I have absolutely no question in my mind now that leaving the Serapeum with him is the right thing for me to do. This academy has taught me much in the way of what I am and about the history of our kind, but it's also kept dangerous secrets that have caused more harm than good, not only for me but for Caleb. If I'm ever going to have true happiness in my life, I need to be away from the toxic places that would keep me confined to my misery and unhinged state of mind. I want a fresh start. A *real* one.

And I'll only get that by going with Caleb.

The school is pitch black as we sneak away from the dorm and retrace our steps down to the underground passage. Caleb walks just ahead of me, tugging me along behind him with one hand while the other is held out before us, the soft glow from the purple edge of his flame coloring his fingers. His fire twists itself into a slideshow of shapes, each one mesmerizing and beautiful. The ebony fire itself doesn't radiate light, and

I've come to realize our Nephilim vision is good enough that neither of us need any help seeing in the dark, but regardless, the sight of Caleb's fire is a comfort to me, and I'm certain that's why he chose to conjure it—so the darkness and the task ahead wouldn't feel quite so frightening.

As the deep violet hue of Caleb's flame casts faint flickers of color across the stone walls, I'm determined to test out my own powers again. It's been weeks since we practiced together, and I've been too afraid to summon my fire out of fear my visions might become reality. Since deciding to release Alexander, that fear has subsided a little, putting me more at ease with the idea of connecting with my true nature again. So, I recall what Caleb said in Vesta's class, and this time, when I think about being a Nephilim, I picture myself as I truly am. Not wholly Light or Dark, but a combination of both.

A Gray.

Ruby fire spurts up from my palm, and I smile as the light from it licks across the floor like a wave of lava stretching through the long corridor. As it reaches the dead end, the Enochian symbols etched into the wall glow white in greeting, and a tall figure emerges from the diminishing shadows, stepping into the haze of red light.

My breath catches at the sudden movement, and I squint, focusing on the distant face still half cast in darkness. She's as stunning as she is intimidating, like a hungry tigress on the hunt for food. Her eyes narrow, as if trying to decide if I'm prey.

"Who is that?" I hiss at Caleb, tightening my grip on his hand.

"One of my teachers from Babel," he says, his tone soothing. "Don't worry, she's here to help."

A chill of doubt cripples my senses as Caleb leads me the rest of the way through the passage. As we near the dead end, my flame sputters out, the red glow fading away into darkness. In its place, a purple light reflects off the stone, drawing my gaze to the ball of black fire now hovering over the palm of the woman's flattened hand. The flames spasm as we approach, as if tempted to reach out and devour me whole.

A cutting smile curls her lips as Caleb gestures toward the statuesque stranger with a jerk of his head. "Luna, this is Ishtar. Mesopotamian goddess of love and war."

"H-Hi…" I stammer, unsure what else to say. The woman before me—striking in beauty with her brown skin and the thick, sable braid hanging over one shoulder—is only slightly less terrifying than Gabriel, which is saying a lot, since I'm fairly certain Ishtar is a Nephilim. There isn't enough variation between her aura and Caleb's to make me think she's a full-blooded celestial being, and if the other academies are anything like the Serapeum, the only angels and Fallen working at these institutions are the ones in charge of them.

The longer I stare at her, the more certain I am that Ishtar is a Nephilim like us. Though, if I had to guess, I'd say she's probably a first generation based on the power exuding from the shadows swathing her body and the confident look smeared across her beautiful face.

As her eyes lock on mine, it strikes me that her name is familiar, and suddenly, it registers where I heard it before. Caleb mentioned her once during *History of the Fall*, when he made a jab at Gilgamesh about their relationship. It didn't click with me until now that the woman Caleb was referring to was a Dark and Gilgamesh is a Light—a forbidden pairing, just like Caleb and me. To the Lights, the divide between our kinds is law.

Strange. I never would've taken Gilgamesh for a rule breaker. The thought of him liaising with a Dark is especially jarring, given his frequent warning glances at me and the nasty things he said to Caleb in class.

Ishtar's onyx eyes assess me with a fleeting glimmer of interest. "Hello, little one," she trills before turning her attention to Caleb. "Dear boy, we really must be quick about this."

"Right." He extinguishes the flame in his hand and turns to face me, taking hold of my shoulders. "Luna, Ishtar is going to teach you how to say what's written here in Enochian." He looks at the wall, his eyes darting across the stone, as if searching for something to look at. The symbols—which I can see clearly—remain invisible to him. "All you have to do is repeat after her."

"It will be painless, I promise," Ishtar says, pulling a cell phone from the pocket of her high-waisted black pants. With an elegant flick of her wrist, she taps the screen, the light illuminating her features, and gently clears her throat. Caleb must have texted her a picture of the symbols I drew for him last night.

"If she can speak Enochian, why can't she just do it?" I ask, casting a wary glance at the goddess.

Caleb shrugs as if the answer is obvious. "Because you're the only one who can see the script, which probably means my grandfather's tomb can only be unlocked by a Gray."

"And you're the only Gray we have," Ishtar interjects, "unless you know of another lurking around here?" She gives me an indulgent and patronizing smile, as if I'm a witless child.

Irritation curls my fingers into fists, and I scowl as resentment forms around me like an extra layer of skin. Ally or not, there's something about this woman I don't like.

My eyes narrow. "I thought Nephilim weren't taught Enochian."

Her nostrils flare, a sneer forming at the edges of her sculpted lips. "*You* aren't, but fortunately for us, I was."

Even Caleb seems stunned by this admission, and while I'm curious to know how Ishtar knows Enochian when the academies make it a point not to teach it, I know we don't have time for such questions. Every second we spend down here is one moment closer to us getting caught.

Out of protests, I let out a soft sigh and nod, resolved to help Caleb and finally get answers about the voice plaguing my mind. "I'll do my best."

Ishtar positions herself to one side of the wall and murmurs a string of lyrical words that sound like a beautiful song on her tongue. It takes me several attempts to get it right, and Ishtar's impatience with this situation—and with me—becomes more obvious each time I pronounce the words wrong. Finally, the correct phrase leaves my lips, and as it echoes around us, the script turns molten gold and the corridor rumbles in answer.

Caleb stumbles back, yanking me close to his chest, as the wall marking the dead end splits in half, a perfect vertical line cutting down the middle of the iridescent symbols, forming two identical slabs. Or doors. A thick layer of dust tumbles down onto us from the ceiling as the stone slides apart, separating like jilted lovers and disappearing into hidden crevices in the walls on each side of the passage. Beyond lies another, shorter corridor, and I can tell at a glance that something is different about it. I can feel the change in the air. Although there is no visible source of light, the passage is bright, as if some unseen magic is illuminating the space. At the end of the path awaits another dead end.

I peek over at Caleb, who just nods and grabs my hand, interlacing his fingers with mine.

In front of us, Ishtar mutters, "He's close. I can feel it."

We step forward in a straight line, Caleb lingering close on my left and Ishtar keeping her distance on my right. As we move into the hidden passage, the air presses in around us, hugging my body like a dense mist. The coolness of it makes me shiver.

"What the hell?" Caleb jerks to a stop, yanking me back. My brow furrows as I pull on his hand, but the meeting point of our fingers stops at the same point as before, as if an invisible wall stands between us.

On my other side, Ishtar has stopped walking as well. "Wards," she says with a tsk. A sound like crackling static cuts through the tense silence when her fist collides with the boundary preventing her and Caleb's advance. "I felt the first one as we passed through it, which means it was created by one of the Fallen. But this one…this was made by a Light."

"Meaning what?" Caleb's tone is anxious as his eyes search my face, our fingers still touching on his side of the transparent magical barrier.

Ishtar cuts her gaze to mine. "Meaning Luna must travel the rest of the way alone. I can only assume these wards were placed as such so a Dark could never reach the Great, even possessing the knowledge of his location. Clever traitors. And, of course, a Light could never pass through the Dark ward, not that they'd have cause to release Alexander. But as a Gray, little one, you are allowed to surpass both Light and Dark boundaries. It's the reason you have made it this far. The Dark ward was a few paces back, near where the stone split at your beckoning."

"Are you saying I walked through some sort of wall and didn't even know it?" I ask. My attention shifts to Caleb. "Did you feel it?"

He gives a half-hearted nod. "I felt…something, but I've never walked through a ward before, so I didn't know what it was."

A saccharine smile upturns Ishtar's lips. "No need to be concerned, sweet girl. The door to the tomb is only just ahead, so we'll be able to see you clearly from here. Caleb isn't going anywhere, the besotted boy that he is. And neither am I."

I peer over my shoulder at the dead end behind me. Deep grooves are embedded in the stone in the pattern of three circles—one larger and the second only slightly smaller, situated a few inches within the outline of the first. The third is a fraction of the size of the other two, positioned in the exact center of the wall. They don't appear to form any defined shape that I would remotely consider a door, but then again, the wall with the script didn't look like a secret entrance either.

Caleb squeezes my hand, drawing my gaze back to his face. "I'll be right here. I'm not going anywhere, I promise. Just open the door and come back to me."

The silence is heavy as our fingers drift apart, and holding my breath, I continue onward, leaving Caleb and Ishtar on the other side of the Light ward. Every time I glance back, Ishtar urges me on with a wave of her hand, her expression pinched, as if she's restraining herself from screaming at me to hurry.

"Fear not," the voice says in my head, sensing my doubt, *"and remember my promise to you. Set me free, and the control you so keenly desire is yours."*

My feet slow to a faltering stop underneath me, the creamy wall of the dead end so close I can touch it. My hand trembles as I reach out and press my fingertips to the divots in the stone.

"What do you see?" Ishtar calls, her voice distant, as if she's speaking to me through thick glass.

My eyes sweep over the stone, but unlike before, there is no Enochian I can read aloud to trigger whatever locking mechanism was placed on the tomb. The stone is bare aside from the three carved circles, the smallest of which transforms at my touch, swinging inward to reveal a steel spike protruding at an angle from a small ring of gold. The sharp tip practically glints with threat.

The breath I'd been holding punches from my lungs. "There's something here. It...looks kind of like an old sewing spindle, but I'm not sure what I'm meant to do with it—"

Ishtar's voice carries down the passage in a commanding hiss. "Cut yourself."

"What?" I spin on my heel, my voice rising an octave.

Rolling her eyes, Ishtar crosses her arms. "The door obviously requires a blood sacrifice. If I had to guess, the tomb was sealed using Alexander's blood and only another Gray's will unlock it. If that doesn't work, perhaps a bloodline sacrifice is in order, in which case, Caleb is waiting right here. If your blood isn't the key, surely his is." With a sway of her hips, she sidles up next to Caleb and slides her hand through the crook of his arm. Her hooded eyes shift to his face as her voice drips with fondness. "He is the Great's grandson, after all."

A grimace twists my mouth. I know what she's doing. This so-called goddess is trying to get under my skin to force my hand and is using Caleb to assert her dominance. To make me feel threatened and insecure. Little does she know she doesn't need to make me jealous to push me to go through with this. I would do anything for him, even at the cost of my own life.

Caleb disentangles his arm from Ishtar's and bares his teeth at her, grinding out, "We have *no idea* what that will do to Luna!" Apprehension shines in his eyes as he raises his hands, planting them flat against the ward. "Forget it, Goldilocks. We'll figure out something else. Just come back!"

Ishtar swipes her hand out to the side, striking Caleb hard across the right cheek. His skin burns red from the contact, and he staggers back, his shoulder slamming into the wall. "Don't be a fool, Caleb. He is your blood and blood *always* comes first. This will be our only chance to save your grandfather, and you're risking it, for what?"

"That could kill her!" he shouts back, pointing at me. "There's no way Gabriel and the other Archangels and Archdemons involved would only require a measly drop of blood to set my grandfather free. For all we know, it'll drain her of everything she has."

"A worthy sacrifice," Ishtar croons.

Caleb straightens and clenches his hands into fists. "I told you I wouldn't just use her and then leave her behind."

Time seems to slow as I watch the two bicker, my heart beating into my ribcage as I realize within the space of roughly ten seconds what will happen if I don't open this door. I can see it in the way Ishtar stands, her hands spread wide like claws ready to slash. Her dark eyes betray how she views Caleb's protests.

She thinks he's being disloyal to her—to his grandfather.

She believes he's choosing me over them.

"Caleb." His name falls from my lips in a ragged breath, and his eyes find mine, the deep brown irises a thin ring around black pupils dilated with fear. I shake my head. This isn't what I want.

I never want his life to be at risk because of me.

Without another thought—and not caring about the price—I reach out and slice my hand on the metal spindle, wincing as a flash of pain ripples through me. Exhaustion overtakes my body, and I struggle to hold myself up, lightheaded as blood pours out of my palm and a searing heat spreads out across my pierced skin like fire. Gradually, the searing sensation passes, although the weakness in my limbs remains. Clinging to the nearest wall for support, I risk a dizzy glance over my shoulder, searching for Caleb through my blurring vision.

His stunned expression is the last thing I see as the passage is swallowed by a blinding white light.

twenty-eight

CALEB

ISHTAR AND I SHIELD our eyes with our hands as the corridor lights up like it's on fire. Blinking, I let my hand fall to my side, my jaw slack in shock. Symbols burn in gold on the ancient sandstone, almost blinding in their intensity. Circular fissures illuminate the end of the hallway, and the wall shifts back and in, dust from the grinding stone briefly providing a respite from the harsh light. A massive figure steps out of the doorway and I gasp, my hand covering my heart as it bucks in my chest. There's a roaring in my ears as the blood in my veins recognizes the man emerging from the tomb. *Family,* my blood seems to whisper. And I know without a doubt that this is Alexander the Great, my grandfather. Anticipation grips me. After all these years, after my father's rejection, I will finally meet my grandfather. I will finally know my true Nephilim heritage.

As I focus on Alexander, shock freezes my heart. Blond hair falls to his ankles like a cape, and I can see his eyes, one blue and one brown. They blaze with triumph and fury. We have little in common in appearance except we share the same nose, straight and noble. But that's not what clamps my attention in a vise, refusing to let go. The enormous, silver wings flaring from his back cast wide shadows in the bright hallway. *Wings.* Time seems to slow to a crawl as I stare at the pewter-colored feathers, mesmerized by their meaning.

My whole life, I've been fed stories about Alexander being a powerful, first generation Nephilim. How he almost conquered the world with his ambition. But if he has wings, that's impossible. Darks don't Ascend, which means my grandfather is a fucking *angel*. Why didn't anyone tell me? All this time, I've believed I'm a third generation, my blood diluted. Instead, my gramps is an angel, with power rivaling the Faithful and the Fallen.

The enormity of that revelation feels like a boulder has been dropped on my chest, pinning me in place. Blood rushes to my head, making me dizzy. My entire life is a lie. Everything I know is a lie. I rip my gaze away to stare at Ishtar in accusation. How could she know and not tell me? But the Mesopotamian goddess is just as stunned as I am. Her dark eyes are shiny with fear and wonder as they roam over Alexander's wings. Tears glisten in her eyes, and that's almost as shocking as the fact that my grandfather is an angel. An *angel*. I can't wrap my mind around it. How did the Council manage to entrap an angel… and why is no one else aware of what he is? And why did they imprison one of their own? All over some half-baked prophecy?

My gaze falls on Luna. She straightens and stands in front of Alexander, her slender figure overshadowed by his tall frame. With my hawk's vision, I can see the tremor running through her body. Is my Goldilocks afraid of him? My eyes dart to my grandfather who stares at Luna with an intense, unreadable expression. I can't tell if he's grateful to her or if he wants to kill her. I mean, he's been trapped for thousands of years. That can't be good for someone's mental state, and I begged Luna to set him free. Fuck, he could be living in crazy town right now, and she might look like the enemy. Would Alexander hurt Luna? Terror envelops me, chilling me to the bone.

Alexander's wings flare as he bends down. I tense, helpless because of the ward standing between us, but he just whispers in her ear, so I relax. Until Luna screams. A horrifying, pain-filled wail I feel down to my marrow. Shocked, I watch as she drops to the floor, writhing in agony, hands grasping at her shoulders and tearing off her backpack. I throw myself against the barrier, bouncing off the invisible shield, shouting her name. My grandfather looks at me and smiles. *Smiles.*

As Luna lets out a blood-curdling cry, an unseen force flings Ishtar and me in opposite directions from each other, hurling me forward while dragging her back. Tossed aside like a rag, I hit the Light barrier, and I fall to my knees, shaking my head clear of its daze.

Confused, I glance back the way we came to find Ishtar now resting outside the confines of the Dark ward, where she pushes herself to her feet. I start to search for the source of the attack when I hear my teacher shout, "Gabriel!"

Behind Ishtar, I see the Messenger step into the light, eyes brimming with wrath, as she stares past us at Alexander. I glance between them, and he lifts his upper lip in a silent growl. I remind myself that it took several Archdemons and Archangels, if not the whole Council, to lock Alexander away, but my heart still races. Two beings with that kind of power can destroy this city fast. And we're all standing directly in Gabriel's path to my grandfather, with Luna right in front of her target. Who knows how long the wards will stand now that the tomb is open?

"Caleb," Ishtar calls to me. Whipping around, I watch as my mentor begins circling the Archangel, distracting her from Alexander. "Take care of them. I have unfinished business I need to attend to."

Take care of them *how*? But I nod, my mind rapidly trying to find a good plan and failing.

With a savage smile, Ishtar leaps at Gabriel. The Archangel leans away, back curved almost in an upside down U. She grasps my teacher and slings her against the opposite wall, thrusting her back into the previous corridor. Ishtar shakes her head, as if to regain her senses, and then scrambles to her feet, dodging as Gabriel's fist hits the stone wall, a spider web of cracks spreading from the impact.

"Goddess of war," Gabriel says, sneering. "I'll enjoy tearing you apart."

"There's your true nature, Messenger," Ishtar taunts. "All that light is just to disguise your darkness."

Gabriel snarls, attacking Ishtar. The two women move so fast I can barely follow them. Living up to her name, Ishtar manages to land a few good blows on the Archangel, ducking and weaving, but despite her strength, she's a first generation Nephilim fighting a full-blooded angel. She can't quite block a knee to the ribs, and I hear bone crunch.

Shit. I turn back toward the Light barrier and bang on it with my fists. "Grandfather, bring Luna to me, and let's get out of here. Please!" My gaze clashes with Alexander's, and it's like being shocked by a live wire. Power simmers behind his eyes along with recognition. He tilts his head, studying me for a brief moment before nodding, acknowledging our blood bond. He then focuses on the battle behind me.

I beg over and over for him to help, but Alexander ignores my pleas, his clashing eyes tracking the fight between Gabriel and Ishtar. Luna convulses on the floor at his feet, and I have never felt so powerless. What the hell is he waiting for? Why isn't he confronting Gabriel?

A stifled scream sounds behind me and I flinch. Half turning, my eyes flick to Ishtar and then back to Luna. I hear flesh strike flesh in the background, along with grunts of pain and cursing, but Alexander hasn't moved. Goldilocks still screams. I face fully away from my grandfather, my jaw dropping for the second time. Blood drips down Ishtar's face from a gash above her left eye, which is swollen shut. She's slow as she tries to evade Gabriel's assault, one hand clutching her injured side. Ishtar is a fierce warrior and has always seemed invincible to me. Now, she resembles a broken doll, and Gabriel—having the advantage of being an angel—doesn't have a scratch on her. *Bitch.*

It's all happening too fast, and everything feels like it's spinning out of my control. Ishtar is my teacher and mentor, and I realize as I watch Gabriel close in on her that I love her like she's my family, my blood. Ishtar is that badass aunt you always look up to, and who you know will get you out of jail if you call her. And Gabriel is going to kill her.

Glancing back at Alexander again, I hope he'll intervene. He's a damn angel, with all the power to take on Gabriel. I'm sure he's stored up millennia of rage and wants to get his violence on. But when he still does nothing but watch, rage boils through me. He and Ishtar are supposed to be friends, comrades. She's always been loyal to him, and he's just going to let her die. And then I remember. I came to this party prepared for anything, even though I hoped it wouldn't come to this. In a sheath resting against my lower back is the special dagger Hammurabi gave to me when I left Babel. The angel-killing dagger.

When I free the blade, it hums again, just like the first time I held it. I stare at it, swallowing. I've been in plenty of fights, but I've never killed anyone—especially not an immortal being. I feel shame when my hands tremble. Some badass I am. I need to find my balls and get this done. At Ishtar's cry, I look up. Gabriel has her pinned against the wall, nails digging into her throat. My teacher is gasping and bloody. So bloody. The Messenger's head swivels, and she meets Alexander's hard eyes.

"Just as it was before, Conqueror," she says, teeth bared. "I'll hunt your allies down and kill them one by one until you're imprisoned once more."

Gabriel is so focused on Alexander, she doesn't see me move. Leaping, I clear the safety of the Dark ward between us. She startles but regards me as if I'm a bug that's next on her list to swat. Until she sees the gleaming blade. Mouth dropping, surprise fills the Archangel's beautiful, terrible face. With all my strength, I ram the dagger in her side and pull it free. Her mouth pops open, and she releases Ishtar, sinking to the floor, her shaking hands covering her gushing wound. I hesitate as Gabriel's fearful gaze meets mine. I could do more damage. I could plunge my blade over and over again in revenge. But I can't. I slip the dagger back in place and rush to Ishtar, throwing one of her arms over my shoulder and propping up her weight.

I have to get her out of here. I have to get Luna out of here. My eyes return to my grandfather to find him rushing toward me, wings extended. Now, he decides to help. Asshole. But he's alone. Goldilocks is still on the floor, locked in her own private nightmare.

Alexander stops in front of me, gripping my shoulder with one hand and Ishtar with another. Shit, I know what he's going to do, and I can't let him. I can't leave Luna here. I promised her.

She's mine, and I have to keep her safe.

"You have to go back for Luna!" I shout at my grandfather, desperation clawing at my throat. "We can't leave her behind. We have to take her with us."

Alexander's face is cold as he regards me, his voice a deep baritone. "All in good time."

"*No!*" I scream as the Shadow Road envelops me.

I keep screaming long after our escape, my throat raw with grief, my heart in shreds. Luna is at the mercy of Gabriel and the other traitors. I have failed my Goldilocks.

twenty-nine

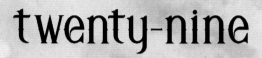

LUNA

PAIN. THAT'S ALL THERE is. An inescapable, nauseating agony spreading over my back like red-hot irons branding into my flesh. My fingers claw at my shoulder blades, as if by doing so, I'll be able to find the cause of this torment and make it stop, but there's nothing there to grab hold of and pull free of my screaming skin. There's only the endless pain cutting through me.

Swallowing a sob, I peer through the haze of my tear-soaked vision at the spot where, only moments ago, Caleb stood at the end of the passage on the other side of the wards. Reality crushes my heart as it fully sinks in that he left without me, even though he promised he wouldn't. His protests had reached my ears past my own cries of pain, but he still left with his grandfather and Ishtar, their bodies engulfed by a bubble of shadow. The weight of that realization pierces my chest and squeezes my lungs, making it impossible to breathe.

Caleb is gone and I'm all alone. Again.

Just like I've always been.

The metallic taste of blood floods my mouth as I bite down hard on my tongue, choking back a shriek when another rush of pain radiates over my back. The sound of tearing fabric sinks into my eardrums, and my shirt goes slack around my torso, exposing my skin to the cool air of the corridor. It feels like all the bones in my back are breaking and like knives are etching lines in my flesh, starting at the top of my spine and carving downward, over and over again. When I reach around to touch my shoulder blades again, the inexplicable presence of feathers grazes my fingertips, poking out of my skin.

What's happening to me? That thought is cut short when another strangled cry rips up from my throat, my windpipes burning and sore from screaming. A deluge of tears streams down my cheeks.

Desperate to escape the pain, I curl into a ball on my side and let my mind drift back over the events that led up to this moment and this inexplicable, unending torture. After I cut my hand on the spindle, the passage had erupted into a flood of white light, and the wall had slid open to reveal the towering figure of Caleb's grandfather.

Alexander the Great.

The fear that overtook me when he stepped out of the thick pocket of shadow and into the light of the corridor nearly brought me to my knees. I barely had the time or sense to understand what I was seeing before he leaned over me—his aura like gleaming shards of razor-sharp glass, every piece reflecting back my terror—and breathed in my ear, his voice deep and hauntingly familiar after hearing it for so long in my head.

"You have my gratitude, little dove," he said, placing an ice-cold hand on my shoulder. *"And in exchange for my freedom, I shall now give you yours."* A string of beautiful, nonsensical words followed this sentiment.

Then there was only pain, all consuming and ceaseless in its brutal assault.

Is this what he meant? The feathers emerging from under my skin, shrouding my body in the worst sort of agony…

Is this what he meant when he said he'd give me the liberation I desire?

If so, I've been duped. Alexander promised he would teach me control if I helped him, and yet, as soon as I opened his cell, he abandoned me with the same ease and speed as everyone else in my life before him. This pain isn't the freedom I bargained for.

Fresh tears prick at my eyes and course down my cheeks as a sob parts my trembling lips. I was foolish. Foolish to think it was wise to help Alexander.

Foolish to ever allow myself to believe Caleb actually cared about me.

"Luna…"

I tilt my head and glance toward the far end of the corridor, past the wards where a figure is curled on the floor near the beginning of the passage. When I squint, Gabriel's face slides into sharp focus, her ivory skin pallid and mouth hanging open as she stares at me with bulging eyes, her chest heaving with strained, uneven breaths. How long has she been here? The seconds that have passed since opening Alexander's tomb are a blur. I vaguely remember Ishtar shouting her name, but I wasn't able to see what was happening through the disorienting fog of pain obscuring my vision.

"You—" Gabriel pulls herself up enough to inch toward me, wincing at the effort. Her eyes never break their unblinking hold on me, not even when the Dark ward stops her advance. She lets out a frustrated scream, collapsing back to the dust-coated stone.

My eyes drift down to the source of her pain, and regret burns deep in my chest when I glimpse the crimson stain darkening the side of her shirt, spreading onto her hands and coating her long fingers in blood. At the sight of it, my mind recalls the memory Alexander showed me of Michael's murder. Alaric had said it's possible to kill angels, but it's still disconcerting to see someone so powerful and capable of imparting fear now injured and weak.

Vulnerable.

As that thought passes through my head, it dawns on me that this is all my fault. I did this. Me. I chose to free Alexander instead of trusting the Archangel, and now look at us—both likely inches from death. At least, in my case, that's what this pain feels like.

Gabriel rolls over onto her back and shoves up her shirt sleeve to her elbow, pressing a bloodied finger to a just visible white tattoo on her forearm in the shape of a thin crescent moon. Her lips move in a blur, muttering something I can't quite make out from where I lie at the opposite end of the hallway.

As she drops her hand, her face scrunching into a grimace of pain, a pool of darkness spreads over the wall beside her and expands over the floor, forming a doorway identical to the one Caleb, Alexander, and Ishtar escaped through only moments ago. I narrow my eyes, staring hard at the dense patch of gloom as a tall figure steps out of the shadows.

Hair the color of antique gold, blinding in its beauty, encases the newcomer's head in a crown of loose curls, the locks cropped short but still long enough to brush the rims of his ears. His eyes, the same blue as the ocean on a clear day and ringed with a circle of citrine, fall to the injured Archangel with worry.

"Gabriel." Her name is a hurried breath parting his lips as he kneels beside her, drawing her head into his lap. Her hand reaches up to touch his face, leaving a smear of blood on the flawless fair skin of his cheek.

"He…" She flinches, dropping her hand back to her wounded side. "He's gone."

"What happened?" the man asks, his concern clear in the way he cups Gabriel's chin in one hand and brushes her raven hair back with the other. Anger darkens his gaze. "Who did this to you—"

"That's not what's important!" Her words are high-pitched and manic, and when she turns her head, the stranger follows her unnerving line of sight to where I lie, shaking beneath the joint weight of their stares.

A humming sensation comes alive in my chest when my startled gaze locks with the man's, my heart filled to the brim with a strange, wordless song, the crescendo building until it reaches a deafening pitch. His eyes are wild and alert as he gapes at me, and in the space of only a few seconds, I watch as every conceivable emotion flashes across his face, starting at shock then moving on to betrayal and ending with the unmistakable facade of grief.

I only look away when the feathers pushing their way out of my skin coax another shrill scream from my lungs. Gabriel blanches at the sound.

"She can't stay here. You have to help Luna," she pleads, grabbing at the man's black collared shirt and yanking him down until her lips graze his ear.

He stills at the words Gabriel whispers to him then climbs to his feet, first taking care to place her in a more comfortable position, upright against the wall. As he straightens, it occurs to me I've seen him before. My mind races back and forth, combing through memories and trying to pinpoint where from, but to my frustration, I come up blank. He steps through the barrier of the Dark ward, shifting closer to where I'm sprawled, unable to move. Panic swallows my thoughts when he crouches on the other side of the Light boundary.

An understanding smile hooks up one side of his mouth. "I know you're tired," he says, his voice soft and consoling. "I know you're in pain. But I'm here to help, and I can't do that unless you make your way over to me. Can you do that, Luna?"

My stomach clenches at the sound of my name on his lips, and before I can even think it through, I find myself dragging my aching body forward, toward the only thing separating me from this stranger and his unknown intentions. All I'm aware of is the peculiar feeling in my chest and the way his aura seems to reach for me as I crawl inch by agonizing inch, grinding my teeth in an effort to redirect my focus from the pain in my back. The black shadows surrounding him are laced with purple and blue and are entrancing to watch as their wisping movements encourage my advance.

It takes all the remaining strength I possess to push my shaking body through the ward. The man immediately draws me up into his arms, his hands skimming my bare back, making me shudder.

"Gabriel…" I lick my lips. "Is she—"

"She'll be fine," he cuts in, his tone curt but not unkind. "For now, let's just worry about you, all right?"

When he offers me a gentle smile, it suddenly hits me where I've seen him before.

My mouth goes dry as the memory of my first day at the Serapeum rushes to the forefront of my mind. When I first approached the entrance to this school, I was captivated by the depiction of the Fall carved into the golden surface of the towering doors, but one face in particular among the heavenly creatures caught my attention far more than the others. The recollection of his beauty is burned into my head.

"You… You're—"

The Morningstar.

He silences me with a firm shake of his head. "Preserve your strength. There will be time for introductions later, once you're safe."

That word sends a snap of electricity racing over my aching skin. *Safe from what?* But I can't find the will to ask as the Archdemon carries me back through the Dark ward.

The moment we cross the boundary, a burst of light blinds me from my left side as a pool of shadow forms on my right. Six figures emerge from each, twelve in total, and my Nephilim instincts tell me the men and women before us are the Archangels and Archdemons responsible for overseeing the Light and Dark academies. Their auras twist and thrash with menace, and I realize—remembering my first lesson with Gilgamesh—this is the Council Alaric spoke of with such fear and disdain in Gabriel's office.

A man with deep brown skin steps out of the light, which fades behind him as if the magic permeating the corridor has extinguished it. "Lucifer Morningstar. How noble of you to show your face. Your absence is always noted whenever we are all called together, so for you to appear says much about the circumstances."

Lucifer dips his head in greeting. "Uriel. It's been a while."

"So, it's true." A fair woman with cardinal-colored hair hanging down her back in a silky curtain moves out of the shadows. As she talks, she tugs her shirt off her left shoulder to reveal a glowing Enochian symbol on the top of her arm in the shape of a backwards, upside down L. "When the brand activated, I didn't want to believe it. But this proves our worst fears have been realized. Alexander's tomb has been opened."

Her green eyes—reflective in the shadows—flick toward the end of the passage at the black hole where Alexander emerged from, then to Lucifer, and finally to me, a perfectly sculpted brow lifting in question. Sweat beads along my hairline as I fight to cling to my weakening control, which slips a bit more out of my grasp under the Archdemon's probing gaze.

The last thing I need right now is to accidentally set fourteen celestial beings on fire.

Keep calm, I tell myself. *Keep it all in.*

A slender Light with black hair and dark golden skin, androgynous in looks and clothing, steps forward and thrusts an accusatory finger at Gabriel. "Have you betrayed us, Messenger?"

"Hold your tongue, Serathiel," Lucifer snarls, stepping in front of Gabriel where she remains on the floor, bleeding from her injury. His voice reverberates from deep in his chest and vibrates against my side, making me shake in his arms. "Can't you see that she's hurt?"

I might not be Gabriel's biggest fan, but it shocks me that no one other than Lucifer, not even the Archangels, seem concerned about her wound or the worrying pallor of her complexion. Are these angels and Fallen so detached from mortality that they don't even care if one of their own dies? Is bickering more important than life?

"A Dark defending a Light?" Serathiel cocks a dubious brow. "How unheard of."

"Silence, all of you." A glowering Archdemon narrows his eyes at me, drawing the collective gazes of the other angels and Fallen. I shrink against Lucifer, wishing more than anything that I could just disappear. "Are you blind? Can't you see the girl in the Morningstar's arms is the culprit? Her palm bears the mark of the seal, not the Messenger's."

I blink in confusion and glance down at my hand, uncurling my fingers to get a better look at the gash from when I sliced my palm to unlock Alexander's tomb with my blood. The wound glows gold at the edges, exposing my part in this chaos. As much as I want to run away or deny it, there's no hiding what I've done. Like the Archdemon said, my decision has left its mark.

"Impossible!" shrieks an Archdemon so tiny in posture he almost resembles a child. The man's features remind me of the cherubs in old Renaissance paintings with his fair mop of hair and bright sapphire eyes. "That lock was designed to kill any who try to open the door, except those who bear the blood of the one who sealed it." Gaze cutting to Gabriel, he grinds out, "*Your* blood sealed this tomb, Messenger. Explain yourself!"

"It's not often I would agree with a Dark, Beelzebub, but Mammon is right about this," Serathiel chirps to the petite Archdemon before Gabriel can utter a word. "The child's palm does indeed bear the mark, which poses a very curious question. And are those wings I glimpse sprouting from her back?"

A collective gasp breaks the ensuing silence.

"How is that possible?" An Archangel with features so light in color he could be albino raises a hand to his lips in stunned shock. "Surely, she isn't Ascending? The Creator would never reward such treachery. It's unheard of. Unless—" His ice-blue eyes widen as a realization stretches across his pale face.

"Unless, she is the product of two of our own," Beelzebub finishes, the hysteria in his youthful tone giving way to somber understanding. "How else could the child have opened the door unless she shares the Messenger's blood? Not to mention the Enochian barring the passage. Only an angel's eyes could have seen it."

Shocked glances from both sides narrow on Gabriel at the same moment disbelief and confusion rip through me. I share Gabriel's blood? And the script on the wall... They're saying only an angel could have seen it, but *I* saw it and I'm a Nephilim. Nausea turns my stomach as the thoughts whirring around in my brain spin like the rotating cogs in a clock. I assumed my powers manifest the way they do because I'm a Gray and not a

Light, like everyone believed. But what if I'm something else, too? Could Alaric have been wrong about me being a Nephilim?

On top of being a Gray, could I also possibly be…an angel?

If so, then Gabriel…does this mean she's my *mother*?

My head goes fuzzy at these notions, and for a second, I think I'm going to pass out from the rush of information assaulting me from all sides. The only thread keeping me conscious is the question now gripping my brain, screaming at me for an answer.

If Gabriel is my mother, who is my father?

"Is she the Gray you spoke of, Gabriel? The one you claimed you had well in hand?" Uriel seethes, a pointed frown sharpening his already harsh face. "How dishonest you've been with us. What danger have you placed us all in with your lies?"

A tall female Archangel with short, strawberry-blonde hair places a hand on Uriel's arm. "If this girl is indeed the one who freed Alexander, then we have no choice but to imprison her and find out what she knows."

"I agree with Raphael," Mammon says with a glance at the angel, his expression pinched, as if ashamed of this admission. "We cannot risk a repeat of last time."

"You can't—" Gabriel pushes herself up in a panic, then cries out, and falls back down to the floor.

At the same moment, Lucifer bites out, "That won't be necessary."

Raphael glances between him and Gabriel, trailing a slim finger along the sharp line of her jaw. "Your protests are bewildering,

Morningstar. Why do you extend such support for our Gabriel?"

The same question spirals through my head on a loop. The possibility of her being my mother aside, why is Gabriel so determined to defend me after I betrayed her by setting Alexander free? I suppose it's possible she wasn't aware of our connection until now, that she didn't recognize who I am to her. Even so, surely, she doesn't feel any loyalty to me, otherwise she wouldn't have given me up when I was born, regardless of me being a Gray. Then again, Gabriel hates the Darks. Of course, she would despise her half-Dark daughter.

But, if that's true, then why is Lucifer—an Archdemon—helping her? Why is he helping me? Unless—

"This girl isn't a threat any longer," Lucifer thunders, an unspoken threat booming behind every word. "I will deal with her. The rest of you may go."

Uriel's hands squeeze into fists as he snarls, "Who gave you such authority, Morningstar? You forget, not all of us followed you during the Fall."

Lucifer takes a careful step toward the Archangel, tightening his hold on me. "Get out of my way, Brother. Or I will be forced to move you."

A smirk peels back Uriel's lips, revealing perfect white teeth. "I will not be intimidated, and you will not leave here with that girl in one piece. Surrender her to us or suffer us all."

"Be smart, Lucifer," Raphael adds. "Hand her over. You might have once been the Creator's favorite, but you are Fallen now and you are outnumbered."

"Or perhaps we should punish the Messenger instead for your insubordination? She's certainly earned a thrash or two for her part in all this." Mammon reaches down and plucks Gabriel up off the floor as if the Archangel weighs nothing.

Rage burns behind Lucifer's eyes as he scoffs. "I don't know what you're insinuating—"

"Don't you?" Raphael counters, cutting him off. "Not all of us are so easily fooled."

Uriel extends his arms and nods for Lucifer to hand me over to him. When he doesn't, Mammon places a hand around Gabriel's throat.

A rush of wind dampens the air with a chill, and I stare up in wonder as two giant black wings fill the width of the passage, extending outward from Lucifer's back.

Fury creases his face. "If you hurt her—"

"Careful now, Lucifer," Uriel warns. "The last Archdemon who dared to make threats was stripped of her position. And her wings. We wouldn't want to have to make an example of you."

The Archdemon with hair the color of garnets places a hand on Lucifer's shoulder, and they exchange a swift, silent glance. An entire conversation seems to happen in that single, grave look shared between them. As she retreats backward into the shadows, the Morningstar's gaze drops to mine, his pupils blown wide, revealing his remorse and anger.

I know without having to ask what he's thinking—I see it in

the regret creasing his otherwise faultless face. *Just like everyone else in my life…* I choke on the thought as Caleb's face forms in my head. Just like everyone before him, Lucifer is giving me up.

Please, don't, I try to say, but the words catch in my throat.

Uriel steps forward to take me from Lucifer, and as his arms brush the sore spots on my back where feathers continue to carve holes in my skin, the Morningstar brings his mouth to my ear. The low timbre of his voice is the last thing I hear before Uriel presses a cold hand to my face, and the darkness of sleep rises to swallow me whole.

"I will find you again, Daughter. I promise."

epilogue

SOFT SPOTLIGHTS ILLUMINATE THE tomb of Alexander's human father, King Phillip II. After thousands of years, it remains well intact. He supposes it is a small mercy it wasn't robbed by the tomb raiders like so many of the royal necropolis, despite all of them being hidden under giant mounds of dirt resembling hills. The scene painted along the top of the tomb is faded but still beautiful, celebrating the thrill of the hunt. Bright blue stripes the white marble under the mural. The tomb is a marvel, a work of beauty only fit to house a king on his final journey. Alexander made sure of that.

Only now, of course, his father's resting place was disturbed. His gold and silver put on display. His crown behind glass for humans to gawk at in awe. Not that he resents the humans for that—Macedonia was a place of wonder and power. The crown jewel of the ancient world, a sparkling diamond amidst the chaos. Alexander ruled that diamond. He built upon the

346

foundation his adopted father laid down and conquered.

Until *he* was conquered.

Bitterness swells within him at that betrayal. As Alexander looks around the chilly museum his father's resting place has become in the north of Greece, he wonders about the identity of his real father, which remains unknown, as does the face of his angel mother. Their blood never sang to him, but the Creator might have a hand in that. Despite the mystery shrouding his celestial lineage, he loved his mortal parents, his loyal mother more than his philandering father, but love them both he had. He sorely misses them. They knew he was special, kissed by the gods, they said.

Alexander shoves aside the curtain of his hair—another reminder of his imprisonment—to regard Ishtar, his loyal companion. Such a fierce warrior of the ancient world, earning the title of goddess. He admires her beauty as she is stretched out on the wooden landing, sleeping. Her injuries were grave but he healed her. When that shiny, golden girl, Luna, freed him from his tomb, he wasn't at full strength. Weak from the angelic power sealing him in, he hadn't been able to heal Ishtar immediately or intervene with the Messenger on her behalf. Now, power surges through him, like being drawn up from a never-ending well, and her injuries fade before his eyes. She will be well, and they will conquer again.

Icy rage frosts his veins as he remembers her awe at his wings, how she reached out to touch them as they traveled along the

Shadow Road as if she never beheld them before. Ishtar didn't recall his true nature, which means that treacherous, traitorous Council must have altered her memories. How much other history did they alter? Do any of his old allies remember him? Are they still alive like Ishtar or were some disposed of?

Pain spears his heart. And what of Alaric? His closest friend and his... Such sadness in Alaric's voice when he spoke of the past to golden Luna. He ponders if Alaric remembers the aid he gave Alexander in his rise to power. How the Nephilim showed him the path to unlocking his Light side, much in the way he unlocked the girl's Dark side. The girl was splintering, her true nature breaking through, forming cracks in the bind over her power. He just tugged hard, and the bind shattered completely.

Alexander folds his gray wings around him like a cloak, his eyes on the silver feathers. The color is a beacon of fear for the Archdemons and Archangels. Something they thirst to eradicate—an imperfection in their perfect, crumbling system of segregation. He didn't understand before—not fully—but now he knows. And he won't be trapped so easily again. He won't be trapped at all. He'll burn the world before that happens.

And from those ashes, humans, Nephilim, and angels alike will experience true freedom. He will lead them into the next era.

His eyes flick to his blood...his grandson. Alexander was young when he was entombed. The idea he has a grandson is bizarre. He knows he has a son—if the boy still lives—but the child was barely walking when he was imprisoned. This boy,

Caleb, does not resemble him, except for the nose, perhaps. And the strength. As a Nephilim, Caleb's blood is diluted, but it still boasts the power of his lineage. His grandson sits on the wooden steps leading to the viewing platform, his hands in his hair. He appears utterly mad and grief-stricken.

Frowning, Alexander's eyes rove over his grandson's appearance. People dress so differently in this time period. Slashes in his faded pants reveal the skin of Caleb's knees, as if he's a pauper and not the descendant of royalty. Is this normal for the time period? And ancient Greek is no longer the common tongue. This English is prevalent, which he had to adapt to during his time spent in Luna's head. Alexander feels foggy and out of touch, but that will soon be rectified.

Caleb looks up, their gazes clashing, and Alexander feels the boy's rage from where he stands, a living, fiery snake coiling between them.

"Why did you leave her there?" Caleb demands again, as if they are on an endless time loop, and this is all he can think to say.

Alexander owes him no explanations. He is a king, but if he wants loyalty, he has to give something in return. Debts must be paid. His grandson brought Luna into his service to free him. That took skill and cunning and perseverance, as they did all this under the Messenger's nose. He swallows a malicious grin at that.

Flaring out his wings, Alexander flaps them once, the muscles of his shoulders protesting at the motion, and lands on the step next to his grandson. Caleb rears back, wariness painting his face. One of his fists closes over the dagger resting by his side—the dagger he stabbed Gabriel with, the dagger Alexander killed the Archangel Michael with—and Alexander admires his bravery and his instincts. He raises a brow and gives his grandson a pointed look, eyes darting from the dagger to Caleb's eyes. The boy just gives him a hard stare, not moving an inch, and Alexander laughs, startling his grandson a second time.

"You truly are my blood," he says. "How did you come by such a lethal weapon?"

Caleb presses his lips into a thin line. A few moments pass by before he answers. "Hammurabi."

Now, it is Alexander's turn to be surprised. He wonders how the fierce Babylonian king and warrior came into possession of his weapon. Although he and Hammurabi were friendly, they were never friends, but they had great respect for one another. If Ishtar ended up with Alexander's dagger, that is a puzzle piece that would fit, but she hadn't. Perhaps it has something to do with the erasure of her memories. He'll turn that over in his mind later.

"It's fitting that you should have it," Alexander murmurs. "It belonged to me."

Caleb's jaw slackens as he glances down at the dagger, but he doesn't offer the weapon back to Alexander. He feels pride in his grandson. Blood bred true, and he has a budding warrior he can mold.

"She couldn't come with us, your golden flower," he says to Caleb. When the boy begins to shout in protest again, Alexander holds an imperious hand up, treating his grandson to the same fearsome look that kept hordes of unruly, bloodthirsty soldiers in line. The boy quells under his glare. "We traveled the Shadow Road, and her transformation was not yet complete."

"H-Her transformation?" Caleb stutters, his eyes focusing on Alexander's wings. "She's an… I mean, I know she had some Dark abilities, but are you saying…" His voice gutters out, and he shakes his head, disbelief sewn across his features.

Alexander smiles. "Her Dark side has been repressed, yes, but that's not all. Her entire life has been a lie, Caleb. I set her free, just as she set me free. Soon, she'll have wings to fly away."

Caleb opens and closes his mouth like a fish gasping for air on shore. He shakes his head. "But that's—that means… Shit, do you mean she's an *angel*, too?"

He nods. "Yes. Once her transformation is complete, I will return for her." He places a hand on the boy's shoulder. "I owe her a debt that I will repay. So calm yourself, she will be with us again and soon."

As a Gray like him, Luna poses a threat to Alexander. One he can't let lay idle, waiting to be used against him. He owes the girl, yes, but he must keep her close. He needs her as an ally. And as she's so young and confused, so mistreated by those who should care for her, it will be easier to convince Luna to join him. Easy to promise her that he values her blood and her talents, which isn't a lie.

"But she's all alone now. With *them*," Caleb whispers, his voice breaking. "They'll do the same thing to her that they did to you."

Alexander gives Caleb a calculating look. His grandson's feelings for the golden girl are obvious, the inky indigo strands of his aura twisting and bouncing in agitation. Alexander will use that connection to corral them both, bonding them tightly to him and his cause.

"Yes, they will try to entomb her," he says, "but they will not succeed for long. I will rescue her, Caleb. I vow it."

Caleb gazes up at him, eyes mournful. "But how can you go up against the Council alone?"

Alexander's smile is vicious. "It took all of them to entomb me before. Now, I know their tricks. And I won't be alone. I have you, my blood, and Ishtar, my general. I will raise my banner and call my allies to me. With our cunning, we will free Luna and crush our enemy." He points to Ishtar. "Get her and come."

Caleb scrambles to his feet, tucking the dagger into a sheath at his back. He goes down a few steps and scoops Ishtar off the floor. Alexander turns from him and enters the main floor of the museum, finding his father's crown with unerring accuracy among the artifacts of silver and gold. With a thought, the glass shatters. Shrieking pierces the air and his ears. Growling, he waves a hand and the noise stops.

The crown is made from delicate, hand-carved gold, the cluster of individual oak leaves each a work of art, shining like a yellow beacon in the darkness of the museum. Some of the leaves are melted, from where his father was burned in the funeral pyre. Alexander reaches for the crown, placing it on his head. Closing his eyes, he basks in the rightness of it, in the symbolic power encircling his brow.

A gasp sounds in the silence, and he turns to find Caleb and Ishtar—awake now—both watching him. Ishtar pushes against Caleb's chest, and he puts her down.

The goddess of love and war stares at him with shiny eyes. "My king," she says, sinking into a deep bow.

The boy looks uncertain but gives a shallow bow of his own.

When they both rise, Alexander says, "It is time to conquer once more."

END OF BOOK ONE

THANK YOU SO MUCH FOR
READING LIGHTFALL!

For more of our star-crossed lovers, scan the QR code below
and enter your email to receive a bonus scene from this book!